THE GRIMM LEGACY

Copyright © 2012 by Addie J. King

Cover Art by Melinda Timpone

Edited by Kathy Watness

Loconeal books may be ordered through booksellers or by contacting:

www.loconeal.com

216-772-8380

Loconeal Publishing can bring authors to your live event.
Contact Loconeal Publishing at 216-772-8380.

Published by Loconeal Publishing, LLC
Printed in the United States of America

First Loconeal Publishing edition: July 2015

Visit our website: www.loconeal.com

ISBN 978-1-940466-38-5 (Trade Paperback)

D0879939

ALSO BY ADDIE J. KING

The Grimm Legacy
The Andersen Ancestry
The Wonderland Woes
The Bunyan Barter

THE GRIMM LEGACY

ADDIE J. KING

THE GRIMM LEGACY - BOOK 1

Loconeal Publishing

Amherst, OH

DEDICATION

This book is dedicated to Merlin David Woodruff.
I hope it's twelve o'clock, Grandpa.
I miss you.

CHAPTER ONE

The blonde newscaster was way too perky for me this early in the morning. If I didn't get coffee soon, I'd find out firsthand if perkiness prior to percolation qualified for justifiable homicide.

My ratty old bathrobe and wild bed-head hair just couldn't compete with the polish of the woman on the battered second-hand television. She deserved a smack for that alone, at least in my opinion. I settled for smacking the side of the television when the picture fuzzed at the edges and wished for some kind of supernatural power that would allow me to slap her through the TV.

I stumbled through the half-unpacked boxes and piles of books and papers in my new apartment, yawning and stretching. I hoped I'd unpacked the coffeepot the night before. I'd just moved in yesterday, and everything was still in a jumbled mess.

"This just in; Dayton police discovered a dead wolf in McGregor Park this morning. The wolf's stomach appears to have been cut open and seven heavy paving stones were placed inside, likely prior to death . . . ."

Huh? It must've been the lack of caffeine; the newscaster couldn't actually be talking about something that strange. I was only twenty-two, too young for dementia. And a wolf that close to where I lived? Yikes. The park was right next-door to my apartment complex. I didn't think we had wolves in Dayton, Ohio. I stood in front of the coffee pot, willing it to brew faster and yawning some more, but the newscast caught my attention again.

"And in other news, last night police responded to a break-in at the Dayton Art Institute. A source close to the museum has told us that several pieces for the upcoming German folk art exhibit have been taken, including a red cape, a spinning wheel and spindle, and a glass shoe; but none of the framed art or sculptures from the museum were touched. On a stranger note, the security cameras seem to have been malfunctioning, because there is no record of entry or exit into the building after the museum closed for the day."

The coffeepot finally finished brewing. Thank God.

Now where were those coffee mugs? I must not have unpacked them the night before. I reached for the first open box and rummaged around until I found my *Give Me My Coffee and No One Will Get Hurt* mug. It was my favorite.

Who would want such oddball things, as opposed to valuable art that could be stolen and sold for money? Not that I would steal anything, but the items the newscaster was talking about couldn't be worth all that much. I looked around my tiny one-bedroom apartment furnished sparsely from garage sales and thrift stores and attics. Money was something I didn't have a lot of, either.

My stepmother was going to be furious. Evangeline Kravits Grimm worked as a volunteer at the museum, and I knew she was preparing something big for the exhibit. I really hoped they wouldn't have to cancel it after all her hard work, or I'd be listening to her complain for a good long while. She'd be miserable, and she'd make me miserable with her.

I had to meet Evangeline for brunch today. I winced as I poured myself some coffee. That was not going to be a fun meal. I headed back into the living room, sipping my coffee and trying to orient myself about what I might be able to accomplish before I left for brunch.

As I turned, I slipped on the pile of mail lying on the floor below the mail slot in my front door and stubbed my toe on a nearby box of books before I could catch my balance. Coffee slopped over the side of the mug, singeing the back of my hand and spilling on the sleeve of my bathrobe.

"Ow, ow, ow." I hopped on one foot, trying not to spill any more coffee as I also tried to see how badly I'd stubbed my toe. I didn't see any blood. It probably wasn't more than just bruised, but *wow* that hurt. I scooped up the mail and tossed it on the kitchen table where I'd sort out the junk and the coupons later. As I set down the coffee mug on the counter and wiped the coffee off the back of my hand, I noticed that the envelopes were marked "occupant". I wondered how long it would take to start getting mail with my own name, Janie Grimm, on the label.

What to wear? My version of acceptable brunch clothing was nowhere near as particular as my step*monster*'s. If left to my own devices, I'd end up in a t-shirt and a pair of jean cut-offs. It took several wardrobe changes before I finally settled on an outfit. If the newscast was to be believed about a break-in at the museum, she'd be extra picky today. She was always hard to please when she was in a bad mood, and thieves inconsiderate enough to ruin her hard work and steal her exhibits would affect her mood for sure.

I got dressed in Evangeline-approved gear: tan slacks and a pale-blue sweater set. I hate clothing like this. It makes me look like one of those people in high end shopping malls, all wearing the same outfit and carrying the same giant paisley purse, with fake acrylic French manicures and perfectly coiffed hair. They're like poodles; primped and pressed within an inch of having a life.

Speaking of primping, I'd have to find my makeup. I hate wearing it, but I needed to go the extra mile today to prevent a stepmother scolding. I always felt like I was wearing a disguise when I wore makeup; it was like I was wearing someone else's face instead of my own.

"Where did I put that makeup kit?" I asked aloud, speaking to no one in particular, since I lived alone. After several minutes of frantic rummaging, I found it in exactly the place it shouldn't have been; jammed in a box of Dad's old books, between the leather bound family Bible and the photo album of my father's wedding to Evangeline.

I shouldn't have taken the time, but I cracked open the photo album to see a picture of my Dad. Mom took off when I was eight, and two years later Evangeline married Dad in a ceremony so sickeningly perfect that Martha Stewart herself would've cringed. I'd worn a scratchy pink crinoline dress that day without complaint, because it made my dad so happy.

I missed him. Dad got sick just after the wedding, and spent the next twelve years fighting the cancer that finally killed him six months ago. I was, at least, able to announce my acceptance to law school before he died. He made Evangeline promise to help and support me since he couldn't be there himself, and she had, albeit reluctantly, agreed. She was my only family now, and I was stuck with her because she held the purse strings. The relationship she and I had didn't come without obligation.

It's not that I can't pay the rent, I thought, as I put the album on a shelf beside the Bible. I don't mind hard work. I could get a job, but first year law students aren't supposed to work. The law school was adamant all through the application and acceptance process and through orientation, telling us the workload would be too heavy to take on a job, even a part-time one. I hated the idea of putting myself in debt to Evangeline, but all she'd asked for in return for paying my rent was a promise to meet her for a weekly brunch, on her. At the time it seemed like a small price to pay.

Now I was spending the day before my classes started meeting her for brunch instead of figuring out which boxes held my notebooks and highlighters for tomorrow. I grabbed the makeup bag and hurried to get ready. As it was, I'd taken too much time looking at old pictures, and ended up rushing to finish my makeup in the parking lot when I arrived.

When I got to the restaurant, a chi-chi bistro I couldn't hope to afford on my current budget, I caught sight of my reflection in the glass door and groaned. My chin-length brown hair was not being cooperative. It was mid-August in Ohio and the humidity was making my hair look like I'd combed it with a pitchfork. I reached for a headband in my purse and hoped Evangeline wouldn't complain too much. It was too late to do anything about it now.

And there she was; a vision in a pale yellow sweater set, her blond hair shellacked into place with enough hairspray to make me consider buying stock in Aqua Net, her long manicured nails click-clacking as they drummed an impatient rhythm on the table. Okay, so I was late. It was only ten minutes. I swear it wasn't on purpose.

Evangeline's gravelly voice didn't match the perfect, falsely youthful, exterior. "Didn't you promise to meet me at eleven? At least you made it here while they're still serving brunch. My dear, you really must start wearing a good watch, especially if you're going to be an attorney. How will you know how much time to bill a client if you don't get used to checking your watch?"

I wondered if I could buy a reliable watch for less than ten dollars.

That was just about all the money I could afford for it. I muttered an incoherent objection, not expecting to win any arguments with her but physically unable to agree with anything she said. It was a reflex after years of digs and disagreements.

And, as usual, she waved off petty concerns like money. "You have plenty of money. Your father's estate had money and a watch is an investment in your future."

Yeah, I'd inherited money from my dad in the form of the proceeds of selling the house we'd lived in before Evangeline married Dad, but law school tuition was the investment in my future I'd chosen to make, rather than fancy jewelry. Between tuition, books, supplies, and all the expenses other than the rent, I didn't have much extra cash left to get through law school without running out of money, especially if I couldn't work for the first year.

"Evangeline, how's your work with the art institute going?" *Better get it out of the way now.*

The waiter came by to take our drink order before my stepmother got a chance to say anything else. Evangeline ordered a soy milk latte and I ordered a mimosa. This wasn't starting well.

The waiter, a cute redheaded guy about my own age, started yammering on about the day's specials. I smiled at him; he had served us at most of our brunch meetings. I never could remember his name, but he wasn't bad to look at and never tried to extend our meetings with dessert or coffee offerings. It was almost like he knew I didn't want to be there and was trying to help me get out of there faster. I caught a glimpse of his name tag: Aiden.

Evangeline looked down, meticulously lining up the handles of her silverware so they were even with the edge of the table. She then refolded the napkin on her lap twice before pulling out a small jar of lotion, which she proceeded to rub into her hands while she complained to the waiter that there were spots on the silverware. Okay, Evangeline was anal retentive, and the hand lotion thing was an obsession with her, but that was way overboard.

I shooed the waiter away, despite the insane urge to keep talking with him instead of my stepmother. He seemed nicer than Evangeline. He tripped on his way back into the kitchen, knocking over a tray of dishes that crashed to the floor as he fell. I definitely would have preferred to go over and see if he was okay rather than stay at my table. Instead, I asked her the question I knew I was supposed to ask.

"Are you all right?"

"Oh, I'm fine. Thank you for asking," she said, clearing her throat and looking up from the pristine napkin in her lap. "I suppose the news last night shook me up a bit."

Huh? The plastic Barbie of Botox shook up? This I had to hear. "What happened?" Ice queen, clenched-teeth pique, I expected. Frostily annoyed? Sure. Shook up? I'd never seen her antsy or distracted like this. Maybe I shouldn't have brought it up.

"Someone broke into the art institute last night and several of the exhibits were taken. There was to be an exhibition of German folk art and historical artifacts to open right before Oktoberfest and now they must cancel, because the cornerstone pieces were taken."

"What pieces?" I asked, wondering if the news had gotten it all correct.

"There was a horn mouthpiece made of bone, a glass shoe, a red cape, a spinning wheel and spindle, an iron stove, as well as twelve worn out pairs of dancing shoes. And they cannot be replaced!"

It sounded like an overreaction to me. But then again, Evangeline had perfected the art of genteel melodrama. "I'm sure it'll turn up. At least it wasn't a Monet or a Van Gogh. I'm assuming the exhibit had more pieces to display than that, so those six things shouldn't stop the show, should it?" Our drinks arrived and the waiter asked for our order again.

I sipped my drink and started to order. The cute waiter bolted, babbling incoherently about needing to get more water. I looked at our full water glasses and began to call after him, but I caught sight of Evangeline's expression, and gaped at her uncharacteristic show of emotion.

Her face flushed, her eyes went red, and she was gritting her teeth as she spoke in clipped bursts of tight-lipped pique. "Don't you dare belittle the value of those precious items, you ungrateful thing. They may not be traditional art, but they're irreplaceable cultural treasures and you'd do well to remember it. Someday you'll understand the true value of things."

I must've looked shocked at her outburst, my glass halfway to my mouth. She took a moment to run her hands over her hair and smooth back the nonexistent flyaways as she took a deep breath to compose herself. Evangeline didn't lose her temper, not ever. I'd seen her be frostily annoyed. I'd seen her nag without a crack in her polished veneer. But visibly angry? Never. And lecturing me about the true value of things? From Evangeline? Was she kidding me?

CHAPTER TWO

I tried to apologize. Just the idea that Evangeline had actual emotions had thrown me.

I could've slapped myself for that ungrateful thought. If I'd managed to piss off my stepmother, I wasn't sure how I'd get the rent paid this month. She let me stew about it a moment, and then her face relaxed as much as it was able with all of the Botox. After she collected herself, she pulled a check out of her purse and slid it across the table. I grabbed for it before she could snatch it back, and noticed that she'd written it for three hundred dollars more than my rent. Now I really felt bad. "Evangeline, I did tell you that my rent was only five hundred dollars a month, didn't I?"

She gave me a serene smile, a one-hundred-and-eighty-degree change from just moments before. "Of course I know what your rent costs, my dear; I was there when you signed the paperwork. I just felt your father would want me to look after you better than that. After all, he did make me promise to take care of you."

I stammered something that sounded appreciative, still in shock at her turnaround.

She continued. "You'll have some expenses getting started that I'm sure you weren't expecting. Of course, I expect you to buy a decent watch, as well. You'll need to be sure to get yourself to class on time. I can't imagine how you made it through college without someone to ensure you went to all of your classes without being late. And someone certainly needs to look after you if you don't have the social graces to think about what you say before you say it."

And there it was. The dig. Not that I wasn't grateful for the money. Setting up house was more expensive than I'd budgeted for, and my savings were taking quite a beating. Who knew just how fast bed linens, and brooms, and pots and pans could blow a budget? I certainly hadn't realized how expensive it would be.

I felt bad about belittling something that obviously meant so much to her. "I appreciate it, Evangeline. Is there anything I can do to help you this week?" It'd be hard to juggle my first week of law school with keeping her happy, but I'd fouled up, and I knew it.

"Well, if you would be a dear, the art institute is having a fundraiser on Friday night. If you could show up in an appropriate outfit and pass out programs, I would appreciate it; and you'd get a free meal out of it as well."

Done. It was the least I could do for her when she'd covered the extra expenses that had kept me up late last night budgeting and recalculating in my head, worrying about how I'd afford food for the next two weeks. There's only so much Top Ramen a person can eat. "I'll be there."

As I left the restaurant, I was congratulating myself at giving her what she wanted. The whole meal hadn't lasted long, so I still had time to get back to my place to unpack a few more boxes and get a good night's sleep.

I went home and straightened up my apartment, then began organizing my backpack and my notebooks to embark on my first day of law school. This was what I'd been working for. I wished Dad could be here. He used to send me off to my first day of school with a hand-packed lunch, complete with goofy I-love-you note and cookies, even when Evangeline hadn't approved.

I went to bed early that night, trying not to fantasize about how interesting law school would be, how much I was looking forward to it. I couldn't wait to join the clinic program the law school had. One day, I'd represent people in court and make a difference in their lives.

Yeah, I know. Real life isn't all hearts and rainbows.

I had set the alarm, set a back-up alarm, had my things all packed and ready to go, as well as organized for note-taking frenzy. I was ready.

Or so I thought.

The next morning, I woke up early and made it to class with plenty of time to spare. I got organized, opened my notebook to the first page and was ready to take notes. I was well-rested, ready, and eager to see what would happen next. I was looking forward to law school, ready for the challenge, and I couldn't wait.

Within five minutes, I was in trouble. And it had nothing to do with my stepmother.

"Ms. Grimm, do you mean to tell this class that you failed to check the assignment board for the first day assignments?" The contracts professor snapped at me as the entire class watched. I frantically skimmed the case as he waited for an answer. It had something to do with one party offering a contract to another, but it just didn't make a lot of sense to me. I was toast.

"I apologize, sir. I didn't check the board, because I didn't realize that we'd have homework for the first day of class." Could I sink any lower in my seat? Maybe if I just fell over dead, the embarrassment would be over and I could go home to cry.

He huffed at me, and the class tittered. "Ms. Grimm, you realize that I only allow four unexcused absences before I fail a student?"

Gulp. "Yes sir, I do." He'd announced it the moment he started the class, less than fifteen minutes ago. I written it down at the top of the notes I'd been trying to take, but it's impossible to take coherent notes when I didn't understand what he was talking about. It was like taking notes in Martian and expecting those of us living on earth to understand it.

"Being unprepared is as bad as failing to appear for class; this will count as an unexcused absence. The same goes for any other student in this class for the rest of the semester. Be prepared, or don't waste my time. Exciting careers in other fields await you if you cannot move yourself to do the work. Mr. Templeton, could you save Ms. Grimm and give us the facts of the case in the assigned reading for today?" he asked, as he turned to someone else.

My face was on fire, the blood pounding in my ears. I buried my face in the textbook and tried to follow along as Professor Higgenbottom raked Mr. Templeton over the coals. The class continued, but I just wanted to go home. This wasn't what I'd imagined law school to be. I'd thought that we'd debate the law, rather than be chastised like misbehaving children who'd failed to do their chores. Was I wasting the money I'd inherited from Dad by spending it on law school tuition? Did I really belong here?

Croak. "Wow, some people are really clueless," a deep voice

coming from somewhere in front of me muttered.
What the hell? The person directly in front of me was a petite
blond woman. That couldn't be her voice, could it? Who was talking?
I couldn't figure out where the sound was coming from. I didn't
see anything, and I didn't want to draw any attention to myself. I tried
not to respond, hoping I hadn't already been noticed.
    Croak. It sounded like a frog. And a really big one, at that.

CHAPTER THREE

People were starting to look around, but no one wanted to be in the line of fire.

There had to be a window open. The frog kept croaking and ribbit-ing as the class continued, but no one got up to close the window. I suspected that the rest of the class was trying to avoid coming to Professor Higgenbottom's attention. Maybe I wasn't the only one who'd screwed up by missing the first day assignments. I hoped the next person called on would be the mysterious mutterer, and I hoped they hadn't done the work. That would serve them right for making me feel like I'd lost my mind.

The whole class breathed a collective sigh of relief at the end of the hour, and the professor's parting shot that he'd taken it easy on us wasn't helping the general stress level in the room. I bolted away from my humiliation and that weird noise as fast as I could, but I wasn't quite fast enough to avoid everyone.

"Look, honey, don't worry about it. I heard he can be a real bear, but my cousin went to school here and told me he really does prepare students well for the bar exam. That's the bottom line, isn't it?" My good friend from high school, Mia Andersen, was standing there, waiting for me. She pulled her long blond hair back into a ponytail and slung her backpack over her shoulder to head for our next class.

"Thanks, Mia. Seriously, though, I feel like my stomach is about to drop straight through my feet. Why does law school have to be this way? We're all adults; we shouldn't be treated like irresponsible children." I knew I was whining, but I figured I'd earned the right to be a little upset with the humiliation I'd just endured.

Mia grinned at me as we walked out into the hallway. "You just happened to land in the line of fire today. I'm sure everyone will be there at some point. Meanwhile, there's a few of us meeting for coffee after the last class of the day to talk about forming a study group. Wanna come?"

I forced myself to smile back, even though my stomach still felt like I'd drunk heated needles dipped in Tabasco. It did help to think that we were all going through this together. We went on to our next class, Torts, where a similar scene was repeated, although thankfully, not with me. The other student who'd incurred the professor's wrath was just as upset as I was, and when the day was over, Mia and I retreated to a nearby coffee shop to commiserate.

While we waited on the others to arrive, we looked over our schedules. We both had the four core classes–Torts, Contracts, Property, and Civil Procedure– at the same times throughout the week, but we were in different classes for our Legal Writing course. It looked like Tuesdays would be the longest day, five hours of class with the first one at nine in the morning and the last class not ending until six in the evening, but we'd have long breaks in between to get more studying done at the library. Each class met multiple times through the week, so we'd be spending plenty of time at the law school.

Thanks to Evangeline's generosity I had the cash to get a cup of coffee, but I still didn't order the expensive frou–frou drinks on the menu. I like my coffee strong and black; and I didn't think a lot of sugar, whipped cream, or flavored syrups would sit too well on my still-nervous stomach. Besides, with Evangeline's check, I was looking forward to heading to the grocery store later to stock up on something other than store brand macaroni and cheese.

Mia was a natural organizer. Before long, we'd all agreed to meet on Wednesday evenings and Sunday afternoons for study meetings, to talk about the week before, help each other, and generally commiserate. The others in our group were just as scared as we were. David was a middle-aged man with a girlfriend who was a single mom, and was going back to school after being an insurance salesman for the last ten years. Mike was a retired cop, who decided to go to law school when he had to take an early retirement due to a leg injury. Leann was younger than anyone else in the first year class. She'd graduated from high school early and finished college at nineteen. I hoped she'd handle the stress of law school better than I was handling it at the moment.

Croak. "What a bunch of Nervous Nellies." I heard that same deep voice I'd heard in class. *Oh, crap. The Mad Mutterer was in my study group?* I wasn't sure I liked that idea. Wait, I hadn't seen any of their lips move when I'd heard that statement made.

"Do you hear that?" I asked.

They all nodded, and we looked around again, but still couldn't figure out the source of the noise. When we didn't hear it again, we continued our plans to stay on track with the assignments and outlining we'd have to do in order to be prepared for exams in three months. Law school grades were whatever the student got on the final; there wasn't an average of tests and projects and assignments like in high school and college. With everything riding on one exam score, we hoped that the stress of preparing would be less if we helped each other.

Croooaaaaaaak. Ribbit.

I'd had enough. "Am I going crazy, or is there a frog stalking us?"

They all laughed. Leann spoke up. "I heard it in class, too. I thought I was losing my mind. Or maybe it's some kind of prank being played by another student to get us all in trouble."

We agreed that we'd all heard it, but no one knew where it was coming from. We searched again, but still had no luck in finding the offensive amphibian. The noise was starting to grate on me, but we were just about done with our meeting. I tried to ignore the frog, and so did everyone else. If it was a prank, why was it targeting us? Was it some second or third-year law student having fun with the newbies? Or some fraternity prank?

"Where're we going to meet? I can't afford to meet at a coffee shop or restaurant all the time." I was still mentally counting and budgeting Evangeline's check, and worrying about how I'd keep up with expenses once the extra money was gone. I couldn't count on getting extra money from her every month. Our agreement was that she pay my rent, nothing else. I might swing a bit more this month because of the extra funds, but I didn't want to count on it.

"I can't afford to, either," said Mike. "Is there another way to do this?"

"Why don't we just rotate going to each other's houses?" Mia suggested. "That way we aren't tempted to spend too much money.

Besides, a pot of spaghetti or a few hamburgers on a grill is a whole lot cheaper to put together than going out to eat, and if we take turns, the cost shouldn't be too bad."

I jumped in. "Here's another idea; why not reserve a meeting room in the library for a study session right after our last Wednesday classes, and then Sunday afternoon can be more relaxed at our houses. That way we're not stressed about hosting everyone more than once a month or so, we don't spend too much money, and we help each other as much as possible."

We all agreed, and I volunteered to host our first Sunday meeting while I still had the extra cash. Mia agreed to reserve the library study room for Wednesday. As we trudged out to our cars, carrying heavy backpacks and anticipating a long night of reading for tomorrow, my cell phone went off. It was Evangeline.

"I was just calling to remind you of your promise to help at the fundraiser on Friday night, dear. We're shorthanded, so you can't forget, and I don't want the museum to pay for your meal if you can't show up."

I had an idea. "Evangeline, you told me I could eat dinner for free if I helped, right?"

"Yes, of course." She sounded annoyed that I had asked, but I wanted to make sure.

"I bet I could get a few more volunteers to help if I could make the same promise to them." We'd all get a break on Friday night, and get to socialize a bit over something other than cases and lectures. And hopefully, they'd be a buffer from the worst of Evangeline's insults, even as I made up for my insensitivity yesterday. I call that a win-win situation.

"Why, that would be wonderful. Go ahead and tell your friends, but let me know how many so I can keep an accurate head count. It wouldn't do for the caterers to run out of food for the paying guests because they gave it all to the volunteers." She clicked off without saying goodbye, as she usually did when she was done with a conversation. I'd have been annoyed at anyone else, but I was used to it from her. I'd heard her be more polite to people whose opinion she actually cared about, but I knew I wasn't in that category.

I hung up and ran after the others.

"Anyone want to go to a party and get a free meal Friday night?" I asked, slightly out of breath from running after them with forty pounds of textbooks weighing down my backpack.

They all turned around and I relayed my stepmother's offer. David declined, citing child care issues, but the others agreed. Evangeline was ecstatic when I called her back, and I was actually looking forward to it. Maybe it wouldn't be as boring as I'd thought. After all, I'd have people to talk to, free dinner, and distractions from Evangeline. I figured I could handle that without a problem; the week was starting to look up.

Except for the mystery voice following me around, that is. I'd have to do something to figure out who was making me feel like I'd lost my mind. If I didn't, I'd never get any studying done tonight.

CHAPTER FOUR

I headed home that afternoon with a smile on my face. Law school wasn't going to be easy, but I'd made a few friends and we had weekend plans to look forward to. Even working at one of Evangeline's fundraisers was guaranteed to be an interesting night. She always had the city's best caterers, and if nothing else, I'd be able to amuse myself at the sight of the city's upper crust acting like they were hoity-toity society mavens. It's not like we're in New York or L.A. Our concept of big money just isn't all that big; we don't exactly have any Hiltons or Rockefellers in the greater Dayton metropolitan area.

I got out of my car and walked up to the small patio outside of my apartment, my mind chewing over the possibility of a fun Friday night and distracted from most of my surroundings. And I was away from that deep voice that had been bothering me all day.

Ribbit. Croak. " 'Bout time you got here."

There it was again. It had followed me home from the coffee shop. Or at least it sounded the same.

"God damn it!" I yelled. "I can't lose my mind right now." I still had to catch up on the Contracts homework, and do the rest of today's assignments, and to read for Property class for tomorrow. I had a fleeting thought that my priorities were completely out of whack, but I just couldn't face another day like today.

Wait a minute. This was a frog. I shouldn't be able to hear it inside. If I went in my apartment and made sure all the windows were closed, I'd be able to block out the sound enough to concentrate on all the reading for tonight.

A deep voice answered from right behind me as I put the key in my lock. "If you don't want your neighbors thinking you're crazy, then I suggest you stop yelling and cursing in public when you're alone. That's a one way ticket to a rubber room."

"Who the hell are you?" I spun around. There was no one there.

The same deep voice rumbled again, like he was speaking right over my shoulder. "Spinning around in a circle and talking to someone whom others can't see isn't going to help you in the proof of sanity department, either. Besides, you're making me dizzy, as well. Cut it out, or I'll yak on you."

I couldn't help it; I spun around again. There was still no one standing there. I unlocked the door and turned to look back over my shoulder as I slipped inside. I had to see if any of my new neighbors were watching me doing the hokey-pokey on the patio. I still didn't see anyone outside, and there definitely wasn't anyone standing close enough to account for the voice, so I shut the door and dropped my law book-heavy backpack.

"Ouch!" I heard simultaneously with the thud of books hitting the floor.

Huh? There wasn't another person in my apartment; it isn't big enough for a human-sized being to hide and I didn't have enough stuff for anyone to hide behind. There couldn't be anyone here without me seeing them.

I'd been under a lot of stress on my first day. Maybe I *was* losing it. It had to be my imagination. I shook my head to clear it before I started to unpack my backpack for a night of studying and reading.

When I pulled my Torts book out of the bag, there was a frog beneath it. It was no ordinary frog; it was bigger than both of my fists put together. I had to use both hands to pull it out of my backpack, its skinny frog legs dangling over the sides of my palms.

I did the only thing I could think of. I shrieked at the top of my lungs like a scared little girl as I picked up the slimy green amphibian, then ran outside to put him in the grass beyond the sidewalk in front of my apartment. I was happy to note that none of my neighbors were outside to witness my freak out.

I wiped my hands on the seat of my jeans; sure they were covered in some kind of invisible frog goo, and shuddered as I did so.

"Well, that sure looked brave, Janie Grimm. Big tough city girl scared of a little frog? I didn't know you'd be such a wimp, and to think I'd been looking forward to meeting you." There it was again, that deep voice, coming from somewhere near my toes. It was the same voice from class, the same voice from the coffee shop, the same voice from my patio. But there was no one else around.

I looked down, and the frog was blinking in slow motion. "It couldn't be," I whispered.

"And . . . wait for it; she's getting the picture . . ." His lips clearly moved as he spoke.

"This must be what going mad feels like." I wanted to reach up and rub the hallucination out of my eyes.

The frog laughed. I didn't know frogs could laugh. Oh, what the hell was I thinking? I didn't think frogs could *talk*. Amphibian laughter was the least of my problems at the moment.

I ran back inside and slammed the door. No frogs inside my apartment. It was an air pocket of sanity in a bubble of crazy. I sighed and ran my hands over my face. I must be hearing things. No way was this really happening.

After a quick search of my apartment failed to turn up any intruders, and a quick glance out the window showed me that no burglars, bad guys, bogeymen, or neighbors were outside, I figured I'd get my work done and go to bed early. I tried to convince myself the voice was the result of an overactive imagination, extreme stress, and too many meals costing less than a dollar.

Once I'd calmed down, I settled onto the couch to start on my homework. I opened my Torts book and took out my highlighter, holding the cap in my mouth as I tried to concentrate on the reckless standard needed to constitute negligence. I was trying to disregard the nagging feeling it wasn't my imagination making the frog appear to speak.

The next thing I heard was a deep voice singing Kermit the Frog's "*It's Not Easy Being Green*" outside my front door. I tried to ignore it. There wasn't anyone out there. It couldn't be the frog. I peeked out the window again, and the frog was sitting at the edge of my patio, singing his heart out. No one else was around, but it was almost dinnertime. The neighbors could come home from work at any moment to find a slimy green thing serenading me on the patio.

His song finished, he launched into a loud rendition of "*Who's Afraid of the Big Bad Wolf?*" Maybe the newscaster yesterday wasn't wrong; maybe the moon really was made of green cheese, aliens really had landed at Roswell, and winning lottery tickets really do grow on trees. No matter what, though, I didn't have the time to deal with being crazy. I had fifty pages of case law to read for tomorrow, and I didn't understand any of it.

"Will you kindly shut the hell up?" My fists balled at my sides, I hissed softly at him through the window and around the highlighter cap still in my mouth.

He blinked at me slowly and kept singing, "Hey there Little Red Riding Hood, you sure are lookin' good . . ." It took me a minute to place it as "Li'l Red Riding Hood" from Sam the Sham and the Pharaohs, a band Dad used to listen to on the oldies station when I was a kid.

The whole world was going crazy. I saw my neighbor, Chris, a brawny guy stationed at nearby Wright Patterson Air Force base, as he pulled up in his Chevy extended-cab truck. The frog winked at me, slowly turning to face Chris as he came up the sidewalk. Rather than risk Chris thinking me ready for the funny farm—hey, he was cute and had impressive chest muscles that he showed off in tight t-shirts—I quickly opened the door and scooped up the frog and ran inside, barely swallowing the "Ew, ew, ew" that came to my lips when I touched him. I'm not big on slimy things, so sue me.

I got back inside, closed the drain on the kitchen sink, and placed the frog in the sink. Before I got back to the door, he was already talking again. I ignored him until I got the door shut and the lock secured behind me.

"Boy, are you paranoid, Janie Grimm. Makes me think they've already got to you or something. Got a beer in this place?"

"A beer?" I settled one hip against the counter and crossed my arms over my chest. "You've got to be kidding me. You're a talking frog; you know my name; you showed up out of nowhere, but the only thing you can say is 'you got a beer in this place'? And for your information, beer's expensive. I don't keep any around."

The frog belched, long and loud. Great. Not only did I have a talking frog in my apartment, he was also an obnoxious pig. Er, frog. Whatever.

"Are you done?" he asked.

"Who the hell are you and what the hell do you want?"

"That's the first intelligent thing you've said today, Janie, and believe me, I should know. I've been stuck in your book bag all day. By the way, that was pretty embarrassing this morning in Contracts class when you didn't have a clue. Though that professor of yours did seem to know what he was talking about."

I gritted my teeth. I could add know-it-all to the rapidly growing list of things I didn't like about this frog. "You still didn't answer my question."

"I guess I didn't, did I? Well, tenaciousness will serve you well in trial, future counselor. You can call me Bert."

"What kind of name is that?" I pinched my own arm to see if this was some sort of weird dream. It hurt.

"You're gonna want to stop that, or you'll bruise. Besides, I'm as real as you are. My name's Englebert Maximus Jorgenson Horace the Sixth. Bert's about the best I'm gonna get out of that. I swear my parents hated me to saddle me with such an awful mouthful of a name."

What can one say to that? "I guess I didn't realize frogs named their children." Wow. That was lame. Of course, what could I expect? I was making small talk with a frog. That wasn't a situation I was prepared for, and it certainly wasn't something Emily Post had ever covered. On the other hand, it wasn't something Evangeline was around to see and get after me for violating some arcane etiquette rule.

He rolled his eyes. "I wasn't always a frog, you nitwit. I was a human, a prince. Well, a younger prince, anyway. I had four older brothers, so I wasn't getting anywhere near the throne. I was an advisor to my oldest brother on matters that affected our people, including dispute resolution. I gave good advice, so I was popular, and that made me a target for the witch."

"You believe in witches?" I asked.

"I'm sure you don't believe in them, but I do," he said. "It's hard not to, after one turns you into a frog."

He had a point. That'd convince me, too. "So, why are you here?" I asked. I opened the refrigerator door and got out a pitcher of iced tea

I'd made when I was unpacking boxes yesterday. I might not have any beer, but tea bags are cheap. I poured some into a small bowl and set it in the sink next to him. He made a face, but he drank. "I'm not some dumb ass pet. I can drink out of a mug like a civilized person."

"I'm sorry," I retorted, automatically. "How would I know? I've never served iced tea to a talking frog before." I still didn't believe this was real. It had to be some kind of strange hallucination, dream, or break with reality, and apparently I couldn't ignore it away. If I wasn't worried it would get me kicked out of law school, I'd have hightailed it right to the nearest mental health hospital for evaluation. I wasn't sure I'd be allowed to stay if I was psychotic enough for hospitalization, and there just wasn't a better explanation for what was going on.

He shrugged. I couldn't believe he actually shrugged. Of course, I didn't think frogs had shoulders, either.

"There are bigger things to worry about right now, Janie. I'm here to warn you. You might be in danger."

I resumed my position against the counter with my arms crossed over my chest. "The only person I've pissed off lately is my Contracts professor and he just doesn't seem the murderous rampage type." The man wore a polka-dot bow tie for crying out loud. If there's one thing that doesn't scream psycho killer, it's a polka-dot bow tie. Who wears things like that anymore? Maybe it *was* a sign of an unhinged mind.

"This goes back a lot further than just this morning, Janie. It goes back to your father."

"My father had been sick for a long time before he died. He couldn't have been involved with anything that could come up now, and you have no right to talk about him." Rage, like a white hot spear in my belly, rose up in the back of my throat. I fought not to grit my teeth as I spat back at him. "He suffered and he fought as hard as he could, but nothing worked. He's gone. And no one can do anything about it." I caught myself crying, and took a deep breath, hard and fast through my nose. I mopped the tears off my face, trying to shut off the waterworks. I guess I was still mad that my father wasn't here any more.

Bert tried to say something, but I cut him off. "You know nothing about my father."

"Yes, Janie, I actually do. Your father didn't die of cancer. He was murdered."

I was still trying to get a hold on my emotions, and realized my hands were clenched into fists, my mouth opening and closing repeatedly like a fish out of water. It took me a minute to respond in a coherent sentence through the anger and grief trying to shut down my brain. "What the hell are you talking about? I watched him die. I held his hand through chemo treatment after radiation treatment after surgery. Of course he had cancer. No one killed him. And now, just months after he's gone, you have the audacity to show up here, make me question my sanity, tell me I'm stupid, and that my father was murdered?"

Bert nodded his head. "You might not want to hear it, but it's the truth."

I snatched up the bowl of iced tea and dumped it in the other side of the double sink. Petty, I know, but it did make me feel better. "There's no way what you're saying could be the truth. Despite what you might think, I'm not a complete idiot. I know what I saw. I know what he went through. It's time to go. You've said what you came to say. I have work to do." I didn't have the time to lose my mind, and I certainly didn't have the time or the emotional resources to talk about losing my dad with a figment of my imagination. I was done talking to him.

He scrambled around in the sink, slipping and sliding and trying to dodge my grasping hands. I meant to kick him out of my house, though I knew it would be a struggle to concentrate now that I was thinking about Dad. I missed the smell of his cologne, the cheap peppermints he always carried in his pockets, and the smile he always gave me at the end of a bad day, even on his last day. It was time for Bert to go, because the memories hurt on a day I could have used reassurance and a big hug from Dad.

He looked panicked as he evaded me. "Please, don't kick me out there. I won't be safe in this form. You don't understand what they went through to place me with you."

"Place you with me?" I stopped grabbing for him. He slid toward the drain. "Who placed you with me? What do you mean?"

He ignored my questions, but he nodded his head as he spoke, cowering at the back of the sink. "Something's after you. You won't know where to look unless I tell you. They sent me to warn you and to help you spot danger. It's about all I'm good for at this size."

No way was this toad staying in my house tonight. He wouldn't tell me who he worked for, but his fear seemed genuine. We compromised, in that I agreed to let him stay on my patio, and wedge himself on the threshold between the storm door and the screen door if he felt the need. I couldn't quite catch the slippery little slime ball, so he allowed himself to be picked up once I made the promise he didn't have to leave completely. I didn't care, as long as he was outside, and he was quiet. I didn't really want him reciting every line from "It's a Mad, Mad, Mad, Mad World" for my neighbors throughout the night. That would just be the icing on the proverbial psycho-nut cake.

I set him outside, on the threshold, like I'd promised, and gingerly shut the door behind him, throwing every lock, deadbolt, and chain latch I had. It took a while for me to focus on my work, with the barrage of memories about my dad, but I had to be prepared for school in the morning. I couldn't fail when everything my father left me was riding on my performance.

Screw that frog. He was crazy. He was making me think I was crazy. Tomorrow I would wake up and find that he didn't exist. Or at least, I hoped so.

CHAPTER FIVE

When I woke up the next morning, my alarm clock was bleating an insistent shriek in my ear. I sat bolt upright, panicking when I saw that the clock read seven a.m. I'd meant to get up at five, to have another two hours to go over notes for class today. I needed to prove to everyone I belonged in law school after my miserable showing yesterday. And I had a stop to make first.

It turned out I hadn't reset the alarm for five, but instead had left it at yesterday's setting. Too late to fix it now, I dressed quickly and packed my bag for the day's classes. Of course, I had to drop my backpack on the patio and run back inside to make sure I'd turned the coffeepot off. That's something I always forget to do. In fact, the morning stop to check the coffeepot was rapidly becoming part of my morning routine.

Fire hazard averted, I scooped up my backpack and headed to the car. I didn't even turn on the radio. My morning errand was too somber for music or radio humor.

I was visiting my dad's gravesite.

Yesterday had been an abject lesson in humiliation and embarrassment. I needed to talk to my dad, and this was the only way left to me. I'd figured that visiting early in the morning would mean an empty cemetery, where no one would hear me talking to Dad.

I was wrong.

I pulled in and put Dad's old Buick in park. There was a man with flame red hair standing near my father's grave. He looked familiar, but I couldn't place him. I sighed. It was a public cemetery; I couldn't shoo him away or call the police just because he happened to be there. I'd just have to deal with it, and hope he'd either leave quickly or leave me alone. Or both.

I left my backpack in the car and headed for Dad's grave. I'd just say hello and spend some time trying to remember what it was like to sit in a park with my dad. He used to take me to feed the ducks at a park near our house. We'd sit together quietly, but it was peaceful, and I needed a bit of peace in my life. If I shut my eyes tightly, could I pretend he was sitting beside me without wondering if I really was losing touch with reality? I decided that would be pushing it, after all the strange things the day before.

His headstone was a simple black granite marker, stark, with only his name, Robert Jonathan Grimm, and the dates of his birth and death. Evangeline and I'd butted heads on an appropriate marker for his grave. My ideas for something meaningful weren't extravagant enough for her, and her ideas were horrifying to me. Finally, the granite guy had stepped in and told us that we had to decide on something, and sometimes the easiest thing to do was a simple marker. He told us that we could always replace it later if we ever agreed on anything. At this rate, Dad would never have anything more, but it suited him a lot better than the angel wings, lacy hearts, and gushy love sentiments from Evangeline. Gag me.

"Ms. Grimm? My name's Aiden Ferguson. Can I talk to you a moment?"

I kept walking even as I pulled out my cell phone, poising my fingers over the keys to dial 911. My own internal weirdness-meter blared an alarm signal in my head, even as I thought I'd recognized him from somewhere. Wait, how did this guy know who I was? It wasn't like I was wearing a name tag.

"Ms. Grimm, it's really important," he called, tripping over his own feet as he came my way. Suddenly, he fell to the ground, got up, tripped on the nearest headstone, got back up, and slid in a puddle, until he found himself teetering precariously in front of me.

Wow. I've never seen such an uncoordinated display in real life. I've only seen something similar in old slapstick comedies, and I didn't think it was possible for anyone to pull it off without using a banana peel and doing it on purpose. He had my attention for that fact alone. "Can I help you?" I didn't have a lot of time, but it was like a train wreck. I couldn't look away. And I still had my cell phone at the ready to call the cops.

"Ms. Grimm, thank you! I've needed to talk with you ever since I saw you at the restaurant."

That's where I'd seen him before; he was the waiter who'd looked so spooked when Evangeline lost her temper, running off to refill our already full water glasses. I'd thought he was a flake then, even though he was cute. He wasn't doing much to change my initial impression. I turned away from him and took the last step towards Dad's grave. Maybe if I ignored him, he'd go away.

No such luck; he seemed determined to talk with me.

"Ms. Grimm, I know you won't want to believe me, but I can help you. And you're going to need it. It sounds crazy, I know, but you're in a position you won't be able to get out of on your own." He reached up and swiped his hair back from his forehead, putting on a University of Dayton Flyers baseball cap he pulled out from a back pocket.

I turned on him. I didn't need help from a clumsy dork, especially one I didn't know. And the whole "Ms. Grimm" thing was a little too formal for me. Had my morning breakfast been Crazy-Os instead of store brand Wheaties? "What do you plan to help me with? You don't know anything about me; there's no way you could know what problems I might have in my life. So, if you don't mind, I'd like to spend a moment of peace thinking about my father before I have to jump back into my shitty, stressful, and stupid life."

He waited until I'd stepped away and was settling myself on the small bench near Dad's gravestone before he said anything else. "It's Jane, but you go by Janie, don't you? And your dad was a professor of history and folklore here in Dayton. Your stepmother's on the board at the Art Institute, and you're a first-year student at the law school. You just moved into your first apartment, and you live alone."

"Are you spying on me? I don't know who you think you are, but I can file a restraining order against you and have you arrested if you violate it. Stay away from me and don't ever follow me again. And a little advice? Showing some girl how well you've stalked her does not exactly engender trust." I wondered if I still had that old can of pepper spray Dad gave me when I started college. If I did, it probably wasn't in my bag today; it was probably still in a box, one of the ones I hadn't unpacked yet. One of many I still hadn't gotten to yet. And who knows if the spray would actually work when I needed it.

"If I do what you tell me to do, you'll be dead within the next six months. Your dad told us to go away as well, and look where he is."

"How dare you speak about my father like that? Refusing to talk with you has nothing to do with the cancer that killed him. Unless you're some kind of doctor, there's nothing you could've done even if he had talked to you, and unless you're some kind of weird voodoo priest or magician, you can't bring him back either, so go away." What the hell was he talking about? It wasn't like cancer was contagious. And besides, didn't all those cheesy horror movies advise against bringing someone back from the dead?

He sat down on my bench, facing the opposite way.

"My predecessor tried to talk with your father. I tried to talk with him. He didn't want anything to do with us. There was probably some academic bias working against us, too; he'd heard of us, and he'd heard we were a bunch of story collectors. The truth is, however, we're more than that."

"Yeah, you're a bunch of stalker whack jobs. You need to leave." I tried to get up, to walk around him, but he reached up one hand and laid it on my shoulder.

"Your dad thought the same thing at first. My mentor, John Brown, approached him years ago. I can tell you about it, if you like."

As much as I wanted him to leave, if he had a story about Dad, I wanted to hear it. I still would have preferred time alone, but this was a close second. I checked the clock on my cell phone since I hadn't picked up a watch yet despite Evangeline's nagging, and I still had an hour to kill before my first class. I could listen to his remembrances of my father, and then I could leave and never talk to him again. That could work. I sat back down.

He ignored my internal monologue and kept talking. "You'd have still been a kid, and it was just before you lost your mother. John told me your father had just gotten tenure at the university, and he was so happy that he didn't want to listen when we told him something might be wrong."

I wondered what Dad was like when my mother was still around. I didn't remember her well; I remembered the scent of her perfume, the roughness of her corduroy jacket on my cheek, and the softness of her hand holding mine. I remembered my father's smiling face as he wrapped his arms around her waist in the kitchen. They were very happy, but I didn't know my mother as a person. I don't have an independent recollection of any family events prior to Dad's wedding to Evangeline. Then I remembered the ice cream cones, the zoo, and other outings designed to get me away from my stepmother when she was having one of her famous headaches. It seemed like most of my good memories from childhood were from those outings with Dad.

Aiden continued. "From what I've heard, John tried several times to talk with your father about The Legacy, but your dad didn't want anything to do with it. In fact, he told me once, privately, that he thought John was delusional. He'd never found any reference to the Holder or Legacy in his own research, and he thought we were a bunch of crackpots."

I didn't have the nerve to tell him I agreed about the crackpot label, but how do you tell someone they're crazy when they're not listening? Besides, what the hell was the Holder and whose Legacy? I refrained from asking. I didn't want to distract Aiden from telling his story, and I didn't know how long he'd take to answer my questions instead of just talking about Dad. I'd listen to a lot of insanity if it meant hearing more about my dad.

"Well, your father was polite to me when I was just starting out. I first met him as a student a couple of years ago. He wasn't teaching a lot then, but there was an elective class he taught as an adjunct professor just before he went into the hospital that last time. I thought he was a really nice man, and awful smart, but he thought I was nuts when I took up with John's group."

Regardless of what I thought about Aiden, he was saying nice things about Dad. And it was nice to hear that other people thought good things about him.

He handed me his business card. Of course, he spilled a small stack of them on the ground as he tried to pull one out of his pocket for me, but he had them scooped up before I could help him. It looked like he was used to being uncoordinated.

"This is us. We aren't just collectors of folk stories. We collect real stories, but we also try to help people who find themselves in situations they don't know how to resolve. We think you're headed for one of those situations, Janie. We're actually here to help."

Despite the fact I was uncomfortable with the amount of information he had about my life, he looked very earnest. He continued to pack his spilled business cards back into his pocket as he talked. It was kind of cute, even though I thought he must be high on something to believe a word of what he was saying.

"I appreciate your concern, but I'm still not sure what you could do to bring Dad back, make Evangeline rational, or get my reading done for class today. It was nice talking to you, but stay away from me." He might have been a creepy stalker boy, but he had good memories of Dad so it was worth listening to him. Besides, what would their help cost? I didn't think that fees for folk tale collectors were in my budget no matter how much extra money Evangeline gave me.

He let me go; I don't think he really expected me to walk away but I took advantage of it to head toward the car, glancing at his card as I went. Whatever this group of his was—and his card said they called themselves F.A.B.L.E.S., the Foundation for Ancestry, Biography, Legends, Epics, and Stories—I was comforted by the fact Dad had heard of them. He might have thought they were crackpots, but he did know them. I certainly hadn't expected anything like that. I slid into the front seat of the car and started it up when I heard a deep voice again.

"You know, you're going to need to call him soon and get his help."

I screamed, long and loud, twisting around to make sure no one was waiting in the backseat of my car to slit my throat like I'd seen in so many movies. I didn't see anything, so I sat back down in the driver's seat, my heart pounding in my throat.

Bert stuck his head out of the top of my backpack. "Not exactly the reaction I like to get from a woman," he quipped.

"Why are you still here?" I yelled. I'd chalked up last night's amphibian interaction as a bad coffee-and-stress-induced dream. Besides, he was supposed to be gone this morning.

"You said I could stay in your doorway last night, but you didn't say anything about today so I hitched a ride. I'll stay quiet, I promise. I enjoyed listening to the class yesterday, and I think something strange might happen soon. You'll need my advice when it does, so you might as well have me close by."

I didn't know what was worse, that he'd hitched a ride, that I had a frog in my backpack, or that he'd actually enjoyed Contracts class. "I give up," I said, giving him permission.

My life was just too weird. Maybe if Bert kept his promise to keep quiet, I could at least pretend my life was semi-normal. Maybe I could forget all about the last twenty-four hours long enough to get things done today. As it was, I needed to get to class. I didn't really have time to argue. I guess I was feeling magnanimous after listening to someone else's good opinion of Dad.

I put the car in drive and headed for the law school.

Chapter Six

I was early to my first class, and arrived to find Mia sitting in the classroom, looking over her notes for the first Civil Procedure class. I dumped my stuff next to her and sat down.

"Hey there," she said. "Are you letting your hair grow?"

Huh? "What are you talking about?" I asked.

"It seems longer. I just wondered if I'd missed it with all the first day craziness." She capped her highlighter and put down her pen. "It's a different look for you. I don't think I've ever seen you with hair longer than your shoulders. I like it."

I shook my head. I'd just gotten it trimmed two weeks ago. I reached up to find that my hair was longer, and thought my new hairdresser must have been too conservative with my last trim. I shook it off, vowing to be more specific the next time I had an appointment.

We talked about the study group; making plans for that Sunday's meeting, talking about the fund-raising dinner we'd go to on Friday night with Evangeline's friends, and laughing about our fears yesterday. "It seems like hazing, like we're rushing some sort of law related fraternity," I commented.

"I'd rather eat a live goldfish than go through what you had to deal with yesterday. No offense, but this is more like mental boot camp than a fraternity," she responded, laughing at my grimace over the first day debacle.

"At least a fraternity would have some good parties. I haven't heard of anything like that in law school. Of course, it's early in the year. You never know how crazy things might get after we all get in the groove. And there's always the week after finals are over to let one's hair down."

"You're probably right. Anyway, let's hope today goes better than yesterday," she said, turning again to her notes.

The other students began trickling in. The professor wasn't far behind, spouting some nonsense about "fee simple". I didn't know what that meant, but at least I wasn't getting called on. I could handle that.

Professor Talbot, a tall guy with a long grey ponytail, wire-rimmed glasses, and a potbelly, kept looking at me. I couldn't figure out why, but I wasn't ready to be in the spotlight again, so I tried to pay attention without looking like I wanted to answer a question. As long as he wasn't asking me to explain some obscure property term I didn't understand, I was fine. He could make whatever faces at me he wanted to as long as he didn't call on me.

As different students answered his questions, the professor never took his eyes off me. I caught Mia staring at me as well. I had this insane urge to stand up and yell at them to cut it out, but I didn't want to risk looking crazier than I already did after failing to get my work done yesterday.

Oh well, I thought, trying to scribble down notes I hoped would make sense after I finally figured out what all the terms meant. I remembered seeing them in the cases I'd read last night, but I hadn't taken the time to look them up. I wouldn't make that mistake again.

"Ms. Grimm," the professor intoned, cutting off the student who'd been droning on in answer to the last question.

"Yes, sir?" I asked. Oh, crap. Here we go again.

"I don't appreciate practical jokes in my class."

"Of course not, sir."

"Then cut it out right now."

"Certainly," I responded, without a clue as to what he was talking about.

"I don't know how you're doing it, but make it stop."

I was suddenly getting the mother of all headaches. It felt like someone was pulling, hard, on the back of my hair, but when I turned my head, there wasn't anyone close enough to be grabbing it and the pain wouldn't let up. As I turned back, I felt a yank, and saw my hair. It was long enough to touch the arm of the chair, and a couple of strands had gotten caught in the metal joint between the arm and the back. Wait a minute. My hair wasn't that long. It hadn't been that long, well, ever. What was going on?

I was the only brunette sitting there. Mia had blond hair; the girl next to me did as well. The guy behind me had black hair, and it was jock-buzz cut short. It really was my hair. How did my hair grow out a foot and a half in less than an hour?

"I'm sorry, sir. I really don't know what's going on."

"Then someone's playing a prank on you. Get that hair out of my sight; you're distracting my entire class."

I tried in vain to yank back my hair, but I didn't have any barrettes or hair scrunchies or even rubber bands with me; my hair's normally too short to need them. Mia finally handed me an elastic band out of her purse, and I tried to pull my hair back out of the way, so at least the professor and the other students wouldn't watch me sprouting hair at an alarming rate. I couldn't get kicked out of class. I was too afraid I'd fall further behind and wouldn't be able to catch up.

Professor Talbot glared at me, but he didn't make me leave. The headache kept getting worse, and I kept reaching up to tighten the rubber band, hoping to stay in the classroom. The other students were making a concerted effort not to look at me, which was almost worse than the staring they'd been doing earlier.

I tried to ignore everyone, scribbling furious notes about the lecture, but I wasn't paying attention to what I was writing any longer. Bert was good as his word; not a peep, ribbit, or belch came out of my backpack. My head hurt worse as the class dragged on, and finally the professor dismissed us. Mia waited for me, and I waited for the rest of the class to leave. Good thing, too. I stepped on my own hair when I tried to stand up. That really hurt.

The professor came over to us, and told me that if I was the butt of a bad joke, then he was sorry I had to suffer like that. He said, however, that if I was behind the practical joke, then this was my one warning and I shouldn't return to his class if I planned to pull any other stunts like this. I kept a straight face, agreed to his lecture, and waited until he was done. He finally turned away from us, and Mia and I made a mad dash across the hall to the bathroom, hoping to avoid the curious stares of our classmates.

I looked in the mirror and saw that my normally shoulder-length hair was now down past my knees. I couldn't believe it, but there it was. In looks, in texture, in the smell of my apple-scented shampoo, it was my hair. I wasn't hallucinating. I ran my fingers through it, wondering how in the hell this had happened.

Mia, bless her, ran to the admissions office and borrowed a pair of scissors. She helped me hack it off above my shoulders. The headache began to recede as the weight pulling on my tender scalp lessened, but it never went away completely. I could feel the hair growing, in a painful, itching burn across my head.

She kept asking me what was going on. I didn't have any answers. I was choking back tears, and she kept pushing, asking if I needed to go to the health clinic, or if I needed to go home. She even offered to drive me to the emergency room if I thought I needed it. When I declined all her offers, she looked at me like I'd lost my mind, but she helped me bundle up all the hair we'd cut off and stuff it in the trash can in time for us to get to our next class. I just needed to get through the rest of the day and escape before things could get worse. I wanted nothing more than to get home, but I just didn't feel brave enough to skip class.

We headed off to the next class, despite Mia's constant worry over the state of my well-being. Luckily, I was able to grab the rubber band and yank my hair back again before it got too distracting; it was growing again, just as fast as the last time. I mean, I still got a lot of stares, and there were a lot of distracted students, but the professor seemed oblivious. I took notes throughout Torts and counted the minutes until the end of class; it was a short day, with only three classes. My schedule worked out to a free afternoon every week, and it was today, so if I could get through the morning, I could go home and hide.

When Torts ended, Mia and I repeated the same procedure before I ducked into my Legal Research class. Yet again, she met me after class, and we lopped off my hair, giving me a sense of relief as the heavy weight fell from my sensitive head into the trashcan. I had the sudden, irrelevant thought that the janitor would definitely earn his paycheck today if he had to empty out a huge can full of my hair. I wondered what he'd think when he saw it.

Finally, classes for the day were over. We ended the day with another trim, before I tried to head to my car. I hadn't heard a peep from Bert, and I wondered just how much longer he'd be able to hold it in without giving me his opinion. I knew he'd say something the minute I was in the car, but I didn't want him talking in front of Mia. Goodness knows, she probably thought I was losing my mind anyway without introducing her to the talking frog in my backpack. I'd probably end up looking crazier than I already did if Bert decided to make his presence known.

It took a lot of talking to get her to agree not to follow me home. I had to promise that I'd call if I needed to go to the emergency room, and she said she was going to call and check on me later on. I also had to agree to call her if my hair didn't stop growing, and if the headaches didn't stop. I'm not sure what she'd be able to do about them, but it did feel good that someone cared enough to nag me to take care of myself.

I left her at the front of the school despite her offers to drive me home. I didn't even have the key in my ignition switch when Bert stuck his head up and asked if I was okay. Yeah, he was a frog, and I still wasn't ready to believe he was real, but another being caring if I was okay wasn't a bad thing right then. As long as he didn't talk about Dad or magical woo-woo stuff, I was okay.

"Yeah, I'll be fine. I'll just cut my hair every time I start getting a headache. I've really got to get some reading done."

Bert was quiet for a minute. "You know, you really should call Aiden," he finally said, as I pulled out of the parking spot I'd found that morning on the street, just a couple of blocks away from the law school.

I was astonished. "You're on a first name basis with the dork in the cemetery? How well do you know him?" I was rapidly reassessing my evaluation of Bert as harmless if he was involved with Geeky Stalker Boy. And the name of their group? The Foundation for Ancestry, Biography, Legends, Epics, and Stories sounded like a bunch of nerdy teenagers geeking out in their parents' basement like Star Wars fans who debate on who shot first, Han or Greedo. They weren't my idea of qualified help, but I guess beggars couldn't be choosers.

"I've known him since he was a kid. His mom was one of the

council members, and used to bring him around to meetings when he was just learning to walk. He's always been a little on the clumsy side, and he's not the most socially adept out there, but today really took the cake."

"You were watching?"

He chuckled. "You bet your sweet ass I was. Of course, this is his first lead contact, so I shouldn't laugh. He was probably nervous. Aiden's been the secondary on cases prior to this one, and has always done a bang-up job, but he's never initiated contact before. The council probably thought he'd relate to you better than one of their old fuddy duddies; some of those guys have been doing this so long they sound crazy when they talk outside of council meetings."

That assumed, of course, they didn't sound crazy *during* their meetings. "Are you saying there's some grand plan to talk with me? Can't I just give them whatever they want and get on with my life?" My head was starting to hurt again. When I stopped at the next stoplight, I pulled my hair out from under my rear end and flipped it over the back of the seat so I wasn't sitting on it.

Bert hopped up on the door's armrest and watched the passing scenery as he talked and I drove. I couldn't help but think of the dog I used to have when I was a kid. He used to hang his head out the window and let the wind whip through his ears until he puked. I hoped the motion wouldn't make Bert puke. I really didn't want to clean frog vomit out of the upholstery.

Luckily, he showed no signs of stomach discomfort. Instead, he kept talking. "You really don't have a clue what's going on, do you? Why do all these weird things keep happening to you; why did your hair grow like this? Do you even consider what I'm saying is true? No, you want to bury your head in the proverbial sand and forget there's life outside of law school. Never mind that you won't live to finish if you do that. You want to forget the fact people are going to get hurt, including you."

"Wait a minute," I exclaimed, pulling from Brown Street onto the highway to head back to my apartment. "What do you mean, forget that people are going to get hurt? What people? Who? Or that I won't live to finish law school? What does that mean?"

He kept on talking. "Aiden's not wrong. Your father didn't die of cancer. He died from a curse; a slow, evil, insidious curse that invaded his body and was planted by someone who knew him well. Do you remember anything unusual happening in your childhood? Did anything happen that you might not recognize as being odd or strange right away, but in hindsight seems like it had to be a figment of your imagination?"

I thought about it for a minute. I suddenly did have a strange memory of a rumpled little man asking me if I planned to have children. He'd asked me if I knew how to spin straw into gold, and if I could guess his name. I'd thought it was just a homeless man who was off his medication and wandering into the library for story time, but maybe it was more. I couldn't have been more than five or six at the time. I didn't remember Mom being around, but I remember Dad getting really upset about it. Why was this something I was just remembering? Or was it all in my imagination?

"You've thought of something, haven't you?" Bert asked.

I didn't want to share it. I remembered my father steering me away and telling me to be careful of crazy homeless guys and having a panicked look in his eyes. I'd thought Dad was keeping me safe from "stranger danger" as the teachers at my grade school had called it, rather than some whacked-out fairy tale come to life. "Maybe," I said aloud. "But even if I did, what would I do about it? It's not like I have some magic wand that makes it all go away. And none of it brings my dad back."

Bert got quiet again. "You're right," he finally said, as I pulled off the highway. "It won't bring your dad back. But it just might save your life."

"You're kidding me, right? This redheaded dork is able to heal me of all the weirdness in my life except for my dad's death as long as I listen to the goofy, out-of-his-head statements my Dad wouldn't listen to. I'm supposed to do this because Aiden and his buddies, your council, are able to save my life from some random danger no one's ever explained to me and I've never seen. Meanwhile all your weird crap is threatening my ability to handle law school. I don't buy it, and somehow, I'm starting to think you're hurting me more than you're helping me," I concluded, as I pulled into a drug store parking space.

Bert looked up at me, his froggy lips curved in a strange grin. "What do you think you're doing now?" I swear I just wanted to hit him. Or at least throw him out of the car. Either one was fine with me, but I just didn't feel up to a shouting match in public with a talking frog. If I got arrested for creating a disturbance, I'd never finish my reading for the next morning. And what kind of crazy attention-getting stunt would Bert create while I was inside?

"I'm going into this drugstore and getting some aspirin for my headache. It's getting worse. Are you going with me, or are you sitting here in the car while I go in?" I held out my purse for him to jump into.

He hopped in. "I'm going with you. I'm not letting you out of my sight for a while. I want to be there when you finally realize the truth in what we're all telling you. And when you realize it, I'll have a few other things to tell you, as well."

"Whatever," I snipped at him, hoping he'd just shut up. The headache was worse, and I wanted some relief, no matter how short-lived or brief it might be. I caught sight of myself in the reflection in the rear passenger window as I shut the door. No wonder the headache was worse; I was going to need another haircut soon.

CHAPTER SEVEN

"Can you tell me where you keep the aspirin?" I asked the teenaged stock clerk as I ran into the store. I just wanted to get some drugs and go home, where I could hack off my hair and read cases I didn't understand for the rest of the night. How long could this possibly take? I'd been looking down aisles for the last ten minutes for headache remedies and hadn't seen them.

He pointed down an aisle and I sprinted towards it. *Little white tablets of pain relief,* I thought. *Where could they be?* Using my finger, I read quickly down the shelves, comparing prices and concentrations of headache relieving substances for the best deal I could find.

"You've got a headache, don't you?" I heard, from a voice that sounded familiar. I spun around to find Aiden's face just inches from mine. I noticed he had a shaving nick right on his jawline. I shoved him away.

"Don't you understand the concept of personal space? Get away from me, or I'll call the cops. Seriously, you're starting to creep me out. Stop following me!" I yelled, hoping the stock clerk would check on me.

Aiden leaned against a shelf, and about a dozen boxes of Advil Cold and Sinus fell to the ground. I wondered if that was supposed to be his suave and debonair move. Instead, it looked like a dorky, uncoordinated, trying-too-hard move. He grimaced. "Yeah, look. I know it's weird. I know it's frustrating. I know I might not impress you. It doesn't change the fact I really need to sit down and talk to you about what's going on."

"No offense, I'm sure it's a real interesting story, but I just need to get rid of this headache, cut my hair, and start reading for Contracts class tomorrow. I've got a ton of work to do, and my life is rapidly turning into crap. You aren't helping; wanting to talk about Dad, following me all over town to the point that it's freaking me out. I can't concentrate with all this going on!" I started to storm away, but my hair got in the way of my flounce. Or the shelf did. Either way, I ended up with tears in my eyes and Aiden gently helping me untangle my hair from the joint in the metal display shelf. I'd been going for dramatic and ended up looking like an emotional fool.

"I'm sorry. I didn't mean to hold you up this morning and I certainly didn't mean to make you think I was stalking you. I'm not a threat to you. I only meant to help."

My hair was getting heavier and my head hurt, but his fingers were quick and light on the tangles caught on the corner of the aspirin shelf. I blinked the tears out of my eyes and swallowed hard to stop the sobs backing up in my throat. Why, oh why, couldn't anything go right today?

He kept talking as he worked on freeing my hair. "I didn't want to disturb you at the cemetery. I didn't know how else to find you; we know you've got an apartment somewhere, but we don't know where it is."

That was a relief. Maybe he wasn't a stalker. Or maybe he was just bad at it. Did that mean he wasn't dangerous? "It's okay. You talked. I got to hear a memory of my dad, and I wasn't late for class. Now I just want to get rid of this headache and go home. Thanks for your help," I added, as he freed the last trapped hair. "Now I need to go." I picked up a bottle of aspirin from the pile that had spilled on the floor and turned toward the checkout line.

"You've been cutting your hair all day, haven't you? And not just once, but probably every hour or so to keep it under control," he added, as he leaned against the shelves and crossed his arms.

"Have you been following me around today?"

He chuckled. "No, I haven't. I'm just smart enough, with the right training, to understand what I'm seeing. This is about the worst case I've ever seen, but I know exactly what it is."

"What *what* is?" I cried.

"Your hair growth is a result of a curse."

I shook my head. "Yeah, tell me another one. Next you'll tell me that angels really dance on the head of a pin, and that UFOs really did land in Roswell and Elvis went home with them. Now go away."

"Well, I just saw you this morning, and your hair was above your shoulders, and now it's getting closer to your knees. You're here for aspirin, so I'm assuming the weight of it's causing you some pain. It isn't hard to put two and two together and figure out that you've got a whopping case of Rapunzel Syndrome."

"Excuse me? Rapunzel Syndrome? I've never heard of that."

"Just because you haven't heard of it doesn't mean it doesn't exist. You've been cursed by a powerful member of faerie royalty. This is one of the potential side effects of infection. We can reverse the symptoms if you come with me right now. Otherwise, this can and will happen again. You don't want to go through this, with your hair growth and headache, over and over again, do you?"

"Faerie curse? Are you kidding me? I'm supposed to just believe this?" I was sure my mouth was hanging open. Seriously, who thinks curses really exist? I mean, I'm a grown up. I'm studying to be a lawyer. I'm not some flighty New-Age-y guru kind of person who believes stuff like that exists. Of course, the hair hanging down to my knees made it hard to ignore the possibility he might be telling me the truth. And he did say something about being able to fix it.

"I know it sounds crazy, but if you let it go too long, we won't be able to reverse it. If you come with me, right now, it's possible to stop the hair growth, or at least slow it down enough that it's manageable. If you think it's something you can ignore, and do nothing, it will quickly become untreatable."

Yeah, right. And then I heard a muffled sound coming from inside my purse.

"He's one of the good guys, I promise," I heard Bert whispering from inside my purse. "He won't hurt you."

"And I'm supposed to just believe that?" I hissed back.

"What are you doing?" Aiden asked me. "Who are you talking to?"

"Nothing. I'm not talking to anyone."

"I thought I heard a voice I recognize. You wouldn't happen to have met Bert, would you? We hoped he might have made contact with you, but we haven't heard from him for a while. Is he okay?" Aiden reached out a hand toward my purse.

The stock clerk stuck his head around the corner. "Is everything all right, miss?"

I stared at Aiden as he swallowed hard, his Adam's apple bobbing. It looked like he was nervous. He cleared his throat.

Before I could believe it, I was telling the stock clerk I was fine, and sending him on his way. What was I thinking? I should have asked the stock clerk to escort me away from Aiden. I should have asked him to call the police. I should have made it clear that I wasn't all right. I didn't do any of those things.

I realized I was probably in more danger from Aiden knocking down the sales shelves than I was from him hurting me. "What do I have to do to get rid of this so I can go back to class looking like a normal human being?"

He reached out a hand to me. "All you have to do is come with me. I promise we'll do the best we can to fix your symptoms, and if we can't fix it I'll buy enough ibuprofen to fill your medicine cabinet, but you need to at least let us try. I don't see how you'll get much studying done if you're constantly cutting your hair and popping pills. Besides, taking enough of that stuff could really be bad for your health."

I considered what he was saying. "Where do you want me to go? How long will I be away? I can't be gone past eight o'clock. I've got class in the morning."

"It's kinda hard to explain, but I need you to trust me. I'll have you right back to this spot no later than eight o'clock so you don't miss your class."

What choice did I have? Besides I couldn't keep chopping off my hair every hour. He was right about that.

I heard a faint, approving ribbit coming from my purse as I agreed. I suppressed the urge to reach inside and strangle Bert. Aiden pointed toward the back of the store, and I turned, following him. He opened the broom closet door at the back of the store, just out of sight of the pharmacists' counter. For a moment I wondered if he was going to knock me down on the way to the door, but he was able to get it open and usher me inside without falling on his face or tripping over my hair. Of course, the broom closet was small and I ended up closer to him than I'd ever been before. He smelled like maple syrup and fresh mown grass. It was intoxicating, and a clean smell. I was fascinated. I'd never met a man who smelled that way, and it was definitely something new. Then I noticed the maple syrup stain on the front of his shirt and I wasn't quite as fascinated any more. He wasn't just a klutz; he was a slob.

He made a waving motion with his hands and opened the air with a noise like a sticky zipper opening an old jacket. I had the sudden thought that I was in a broom closet with the Road Runner, and we were running from Wile E. Coyote by zipping open the landscape in that way. The air marking whatever it was he'd opened was dark purple, undulating in waves, and almost translucent enough to see movement on the other side. I couldn't hear much from inside the, well, portal, for lack of a better word, but I could make out a walkway lit by small twinkle lights along a split rail fence.

"Follow me," he said, as he stepped through the hole in reality and offered me a hand into insanity.

What else could I do? I just wanted the headache gone so I could go home and study in peace. I started to follow him, and my traitorously sprouting hair caught on the doorknob of the small closet as I stepped into the purple, swirling opening. I cried out in pain, and Aiden had to reach back through the portal to help me untangle myself so I could follow. I didn't have a choice. I had to do something to fix this, because it was getting ridiculous. I followed him through the portal and hoped that the cure wouldn't be worse than the ailment.

CHAPTER EIGHT

A cold gust of air slapped me in the face as the sliver of light coming from the broom closet behind me vanished. I heard a soft whisper as the portal sealed itself shut. Was I right to have followed Aiden?

"Where am I?"

He didn't answer; his attention was on one of the glowing twinkle lights on the fence. I walked up behind him and poked his shoulder. He smiled and pointed down the dirt path. I looked closer at the lights.

Pretty and twinkly from far away, up close I could see that they weren't lights at all. There were no cords or bulbs, and they gave off heat like cheap Christmas lights left on too long. They looked more like miniature people winking and waving as I walked by. I heard some high-pitched murmurs of hello, some excited but indecipherable happy mutterings as I tried not to stare at them. "What the hell is this, Aiden? And what are those things?"

"These are pixies," he said, smiling. "They're very happy to see you here, and want to light the way for us. I just offered them a bit of honey for their trouble. Come on, we've got a lot to do, and not a lot of time to do it if you want to get back by eight."

I took his offered arm, more out of confusion about where I was supposed to go than anything else. I made sure my hand was loose enough under his elbow to jerk free if necessary. I wasn't sure how I'd open up the zippy portal as he'd done to get back to the pharmacy broom closet, but I was still trying to keep my options open. "What do you mean, 'pixies'? Like Tinkerbell?"

The little people along the fence tittered with laughter, their bright little spotlights dancing. Aiden smiled at me. "They think you're funny, but they're giving you some slack for not knowing that they see Tinkerbell as a sellout. You might not want to talk about Tinkerbell in front of them; they'll get offended."

I couldn't look away. "What are they doing here?" Three of them came up behind me and began plucking at my hair and shaking their heads in sympathy, or at least I thought it was in sympathy. It was kind of hard to read their reaction when their faces were so tiny.

Aiden kept talking, pulling me along with him. "Most pixies end up as slaves in the faerie courts. These are the ones we freed, and they've sworn to keep our secrets in exchange for our protection. They'll carry messages back to us. In fact, you can tell a difference between our free pixies and the slave-held ones; these shine brighter than the ones still in servitude. Our council thinks it's because they're happier with freedom."

I nodded at him as we kept walking, momentarily distracted from the pain in my scalp by the happy, smiling, miniature faces dancing along the path in front of me. Aiden led the way to a thatched roof hut, and opened the door into darkness. *Lions and tigers and bears, oh my,* chanted my brain with the heavy thud of my heart and the painful dull ache in my head. At least I hoped it was just lions and tigers and bears. The pixies hadn't seemed dangerous, but they certainly weren't normal. I had to be dreaming. None of this could be real. Had he knocked me out or given me some sort of hallucinogen at the pharmacy?

He stepped inside the door and I followed. Aiden shut the door behind me. A single candle flared into brightness. My eyes adjusted to the glow and I made out a handful of people sitting on wooden benches lining the walls of the hut. I was standing in the middle. Aiden pulled down a folding wooden seat from the back of the door for himself. They all stared at me and I felt the pain in my head increase exponentially as they did.

"What do you want from me? Why is my hair doing this?" I shrieked in pain, holding my scalp and the roots of my hair in an effort to relieve some of the pressure of the increasing weight. The growth rate seemed to have doubled from the time I'd left the school, and it caused me to stumble, tripping on the end of my hair. Stepping on my hair pulled on my scalp, and I whimpered.

An older gentleman with a receding hairline and graying ponytail took a step toward me. "Ms. Grimm, we're here to help. We appreciate you coming all this way to talk with us about your problem, but I think we'll need to shift directly to the cure as the curse is progressing rapidly."

I could only nod in pain. My head felt like it had been soaked in gasoline and set on fire. Tears ran down my face, chasing each other, as my hair kept getting longer. I couldn't see through the tears clearly enough to look around the hut.

The older gentleman who had spoken earlier laid his hands on the top of my head and chanted a soft, soothing rhyme in a language I didn't understand. The chanting went on, and the others sitting in the room, including Aiden, joined in. The air around me seemed to levitate my heavy hair off the ground and held it high enough to take the weight off of my scalp.

Aiden stepped into the middle of the circle, holding a strange cup, and continued to chant as I mopped the tears from my face with the sleeve of my sweatshirt. As the pressure and weight lessened, I was finally able to look around inside the hut. There were more people than I thought; close to a dozen men and women sat on the benches around the room. They kept chanting.

There seemed to be no stereotypical members. I saw two middle-aged women who looked the same age my mother would be now if she'd stuck around; one chubby older man who looked like the effort of chanting would stop his heart. Aiden was the youngest, except for me, in the room. Several others looked like they had children at home; some of them old enough to have kids waiting to be picked up from soccer practice or drivers' education classes.

One lady smiled warmly at me while she chanted. She had that Grandma vibe about her. I had an insane urge to throw my arms around her and beg her to bake me a dozen chocolate chip cookies. I managed a small smile in return and she nodded.

The man holding my head squeezed and the chanting got louder. Aiden handed me the huge mug of steaming hot liquid. He whispered that I was to drink it, as it was the cure for the headache and hair growth. "You can't stop drinking. You've got to keep going, no matter how foul, no matter how much you want to stop, no matter how full you're getting, no matter how much you hate it. If you stop drinking, we'll have to start this all over again. It'll hurt even worse while we re-brew the drink, and you won't be able to take anything while you wait, because I don't know how modern medicine could affect this." Oh great. I was going to have to chug steaming hot sludge in one shot. I hadn't been much of a drinker in college, so I wasn't sure I could chug anything, but I didn't have a choice. I had to make this work. I nodded at him.

Aiden held the mug to my lips. "Ready?"

I reached for the mug and tilted it into my mouth, trying not to choke, but wanting to get it over with as fast as possible. He kept me from going too fast, but he also kept the mug in place, pouring liquid down my throat in a continuous stream to keep me from stopping.

It wasn't as bad as I'd thought it would be from his warnings. It wasn't good, but it wasn't terrible. It tasted like tea that had been strained through someone's old sweat socks and sweetened with too much honey to be good for anyone. It was syrupy-sweet, making it hard to keep drinking as the sugary aftertaste built up in the back of my throat. As I gulped my way through the drink it became bitter, like sour lemons and dishwasher detergent. I cringed, but Aiden grabbed the back of my sore head and I kept on drinking. He didn't give me much choice.

The mug couldn't have held as much liquid as I was ingesting. I became aware of an uncomfortably full feeling as my stomach stretched to hold it all. I should have drained it dry, but the liquid kept coming, and tasted worse and worse as he poured it down my throat. I gagged a bit, but kept going. It became salty and thick and I felt like I was gulping hot tar, but I didn't want to have to start all over and do it again now that I knew just how bad it tasted.

The last few gulps tasted like Tabasco sauce mixed with fermented bread dough that had been left to rise in someone's shoe. Finally, I swallowed the last of it and fell to the ground holding my stomach, which felt like it held a three-ton brick of hot lead. Would it work if I threw it all up?

My head was on fire. My stomach felt like it was being stabbed with hot pincers. The people in the circle grabbed my arms and legs to keep me from rolling into a ball against the pain due to the stuff I'd swallowed as it wormed its way through my body. I cried out, tears springing from my eyes as the room spun and Aiden's concerned face rose above mine.

"I'm sorry," he said, as I shook my head and passed out.

CHAPTER NINE

I woke up slowly, the hut deserted and dark. My eyes burned, my stomach was rising and falling as if I was on a psychotic nausea-inducing teeter-totter, and my scalp felt too small for my skull. It was nowhere near the amount of pain I'd been in when we'd arrived at the hut and the ceremony had begun. I reached one hand to my head, and found that my hair was back to my normal shoulder length, curling around my ears. I shook my head despite the headache, enjoying the lack of weight like any woman who'd just gotten a shorter haircut.

Food didn't sound good, but if I could go home and pass out for a few hours then I could get up and at least do the reading for my first class. I sat up and pushed to my feet, then headed outside to find Aiden standing guard outside the door.

It seemed just as dark outside as when we'd come in, so I figured I'd been asleep, or unconscious, for no more than an hour or two. He walked me back down the dirt path to where we'd come through from the broom closet in the pharmacy earlier, and opened an invisible zipper in the air. I'd thought I'd imagined that earlier, but he offered me his hand to step through and then handed over my purse. *Whatever they did, it worked, so I'm not going to question how crazy I must be.*

He turned on the light in the broom closet and started to open the door to the rest of the store, but closed it again indicating a customer was outside. "That's okay, we'll wait," he said, whispering in my ear as he held the door shut. "You're going to have some questions, I'm sure, but I know you have classes. I won't keep you once it's clear. In the meantime, the council has decided to help you out a little more than normal, because we're not sure if you're out of danger. We just don't know for sure how bad this could get."

"What do you mean?" My weird crap-o-meter was off the charts at the moment. "I followed you to the creepy hut of doom and drank your goopy sludge potion. I thought that meant I was cured. See?

Hair normal," I whispered angrily, as I pulled my hair from behind my ear and wagged it at him.

He laughed, opened the door, and carefully peering around before he gave me the all-clear sign. "I'm not talking about anything all that crazy, I promise." He handed me a small box.

When I opened it, I saw a piece of jewelry resting on a cushion of velvet. "This looks expensive." I don't think I'd ever had a guy offer me jewelry before, and this was definitely not how I'd thought it would happen. Isn't it supposed to be some token of love? Not here, wear this to stave off the psychotic break with reality that I was sure the idea of magic must entail.

"It's old, but it's not about that. If you wear this charm on a chain around your neck, it should ward off most curses and evil-wishes. It also protects you temporarily from magic effects. It's not complete protection, and you have to be wearing it for it to work, but it'll help you stay safe enough in order to get things done and not get distracted in class. You really shouldn't wear it for more than twelve hours a day and take it off to sleep if you can; if you don't, it might give you some strange dreams."

As opposed to what I'd seen in the last few hours? "Then what protects me while I sleep?" I asked. Of all the things on my plate, it seemed a minor worry, but I was really going to need some real sleep, and soon. Part of me thought that if I could get home and go to bed, I'd wake up in the morning and everything would be normal again.

"You should be fine inside your own apartment. It's an established threshold, a home, even though you haven't been there very long. It's not as strong as it could be, since you just moved in, but you are someone creating a home for yourself, not just a place to crash at night. It offers some protection from all but those you ask inside, so do yourself a favor and be careful who you invite in. Bert's fine to be there, and so am I, but if you feel even the slightest bit odd about someone, don't let them in. Above all else, be careful what promises you make. Promises bind a faerie creature; they consider the breaking of a promise the lowest form of treachery and punishable by death, and will hold you to the same standard."

I nodded. It wasn't like I was going to be entertaining much at my apartment, other than study group meetings, and I couldn't think of a thing weird about any of my friends. They all seemed pretty normal to me. I kept reaching up to make sure my hair wasn't growing, but I didn't notice any additional length. Thank God.

I'd just have to remember not to make promises to strange beings and not to invite in any weirdos. I could do that.

I hurried away from him, but went ahead and grabbed a giant, economy-sized bottle of store brand aspirin just to be on the safe side. I reached into my purse for my wallet and caught sight of Bert inside, being very good not to comment on anything. I shook my head at him and paid for my drugs before I scuttled outside to my car.

Something was wrong.

It was sunny outside. It really shouldn't be that bright at eight o'clock at night, I thought. I got in the car and started the engine. Bert hopped out of my purse onto the passenger seat as I whipped the car into reverse and began to back out. The clock on the dashboard read exactly eight o'clock as I pulled out of the parking lot. Even in August, as it was now, the sun should be starting to go down.

"You know it's eight in the morning, right, Janie?" Bert asked.

"What?" I stomped on the brakes, sending Bert flying onto the floor. I really shouldn't have done that; my seatbelts aren't big enough to hold a frog in his seat. "It can't be. They promised I'd be back last night!"

He rolled over slowly, as if he'd been bruised. "You made them promise you'd be back by eight, but you never said morning or evening. You said you had classes in the morning and your first class is in about an hour. They wouldn't have been able to cure you in that short amount of time. I thought you knew that, or I'd have said something a lot sooner."

I gnashed my teeth together as I dug out my cell phone to confirm it really was eight o'clock in the morning and changed course to head back to school. I wouldn't be prepared again, and I could only hope the professors wouldn't call on me, or make fun of me for wearing the same clothing I'd had on yesterday. Maybe if I took off my sweatshirt, and just wore the t-shirt I had on underneath, they'd think I was wearing a different shirt. It was worth a shot.

"You know if I'm going to be tagging along with you, we'll have to figure out something better. I can't keep riding around like this without a seatbelt. It isn't safe," Bert commented as he hopped back up on the seat.

"Who says you're going to keep 'tagging along with' me?" I shot back, trying to pay attention to the morning traffic. Somehow, I thought a seatbelt for a pest frog was the least of my current worries.

"Janie, don't be so stubborn you refuse help that doesn't cost you much. Let me stay with you for a week or two. If nothing else happens, I leave. I'm a frog. I don't eat much, and I don't take up much space. I won't make a mess in your apartment. I'll stay out of your way when you need to study, and I'll be quiet while you're in class. In exchange for letting me stay, I'll help you with your classes. Your Contracts lecture sounded familiar, and so does your Property class. I'd be happy to see what I can do to help, especially since you've gotten behind in dealing with all of this stuff."

I considered it. It wasn't a bad offer, despite my crankiness about not being able to go home and sleep. "Anything else?"

"Well, you might consider talking to Aiden, like he said. If you learn more about what's going on you might be able to prevent things from happening later, and if you can prevent it, you might not lose as much study time in the end."

I didn't believe him. I still didn't want to think he might be right, that Dad had been murdered rather than dying from cancer. I didn't want to think about pixies and homeless men wanting gold and talking frogs and magic charms and hair that wouldn't stop growing.

There was, however, some wisdom in what he said. Heck, I was taking advice from a frog after drinking hot lead mixed with honey and Tabasco, spent the night in a hut surrounded by middle aged chanting gurus, and hoping I'd been dreaming the whole sorry mess. I was starting to realize I wasn't going to be that lucky. I agreed to his bargain as I pulled up to a parking spot near the law school.

Bert hopped into the front pocket of my backpack after a stern promise to keep his mouth zipped until we got back in the car. As I leapt up the front steps into the building, I slipped Aiden's charm onto the necklace I wore all the time—a silver locket Dad had given me when

I turned sixteen. I wrapped my fingers around the locket as the charm, a filigreed metal figure I didn't recognize with a red gemstone imbedded in the center, settled next to it. "Sorry, Dad," I said to the picture inside the locket. "I can't risk them being right."

I stepped inside the building and found Mia waiting.

"So there you are! I've been calling your house since you left last night and you never answered. Are you okay?" She looked concerned as she dragged me into the bathroom.

From my reflection in the mirror, she was right to be concerned. I had big, dark, baggy circles under eyes that were bloodshot and dry. My hair looked dirty and unwashed, though it was back to a normal length and hadn't grown since the ceremony I'd undergone the night before. If I hadn't woken up inside the hut where it had all happened, I'd still think it was all a dream. I looked like I'd just graduated from Hangovers 101 and I didn't even have the good drunk story to go with it.

"Have you been drinking?" she asked, clearly reading my mind.

"No. It's too expensive." I threw some water on my face, trying to de-puff my eyes.

"Aren't those the same jeans you were wearing yesterday?"

I groaned under my breath and made some excuse about needing to do laundry, and she seemed to buy it, or, at least, she didn't question it. I realized I wasn't giving my friend enough credit. Maybe Mia could help. I had all of Dad's journals in the boxes I hadn't gotten around to unpacking yet. I wondered if there would be some kind of reference in them to Dad's involvement with this group Aiden was tied up in. Things were happening a bit too fast, and I needed to do some checking of my own. Having Mia's common sense as a fresh perspective to the problem wouldn't hurt.

"Mia, there is something you can help me with." I toweled water off my face and threw the paper towel in the trashcan where my hair had landed the day before.

"You name it and I'll be there." She put one hand on my back.

I still felt like I'd been hit by a truck, but having that small show of support, as well as the cold water waking me up, was a tremendous help. My mind raced as I came up with a plan.

Tonight I had to devote to getting some of the increasing homework and reading done after our study group meeting, or I'd never catch up. Maybe if I got enough of it done, I could spend a few hours getting some of Dad's paperwork organized and grill Bert about what I should do next. If Mia could come over tomorrow night and help me speed-read through as much of Dad's things as possible, we might be able to find something that would help me figure out what was going on and stop it before it interfered any further with my ability to keep up in my classes. Then I'd still have Friday night free for Evangeline's party.

It almost sounded like it would work. I asked Mia if she would come over tomorrow night to help me with a project, and she agreed. I thanked her and she hugged me.

"I don't know what's going on with you, Janie, but there's something taking you away from all your plans. Law school's supposed to be hard, but it's not supposed to be this hard. If I can help, I will. If I can't help, then let's see what help we can find for you. You're meant to be an attorney, and I know it's what you want. Don't lose sight of that in whatever drama is going on in your life right now." She squeezed my shoulder. "And don't forget, we meet today in the library to talk about Contracts."

I had to fight back tears before my next class started. Had I been doing Mia a disservice by not trusting her with what was going on with my life? I'd have to see what I could find out tonight after studying and see what Bert had to say.

Maybe we could figure this whole thing out.

CHAPTER TEN

Throughout the day, I had several students ask me what kind of prank I planned to pull next. They seemed disappointed, as well as disbelieving, when I tried to explain I wasn't pulling anything on anybody. I tried to ignore them as best I could. Hopefully I'd catch up and impress the professors, so they'd all forget about me and my fast-growing hair. Hey, it could happen.

Really.

It could.

I walked through the rest of the day in a fog. I did get called on in one class, but I'd actually had enough time to skim the cases the professor was asking about before class, so I understood enough to survive being in the hot seat one more time.

After my last class, I headed upstairs to the second floor, most of which was occupied by the massive law library. I checked at the desk to find out which room Mia had reserved, and headed for the study room. Mike and Leann were already there with their books out, and arguing about one of the cases from the first day of Contracts, *Hadley v. Baxendale.*

"What do you mean a late delivery of repaired mill parts doesn't have a foreseeable impact on the mill owner's profits? Of course it impacts the mill's profit if they can't do business because the parts haven't been delivered when they were supposed to have been. Anyone could figure that out!" Mike emphasized, rapping his highlighter on the table. "He promised the work. It wasn't done. He's responsible."

"The repairman promised to fix the parts and deliver them. He did that. He didn't promise to deliver the parts to prevent loss, and there's no evidence that loss of profits were ever discussed or even mentioned to the repairman. How's he to know the mill owner didn't have extra parts lying around? For all he knew, the mill owner is using his spare while the primary parts are repaired. Why should he be responsible for losses he couldn't anticipate?" Leann asked, crossing her arms over her chest, her brown eyes twinkling.

I began unpacking my things in anticipation of covering a case that still had me baffled. I kept my mouth shut as I pulled out my Contracts notebook, and added notes about their argument to my confused scribbling from the first day. Sooner or later it might make sense.

They kept arguing about whether a reasonable man would be able to foresee the damages and whether the contract had been breached by the late delivery. I kept on taking notes, soaking up their analysis like a proverbial sponge, as they kept going until the others arrived. Mia wasn't far behind me, and joined in as she unpacked her things. "That's a cool necklace, Janie," she said, as she got settled in. I took it off and laid it on the table in front of her so she could get a better look.

Finally the last member of our group, David, appeared. We were ready to get started in earnest. The problem, however, was that not everyone was ready to start.

David hadn't taken anything out of his backpack besides a notebook and pen; unlike the rest of us, who each seemed to be surrounded by a small mountain of books. He stood behind his chair, and made no move to sit down, preventing the start of our meeting. We couldn't get the door shut because he was in the way. Those rooms were only soundproof when the door was shut, and the library had rules about noise level. "Nice necklace, Janie," he said.

I looked down, realizing he was talking about the charm Aiden had given me, still laying on the desk in front of Mia. "Thanks," I said. I wished I had good dirt to dish with my friends about getting jewelry, but as it was I had no idea how to explain it.

"Where'd you get it?" he asked.

I wondered why he was asking, but there could be a million reasons. I wasn't here to give him gift-buying advice for a significant other. I was here to understand the formation of a contract. "It was a gift from a friend."

It's not like I could explain that a magical boogeyman was trying to kill me with a curse and the necklace was somehow supposed to warn me or protect me or something. I didn't even quite know how it was supposed to work. David eased his way inside and finally sat down, but he just sat there, looking uncomfortable.

Leann piped up. "That looks like an antique. Either it's a family heirloom or it cost a pretty penny. Either way, are you sure it's just a friend who gave it to you? If it's a guy, he probably wants to be way more than a friend. He's got good taste."

I'm not sure that was a better topic than the truth behind the necklace, but at least it was a more rational one. "I don't have a boyfriend, but the friend who gave it to me was a boy. We're just not like that." Boy meets girl. Girl gets cursed. Boy lifts curse. Not exactly romance movie material.

"Are you sure he's just a friend?" Leann kept pushing.

"I thought we were here to work on Contracts and Property. Shouldn't we get to it?" I asked, now desperate to get to work and steer the conversation away from my nonexistent love life.

"Didn't we stop at the reasonable man standard of foreseeable damages?" Mia jumped in, helping shift the topic of conversation back to the reason why we'd taken over the too-small, stuffy study room instead of going home like many of our classmates. I turned back to my Contracts book, hoping she'd diverted them as I swept up the necklace and tucked it in my front jeans pocket.

Suddenly, David jumped up. "I better leave. I forgot I have to pick up the kid from the babysitter."

It seemed odd to me that he hadn't mentioned it earlier. Why had he let us schedule a meeting for a time he couldn't join us? Hadn't we searched our schedules for a time we could all meet? But none of us were heartless enough to argue with a father who had to pick up his kid; besides, everyone forgets an appointment or writes something down wrong at some point in their lives. We were all stressed out; I was sure he wouldn't be the only one to blow off one of our scheduled meetings during the course of the year.

David grabbed his things, then headed out. The group kept talking about the mill owner and lost profits, and whether or not the repairman had made promises with regard to the speed of delivery and the damages of delay, but I wasn't listening. Through the glass panel in the door, I watched David walk away. He seemed upset about something.

They kept debating. I still wasn't sure what they were trying to say, but it made more sense than it had just two days ago. I was glad we were meeting like this, even though I was a bit lost. I took notes. I was still behind on the reading, but maybe after I finished actually reading it the case would make more sense. When I realized how much I needed to get done tonight, I suddenly felt really tired. I had a lot of catch-up to do before going to bed, but I also really needed a good night's sleep.

"What time is it?" I asked. I still hadn't picked up a watch, despite Evangeline's nagging.

"It's getting close to six o'clock," Mia said, as she looked at the slim silver band on her wrist. "We probably ought to call it a night here, guys. There's a limit to what we can get done at our first meeting."

We all agreed we'd been here long enough and began to pack up. My stomach rumbled, reminding me that I hadn't eaten anything all day, which meant my last meal had been Aiden's disgusting hair-curse-curing sludge. I was starving. It was time to go home.

So why did I keep getting distracted by trying to figure out what was wrong with David? Maybe he didn't want to work with us. Or possibly the pressure was getting to him. Maybe he was having trouble with his girlfriend. I couldn't figure out why, but he looked off somehow. I shrugged, and followed the rest of the group out of the library. I'd figure it out sooner or later.

CHAPTER ELEVEN

At the University Of Dayton School Of Law, all the students have lockers, just like in high school. The reason is simple; our books are heavy and thick, and take up a lot of room. There's not always a reason to lug them back and forth if one doesn't need them at home that night, and we don't have the same classes every day. It's also a good place to stash one's coat or lunch or other stuff, taking only necessary things to each class.

That afternoon was the exception. I loaded up most of my books so I could dig into the backlog since I was behind in almost every class. My back and arms were screaming with strain from the weight of the books by the time I carted them all to my car.

I splurged on fast food tacos on the way home, feeling bad for spending the money, but I didn't want to stop studying long enough to cook. When I got home I spread my work out on the coffee table, and then began cramming tacos into my mouth as I read and took notes for class.

When I finished my Contracts reading, it still didn't make sense. I got up to stretch, threw away my trash, then switched books as Bert hopped up on the coffee table. Of course, calling it a coffee table was a bit of a stretch. It was a steamer trunk full of Dad's old books and journals and photo albums, and covered in a few huge scarves so no one would notice the container of stuff that wasn't yet unpacked.

"What?" I asked him, the next book in hand as I headed back to the couch, not really paying attention to him. I seemed to be unpacking my backpack as I studied that night; I was hoping to get it emptied out before it got too late.

"What can I say? I understand you've got a lot to do, Janie, but you can't ignore what's going on. I know Mia's coming over tomorrow to help you, but I'm afraid you'll wait too long to really understand what you're up against." Bert settled himself beside my remote control and blinked.

I gave in. If I took a few minutes right now to talk with him, then maybe he'd leave me alone the rest of the night. "What do you want, Bert?" I put down my things and gave him my full attention.

"I'm not sure how much time you're going to have before something does happen. And don't forget to take off the charm Aiden gave you while you're here at home. You don't need it when you're behind a threshold. It can give you a headache if you wear it too much."

I'd forgotten I had the thing in my pocket. Aiden had told me I shouldn't wear it when I was at home. I assumed that meant anywhere on me. "Aiden used that term as well. What do you mean by 'threshold'?"

"Well, when someone makes a place their home, it builds up a protective energy certain magical and faerie beings can't cross without help or an invitation. Your place hasn't been your home for long, but whoever was before you lived here for a long time. The more you settle in, the stronger the threshold. The stronger the threshold, the safer your home is against things that might want to hurt you." He was looking at my Contract notes while he said this, shaking his head. "You're making this harder than it has to be."

"What?" I asked as I walked to the bathroom to put Aiden's charm in the medicine cabinet so I wouldn't lose it. I wasn't sure I believed in the silly thing having any power, but nothing crazy had happened at school today while I was wearing it. It was worth wearing again tomorrow, just in case.

"Contracts really isn't that hard, Janie. And you're working too hard. You'll burn yourself out if you don't take a break."

"Yeah, actually, it is that hard for me. But I need to read for my other classes to get caught up for tomorrow. I don't have time to take a break. I've got too much to do. Why don't you give me some time to get some stuff done, and then we'll talk about whatever it is you want to talk about for a while." It wasn't that I didn't want to know what was going on; I just couldn't take the time until I got caught up. It was *Dad's* money I was spending to be in law school; I couldn't risk losing everything he left me and not make it through school. I'd never forgive myself.

It took some time to negotiate. Bert wanted to watch TV while I worked, but he couldn't operate the remote control. I stood there flipping channels until he was satisfied with a replay of an old NASCAR race on ESPN Classic. In the end, he settled for the closed captioning with the sound off so I could study.

I settled back into my work, but I couldn't stop the grin forming on my face as I kept catching him trying not to cheer out loud. Who'd have thought a centuries old prince-turned-frog would be a NASCAR fan? I certainly wouldn't have predicted it.

Bert was bouncing with happiness when I turned to him and asked him to tell me what he knew. He looked a bit disappointed, since I was distracting him from the after-race hype, but it didn't take long to compose himself. I had, after all, waited until the final lap was over to ask him. I didn't get a thrill from watching people drive in circles, but I wasn't mean enough to deprive him of watching the winner.

"Janie, I know you've got a lot going on in your life right now, and I hate that you've got to go through this, but I believe you're still in danger."

"What are you talking about? My hair's fixed, I'm at home, and I've got that charm thing Aiden gave me. I'm good."

He shook his head. "That's only a temporary fix."

Yikes. I'd hoped the hair growth would be a one-time thing. That drink was nasty. And what was I supposed to do, pencil into my day planner dentist on Thursday, haircut on Friday, exorcism on Saturday? I shook my head. I couldn't do that. "I talked to Aiden because I had to with the hair problem. See? It's normal length, and it's been that way since this morning. I'm good, unless it doesn't last. And if it doesn't, Aiden and his buddies can whip up more of that stuff, right?"

"You're an ostrich."

"I'm a what?" I asked, hands on my hips.

"You're burying your head in the sand like an ostrich. If that was it, and you really believed it was over, then why did you invite Mia over here tomorrow night to look over your Dad's things?"

Crap. He was right. I knew this was a deeper issue than I wanted to acknowledge, but I'd hoped I could figure it out without all the crazy mumbo-jumbo hocus-pocus nasty potions and captive pixies. I didn't want Bert's opinion to influence my impressions of Aiden, either. Even so, maybe I should just hear him out.

"All right, Bert. You caught me. I'm not sure who to trust, so I wanted to do some leg work on my own before I make up my mind how to handle this."

He belched, long and loud. I'd given him more iced tea to drink while he watched the race, despite his repeated requests for a beer. He said it just wasn't the same to watch a race without a beer. Leaving aside the fact I didn't have any, I was afraid the belching would just get worse if I gave in. "You're right to be cautious, Janie. I just hope that in your caution, you don't wait too long before you take action. I think Mia's a good friend, and she wants to help you. I haven't sensed anything that would make me doubt her or think she's dangerous to you. But it doesn't change the fact she doesn't have a clue what all this could mean."

"Well, of course not," I shot back. "We've been friends for a while. I think I'd have noticed if there was something wrong!" I honestly hadn't even thought to doubt her.

"This isn't a one-time, get-out-of-jail-free card. You don't pass Go. You don't collect two hundred dollars. Your father had no idea what he was facing. He didn't believe it was all that serious, and he ignored what symptoms he had until it was too late for anyone to do much of anything to help him. You've got to understand things aren't as simple as you think, and anyone could be trying to hurt you."

He kept talking before I could get a word in edgewise. "You're doing a good thing by planning to read your father's journals. If nothing else, they might help you determine what symptoms he started out with, so you know what to watch for." He looked a bit embarrassed.

"Well, before I go any further into this web of crazy, you're right. I want to get through his journals and figure out what he knew," I said. "That's why Mia's coming over tomorrow. I'm not trying to ignore it, but I can't get it all done and keep up with the reading, do Evangeline's fundraiser, and everything else without help. I'm going to finish up the Torts reading for tomorrow, organize some of Dad's papers and stuff to be ready for Mia to come over, and then get some sleep. It's been a long couple of days, Bert."

Bert tried to hop from the coffee table to the couch beside me, and he fell. His skinny frog legs were way out of proportion to the rest of his body, and couldn't catch the weight of the rest of his body. He didn't act like he was injured, but I could tell his pride was hurt.

I reached out to help him right himself and tried not to make a big deal out of it. I wondered if he'd ever gotten used to the idea that his frog legs weren't the same as the human legs he used to have. He looked upset, or at least as upset as a frog can look, but after a moment or two to figure himself out on my lumpy couch, he settled and looked me in the eye. "I get that, Janie. I really do. But you still don't understand just how serious this could be."

"I know I've got to get a handle on everything going on in my life to figure out if I'm really in trouble, or whether I need a rubber room, or whether thinking I'm crazy is just a side effect of law school. That means I've got to get my head around the things I understand. Well, maybe not understand, but definitely the normal stuff." I reached up again, making sure my hair hadn't started growing while I wasn't paying attention. I'd been checking constantly all day. It seemed fine; I didn't notice any unusual growth.

"The hair is fixed for now. The only way it comes back is if you get cursed again, but I think someone's been cursing you a little at a time for years. It might take a while for the curse to build back up to the same level in your system for the hair growth to start again. The Rapunzel Syndrome is actually a symptom; it's not the underlying problem. If you continue to interact with whomever, or whatever, is cursing you, it will come back. The only other way to prevent magical side effects is to get the faerie courts to shield you from magic, and the price they'd ask for would be too high. They'd want something like your first born child for a promise that broad."

Yikes. That was a high price.

"Assuming for a second you're right, who could be cursing me? I don't have any enemies. And would that same person be the one who cursed my dad?" I asked. Hey, he *had* been trying to tell me my dad had been murdered. It suddenly made sense in my mind this could be how. No, that couldn't be right. I didn't believe him, did I?

CHAPTER TWELVE

It was late that night when I stumbled into bed. I wouldn't get more than about four hours of sleep before I had to get up for class, but I finally felt caught up. I had a game plan, and was ready to sit down tomorrow night—or was it tonight?—and comb through all of Dad's things. I was ready for class the next morning. I was ahead for Friday. My hair wasn't sprouting at an alarming rate, and I didn't have a headache other than from reading too much. Life was good.

Until I went to bed, that is. Just as I closed my eyes, I heard the worst racket I'd ever heard. I think it was supposed to be music, but it was just noise. It sounded like someone was strangling a cat while their junior high kid was learning four instruments at once and had waited until three in the morning to practice.

I tried holding my pillow over my face, but that didn't drown out the music; it just made it harder to breathe. Bert started yelling from the living room. "I don't know what kind of music you're listening to, but a frog can't get any sleep with that kind of racket!"

I stormed out into the living room and shouted back. It wasn't real mature, but mature just doesn't happen at three in the morning. "It's not me!"

He pointed at the window, and I peered through the slats of the cheap Venetian window blinds that came with the apartment. They made a crinkling plastic sound as I moved them out of the way. "It's a rooster, a cat, a dog, and a donkey, standing in the parking lot, all making noise. What the hell is going on here?" I turned to look at Bert.

He yawned and rolled over from where he was trying to sleep on my couch. "Go put out something for them to eat on the patio and they'll shut up."

"What?" I asked. I ignored his advice, staring out the window at the racket. God, I needed sleep. Why is this happening on the one night I was home and ready to get some shut-eye? What good was getting caught up going to be if I fell asleep in class? Why weren't the neighbors out there complaining? And what would Mia say if they were still making that much racket when she showed up tomorrow? Or was it tonight? Whatever.

"They're singing for their supper. Set out food and wish them luck on their journey to Bremen. That way they get the hint they can't stop here, but you appreciate the music and support their journey. It's the only way to get them to leave." Bert buried his head back in the pillows on the couch, no doubt attempting to drown them out like I'd tried to do a few minutes ago.

"That's all you can say, give them food? What about the neighbors?"

"Well, unlike the Rapunzel Syndrome, which was a buildup in your own body from the curse you've been under and the physical reaction to it, this isn't exactly a corporeal appearance." He poked his head out and grimaced at a sour note sung by the so-called musicians. I think it was supposed to be singing, but it sounded like someone was gargling Liquid Plumber and trying to talk at the same time.

"What do you mean by corporeal?" I asked over the din, shoving my fingers in my ears as I ran into the kitchen to see what I could throw together. I grabbed a loaf of bread, a hunk of cheese, a gallon of milk, as well as a big plastic popcorn bowl.

"I mean that you and I, as people who have a proven awareness of otherworldly things, are now susceptible to the use of magic. Whatever is trying to curse you has also removed some of the barriers to your being able to see magical things around you. I'm not sure exactly how it works or why it happened, but you're going to start seeing some things other people can't, and you're going to have to be careful about reacting to them, or normal people will think you're crazy."

I wasn't sure I hadn't lost my mind. As he spoke, I opened the door and whistled at the animals in the parking lot. They immediately shut up and came over. When they saw the bread and cheese and milk in my arms, I had their attention.

I put down the bowl, and poured as much milk as it would hold. The cat began lapping hungrily at the milk. I tore up pieces of bread and cheese to feed the other animals, tossing a slice at a time at the donkey, who gulped them down and looked for more. I had to run back inside for more food at one point, because they were still smacking their lips and acting hungry. They depleted my grocery haul for the week without batting an eye. Finally, the other animals finished off the milk, and I stepped back, empty bowl, plastic bread bags, and other food detritus in my arms as I wished them luck on their journey to Bremen as Bert had instructed.

They all seemed very respectful, even if they didn't say anything. Of course, I wasn't sure why I expected them to talk. Just because Bert talked didn't mean any other animal I ran into would be able to talk as well. Or would they? It was a question formed in an overtired brain and something I didn't want to stay up all night to find out. Luckily, they walked away before I could say anything else to screw it up. Thank God.

I walked back inside, where Bert had fallen asleep, curled up on the couch against a pillow with an old throw blanket next to him. I couldn't help being glad he was here. If he wasn't, I'm not sure I could have handled the very noisy animals. I probably would've called the police, who'd have bundled me off to the nearest mental hospital rather than listen to a wild tale about the musical barnyard in the parking lot they couldn't see or hear.

I owed him for having the right answer, and I knew it, but I wasn't sure what I could do for him. I didn't know how long I wanted him to stay, but there was no telling how long it would take me to get to the bottom of all this. I'd have to do something nice for him. At least I had Evangeline's check to stock back up with.

I knew instantly what I could do. I could buy him the beer he kept asking for when I went back to the grocery store, which was looking like a quicker trip than I'd planned. I didn't have much left in the refrigerator after I'd fed the animals on my patio.

I wrote myself a note on the pad near the phone reminding myself to buy beer, and hoped I'd have time to pick up supplies tomorrow before Mia came over, at least enough to cook something for dinner. I thought I should probably at least feed her for coming over to help.

I was asleep again almost before my head hit the pillow. Who knew that dealing with figments of my imagination could be so exhausting?

CHAPTER THIRTEEN

It sure didn't seem like I'd slept at all when the alarm clock went off in the morning. It took staring at the clock for a minute or two until my eyes focused enough to tell my brain I'd really slept for three hours. I needed to get moving to make it to class.

I started the coffeepot and stumbled into the shower, hoping a combination of hot water and caffeine would help me get out the door and look a little less like a party girl than I'd been the day before. If I didn't start looking normal and prepared, my classmates and professors were never going to let me live down the hair-growing incident.

Bert didn't look all that awake either, and didn't want to wake up when I'd tried to get his attention. I slipped the charm back onto my necklace and over my head, and left a note on the coffee table. It wasn't like he had anywhere he had to go today, and I figured his quick answer last night had earned him the ability to sleep in, even if I couldn't do the same. Since I only had two classes today and a quick run to the grocery store, I figured I could wing it on my own.

He didn't stir as I bustled around the apartment, and only let out a snort and a snore as he flipped over on the couch when I picked up my keys from the coffee table. I tucked the blanket around him and let myself out, taking extra care to lock up and turn off the coffeepot before I left.

Mia was waiting for me on the front steps when I arrived at the school, with an extra cup of take-out coffee in her hands. I took it gratefully, knowing her budget wasn't that much bigger than mine and I felt better about my plans to provide her dinner tonight. The two cups of coffee I'd had at home made me ambulatory, but I was hoping a third would make me awake enough to get on with the day.

"You okay?" she asked, following me up the steps to the school, past the group of smokers getting in one last hit of nicotine before class.

I told her I was fine, just up late catching up on the reading. How else do I explain the midnight serenade from the night before? I got inside with minutes to spare, and enjoyed the sensation of setting up my notebooks and pens and books and highlighters, secure in the knowledge I was prepared.

The class itself was an interesting discussion of intentional torts; the type of thing personal injury lawyers would make their bread and butter on once they graduated. We talked about assault, battery, intent, and harm. I was able to answer when I was called on, and I wanted to do a little happy dance inside when the professor told me I was correct. Maybe I would fit in here after all. It was a definite improvement over the past few days of confusion.

We moved out into the hallway after class, and Mia and I talked about the fundraiser Evangeline had roped us all into helping with. I kept hoping that Aiden would stay away, that Bert would either stay home or stay quiet, and that nothing else out of the ordinary would cause a scene. Even Evangeline's crazy mother-hen-in-Gucci act seemed like an oasis of sanity in the otherwise insane week I'd been having. And then there was the idea we'd also see a new art exhibit for free, something the public would have to pay for, and before anyone else in the city could get in. I wasn't the world's biggest art buff, but it sounded like a nice break from law school and whatever else was going on in my life.

Contracts passed uneventfully, and I enjoyed the feeling again of being prepared. I still didn't understand what they were talking about, with offers and acceptance and consideration and reliance, but at least I'd done enough of the reading to be able to take coherent notes and write my questions in the margins of my notebook. I'd have to ask someone in my study group if they understood the reading. I felt like I was reading Greek most of the time.

When my class ended, I left the school to get groceries and thank-you beer for Bert. Mia asked for a few hours to get her own stuff done before she came over, so I had a break to stock up. I came home burdened with my backpack and bags of groceries in both arms to find Bert trying to read from the stack of Dad's papers I'd piled up the night before.

"What are you doing?" I asked as I put things down on my thrift store kitchen table.

"Trying to get a jumpstart on all the reading you're going to do tonight," he replied.

Oops. I hadn't thought about including Bert in the research extravaganza that night, because I wasn't really sure what Mia would think of a talking, reading, used-to-be-human frog. I wondered how he'd take that. I tried to think of a reply, or at least an excuse for him to hide in the bathtub or in my bedroom while Mia was here. How much goodwill does thank-you beer buy?

I poured him a beer into a mug so he could enjoy it while I put the groceries away. He crabbed at me a bit for buying domestic beer. "Is this some kind of joke? You bought a frog Budweiser? Have you been watching too many old commercials? You couldn't get something imported?" What a beer snob.

I was saved from making an excuse—because it was on sale—when the doorbell rang. It was still an hour before Mia had said she'd show up, so I looked out the window to see that Aiden had found my apartment. He was alone, carrying a pie.

Pie gets my attention every single time. I'm a bit of a dessert-aholic. I opened the door to talk to him, but I didn't let him in.

"What kind of pie is that?" I asked. Dad would take me out for pie after every report card. There used to be a place near where we lived that served some of the greatest pie I'd ever eaten. My all-time favorite had been their strawberry-rhubarb. I'd cried when I found out they'd closed their doors forever. Of course, there wasn't anything worse than bad pie. It looked great, but how was I to know how good he was in the kitchen?

He held out the pie box to me, smiling. "Don't be afraid. I didn't cook it, and taking it doesn't oblige you in any way to anyone. It's a gift, with no strings attached. Doris made it. You might remember her from the meeting the other night; older woman, hair pulled back in a bun, wire-rimmed granny glasses?"

I shook my head. I didn't remember too many people from that night clearly. I thought I would probably recognize people if I saw them again, but at the moment I was drawing a blank. "You're sure there's not anything funny about it? I'm not going to start mooing when I talk, or wearing tin foil on my head after I eat it, am I? It's not going to curse me and make my hair start growing again, is it?"

He laughed. "Doris would be offended if one of her pies ever did that to anyone. She's like everyone's long lost grandmother at the council meetings. She felt bad for all you've been going through and sent this. It's a Dutch apple pie. She wanted to do strawberry-rhubarb, but strawberries are out of season right now. She just wanted to reach out to you. Trust me, it is good pie. If you don't want it, I'll happily take it home myself. Doris's pies are out of this world."

Wow, that was really thoughtful. I couldn't help but smile. "Please thank her for me. I definitely accept, and it's good timing since I'll have company in about an hour."

His face fell. "Oh. I should have known you'd have a boyfriend coming over."

Did he look disappointed because I was busy or because I might not be single? Hey, I am a girl. I couldn't help giving him a quick once-over. I wondered how long I could ignore the insane magic-using paranoid discussions, but he was cute. And I was single. Did he want to know for himself, or for his file? After all, he'd known about Dad, and his friends had known about the pie. Or had they? Was I really this paranoid? How long could I leave him standing on the doorstep without saying anything?

I shook my head and smiled at him. "Thanks for that, but I'm not dating anyone. My friend Mia is coming over to help me do some research." He didn't need to know what kind of research she was coming over for, so I didn't tell him.

His face brightened at my response. "Well, I won't keep you. I heard you'd had some problems last night, and that Bert was able to help you. He does work for us, you know."

No, I didn't know that, but I wasn't surprised. I took the pie out of his hands before he could drop it. I hadn't forgotten the cloud of clumsy that seemed to follow him around. "Thanks for this. Is there anything else I can do for you?" I asked, still blocking my living room with my body. I didn't plan on inviting him in with Dad's stuff in piles all over the living room. Of course, if Bert worked with them and he'd filled them in on the animal band last night, they'd find it all out eventually, but I wanted a crack at it first.

Aiden looked back down at his shoes. "Oh, well, just so you know we're here to help. I know you've had a lot dumped on you lately, but I think something else is going to happen really soon. Do you know how to handle a weapon?"

That wasn't what I expected, especially if I'd thought he was interested in my dating status earlier. "No. Dad had guns, but I was never allowed to touch them. After he got sick, I never asked and he didn't go hunting anymore. They're in storage, I'm sure, up in the attic."

"I thought you sold the house." He looked confused.

"I did. That's how I'm paying for law school, with the proceeds from the sale of the house. Dad rented out the house after he married Evangeline. It wasn't where I spent my childhood. We moved in with her, and I'm sure there's still a bunch of his stuff up in the attic at her house that never got unpacked in the first place. I took all of his books and papers, but I haven't had the time to go get the rest since I moved. I'm not sure I've got room for it all, anyway, so I haven't brought everything here yet."

He nodded. "I think you'll want to get them soon, and it wouldn't hurt to have a gun here; though it might be smart for you to go to a firing range and take a gun safety class before you do. I've heard your dad had a trunk reinforced with iron. Do you know the one I mean?"

I nodded at him. "Yeah, it's at Evangeline's house. I'll go get it this weekend, after the fundraiser. How'd you know about it?"

"Your dad told me, right before he died. He couldn't talk much, but he said he wasn't sure you would remember it, and he didn't think Evangeline would either. He said something about if I had a reason to contact you, you might need reminding about the trunk and the rest of his stuff. I'm just following up."

Wow. I was a bit shell-shocked, standing there, wanting to ask more about Dad, but the words just wouldn't form the questions I wasn't sure how to ask. How had he known about those trunks? As far as I knew, nobody knew about them. I didn't get a chance to ask.

Instead, Aiden wanted to know about the fundraiser, so I told him. At a hundred bucks a seat, I rather doubted he'd be able to afford it, but at the same time, if I sold a seat, my stepmother would be thrilled with me. That's priceless; a win-win situation either way. He either wouldn't be able to show up and cause a scene, or I'd make Evangeline very happy.

"I'm sorry, Aiden," I said, trying to shoo him away so I'd have some time to get ready for Mia, and to mull over what he'd just said about Dad. "This is just bad timing. I've got a bunch to do before Mia gets here, including some studying."

He looked disappointed, like he'd wanted to be invited in, but I wasn't going there. After a moment of awkward silence, he said goodbye. "Well, I'll leave you to it, then."

His crestfallen look made me feel like I'd kicked a puppy. I had an unbelievable urge to go apologize and tell him to come inside before I remembered I wanted Dad's stuff to myself first. I ended up promising to meet up with him on Saturday, to try to figure out what danger I might be in. "It's a date," I said, when he proposed coffee that morning, on him.

He blushed when I said it, but waved goodbye and headed out to his car just as Mia pulled up early, or so I thought.

A quick glance at the clock on the microwave showed I'd lost track of time, and still hadn't been able to come up with an explanation Bert would swallow without complaint or hurt feelings to keep Mia from thinking I was crazy. Oh well, I might as well tell her all of it; she'd find out eventually if stuff like the Rapunzel hair and the musicians kept happening.

CHAPTER FOURTEEN

Mia approached the doorway to find me still holding Aiden's pie box. "Oh, yum," she said.

"What, the pie? I hope so. Hey, what did you think about Property class?" I asked, hoping to divert her from asking too many questions that I couldn't answer. I opened the door further to let her in, but tried to stay between her and Bert until I could figure out how to introduce him. I was still coming up pretty blank in the explanations department.

She shook her head, stopping to look me in the eye just inside the doorway. "Boy, are you dense. I'm sure the pie's fine, but I meant the guy. He's good-looking, and he brings baked goods. You can't beat that. Where'd you meet him?"

I had to stop and remember she hadn't seen the cloud of catastrophe that seemed to surround Aiden, or heard his absurd theories about Dad's death, curses, magic, or anything else. "Yeah, he's sexy incarnate, if you're into uncoordinated mayhem. He's a walking disaster. He trips over his own feet."

"That's cute," she said, watching as he drove away in his tiny compact car. "I'd still go out with him, but it's nice to have advance warning. Or are you interested?"

I ignored Mia's not-so-subtle question. Bert had made himself scarce as I turned into the living room, so I walked through, wondering where he'd gone, and put the pie in the kitchen. I was grateful he had vamoosed, but I wasn't sure when he might make a surprise reappearance. I didn't want to be unprepared, but I still wasn't coming up with any reasonable excuse for him. Even if I could explain *who* he was, how could I explain *why* he was here?

Mia spotted all the piles of books and papers and scrapbooks I'd tried to organize the night before. "Wow, your dad saved just about everything. Look at this picture. This has got to be you." She sat down on the couch with a loose snapshot from one of the piles in her hand. "Where was this taken?"

I came back into the living room from the kitchen. "I can't be more than six or seven, but I don't remember this picture. It looks like some kind of street fair or carnival. I don't recall ever going to anything like that, and I don't look very happy to be there. I wonder why I seem so scared." If it had been at the top of the pile, why didn't I remember seeing it last night? It must have fallen out of some photo album or journal when I wasn't looking. And why didn't I remember the picture? I didn't know, but there it was, and there was no question I was the kid in the picture. I remembered the pigtails, and the pink overalls; I'd seen them in other pictures of myself at that age.

Mia nodded. "Why would you be scared at a carnival? I'd think a kid would be on cloud nine. Of course, you might have gotten scared of heights on the ride, or sick from too much cotton candy, or do you have some phobia of clowns I don't know about?"

I shook my head. None of this looked even close to familiar, and the look on my face was sheer terror, not some momentary hesitation or junk food nausea. "I don't remember going to anything like a carnival at that age. I must've been too young to remember it. Is there a date on the back of it?"

"There's nothing on the back but your name. Janie, you're not really a little kid in this picture. You're what, nine or ten? I'd think you would remember a place like this."

I picked it up and examined it. The picture was frayed and wrinkled. I didn't know where it had come from. We agreed to set it off to the side for a while as we searched the piles of Dad's papers.

She started on the scrapbooks and photo albums while I tackled Dad's journals. We read in silence for a while, organizing and sifting through Dad's keepsakes. Both of us laughed out loud at the bad fashion choices I wore as a kid, as well as my parents' dated haircuts and clothing.

My father had started keeping a journal when he was just a teenager. It was a habit I'd never picked up, but I smiled as I read about the childhood worries of the man who became my father. He talked about the normal teenage issues of fitting in and peer pressure. I laughed out loud at the entry where he worried about what he would do if he were ever asked to take drugs. When I did the math, I realized he'd been fifteen years old when he wrote that journal entry.

Apparently, he'd smoked some pot when he was sixteen and swore never to do so again. He was convinced the trolls he'd seen in the hallway were a result of some sort of LSD-based hallucinogen laced into the joint he'd stolen from an older boy in his neighborhood. I smiled at that one. If I'd smoked any pot this past week, I'd have thought the same thing. Of course, I'd never smoked pot in my life, so who knows what I'd have thought if Bert had shown up when I was stoned. I had no measuring stick to know what I'd be like when I was high.

I hadn't realized Dad had grown up in a foster home. He hadn't talked much about his own childhood that I could remember.

The only thing he'd had from his parents was an old family Bible with a family tree inside he'd never paid much attention to until he was in college. He'd worked his way through school by way of a succession of odd jobs, getting a double degree in literature and history, and then his masters and his doctorate. He'd met my mother when he was in graduate school, researching what would become his dissertation on the role of folklore providing context for historical study of culture.

Dad never said much about why he'd chosen his field, and his journals didn't explain it for me either. There wasn't a whole lot of discussion here, just the matter of fact way he'd gone about his work. That was my Dad, straightforward and matter of fact. Then there were a whole lot of blank pages, and it seemed, a handful of pages ripped out of his journal.

"Hey, Mia, get a load of this," I called out, as I sat up straight on the couch and began reading aloud.

"June 1, 1998.

One day, I'll need to explain to Janie why I had to leave her. I just can't stand to see her mother's eyes in her face any longer. The police cannot convince me that my wife has run off. We've found no evidence of foul play; they've never found a body, but I just can't believe she was gone. It's been twenty months since she disappeared. There's just no way she'd leave like that, no matter what the police think."

Mia sat up straight. "I don't think I ever heard you say what happened to your mom."

I shrugged. "She took off, and we never saw her again. I never heard anything else, and I don't remember much about her." My mind was racing. The date on the entry was just a couple of months before the perfect wedding to my evil step-monster. Here was my dad, still mooning over the loss of my mother, but he was about to get married again really quickly. That didn't make sense. I didn't remember any of it. Mia put down the photo album she'd been digging through and listened quietly as I read aloud.

"I spent most of last year officially on sabbatical. The truth is I'm still in a mental hospital. I just can't take Abigail being gone. I've started to imagine she's here with me just to make it through each day. My friends filed the paperwork to have me committed. For Janie's sake, I have to face reality; Abby isn't coming back."

I didn't remember any of this. Dad would be the last person I'd have thought could go crazy. He'd always been so rational about anything we'd talked about. Since I didn't have any answers, I kept reading aloud, hoping to stumble on enlightenment.

"I started to imagine little green men waiting around the corner, ready to snatch Janie out of my hands just like her mother had been taken away from me, or so it felt at the time. I saw winged creatures laughing in my face. I saw goblins and hobgoblins and creatures you only hear about in horror movies. I had to be losing my mind. My neighbors, Frank and Doris Wilson, agreed to take care of Janie while I was gone. They're good to her, and she loves spending time with them. I couldn't put it off any longer. I had to seek help with my hallucinations, as the therapists call them."

Why didn't I know that Dad spent time in a mental facility? Nothing had ever been said about it. I didn't remember him going to counseling, or talking about mental problems. Of course, he could have been on some heavy-duty psychotropic medications and I wouldn't have noticed each and every pill bottle there at the end. I almost needed a doctorate in calculus to keep up with his medication schedule in the month before he'd died, and we'd needed a hospice nurse to help keep it all straight. Evangeline hadn't been much help.

I kept reading, moving on to the next journal entry. "I never stopped seeing the hallucinations, but I learned that they couldn't be real. I ignored them. Janie never acted like she saw them. I'm ashamed to admit I use her as a way to separate the real from the hallucinations now that I'm home. Janie, if you're reading this journal, I'm sorry.

"I think I've convinced my therapists I no longer see them, although I flushed the medications they sent home with me. I can't think straight with those heavy doses, and Janie needs me to be a good parent since I'm the only one she has left."

Mia handed me a tissue.

I hadn't realized I was crying until I mopped the tears from my face. "I don't remember him being gone, but he's saying he was hallucinating and paranoid and he refused his meds for me. If he spent that much time in the hospital, why don't I remember any of this? Why don't I remember him being gone?" I couldn't have been too young. I remembered lots of details from his wedding to Evangeline, and that wasn't long after the dates in the journal.

She shook her head and took the book from me, before continuing to read aloud. Neither one of us had any answers. We hadn't become friends until high school. She wasn't around for that period of my life, so she had no memories of the time.

"I came home last week. I'll have the summer to make it up to my beautiful daughter, who hopefully will never know exactly what hell I've been living through. I've gotten better at hiding my grief over Abby. I've learned that the right answer is to make sure no one gets wind of how I really feel. Janie's the important one. I've got to give her a decent childhood. It's not her fault her mother isn't here anymore."

"What did he tell you about your mother, Janie?" Mia asked.

"I'm not exactly sure. I remember him telling me she was gone, but I don't know how. I always assumed she just didn't want us anymore."

"Why do you say that? His diary doesn't read like that."

I didn't get a chance to answer; I was distracted by a piece of paper sticking out of the back of the journal. I pulled it free and stared at it. "Oh. My. God. I've never seen this before." I pulled a clipping out of the journal. It was dated just a few weeks after the journal entry I'd been reading. The headline read, "Housewife Disappearance Solved: Body Found by Highway 35". I read the article to Mia. It turned out my mother, Abigail Grimm, disappeared two years before her body was found on the side of the highway. The police had no leads as to how the body was there and seemed puzzled at the marks, unspecified, on her body.

I broke down, sobbing in Mia's arms as she tried to comfort me. It took several minutes before I could think coherently again. I'd always assumed my mother hadn't wanted me. What was the truth?

When I'd calmed down enough for rational thought, I grabbed my planner and wrote down the name of the police detective handling the case. Had someone killed her? Had she been kidnapped? I knew I'd want to find out more after I finished sifting through all of Dad's stuff.

That reminded me of the heavy trunks in Evangeline's attic I'd been talking to Aiden about. I wiped away a tear and swallowed hard, trying to ignore the thought that my mother was probably murdered. "We'll never get through all of this tonight, Mia, and this isn't all of it. There's some stuff of Dad's in the attic at my stepmother's house I'll need to get. Do you know anyone with a truck?" She didn't.

I could see I wasn't fooling her. She could tell I was still upset, but if there was any truth to Dad's supposed hallucinations, my mother's unexplained death, Aiden and Bert's cryptic warnings, and the curse that was allegedly following me, then I couldn't wallow in my feelings until I'd figured it all out. I wondered if Aiden knew anyone who could help.

Feeling like I was stumbling from one unrelated thought to another, I suggested a break and dinner, trying to get a bit of distance from my emotional upheaval to get a handle on what was going on.

Of course, the suggestion of dinner was all it took to bring Bert out of his hiding place, and distract me from my mental meanderings.

It just wasn't the distraction I'd been looking for.

CHAPTER FIFTEEN

"Well, don't just stand there, Janie, while your friend stares at me in a thoroughly undignified manner. Aren't you going to introduce us?" Bert hopped his way out of the bottom of my linen closet in the hallway, and headed right for Mia, who had frozen in place on the couch. Indeed, her jaw had dropped about as far as it could go and still be attached.

"Um, Mia Andersen, meet Englebert Maximus Jorgensen Horace the Sixth. Also known as Bert," I added, unhelpfully. Buried as I had been by the trip through my father's journals, I'd stopped trying to come up with an answer to the Bert problem. I still wasn't quite sure how to explain him. I was saved from making something up when Mia started to scream and climbed the back of the couch as far as she could away from Bert, as if he was carrying some dreaded disease.

"Mia, it's really all right," I tried to explain when she stopped shrieking long enough to draw breath.

"What the hell do you mean, it's all right? It most certainly is not all right! You have a lizard in your living room. *And it talks!*" she yelled, and started to scream again before I slapped her across the face, trying to get her to shut up. It didn't work.

Bert began to yell something about not being a lizard, but that wasn't solving anything; it was just making things louder. The two of them kept yelling, the noise level escalating. I let out a long piercing whistle to get their attention and get them to look at me.

"Hey, you two, I've got neighbors, and I don't want them to call the cops. You gotta shut up and I'll explain." I left aside the issue I hadn't yet figured out *how* to explain. I was taking this one step at a time.

Mia's eyes were still wide, but she'd stopped screaming. "You've lost your mind, and now you've contaminated me. Is there a gas leak in your apartment? Is the pie guy poisoning pastries to make you go nuts? I take back all the things I said about him. Or maybe you've lost touch with reality with all the grief over your Dad, and decided to take it out on your friends. That thing can't really *talk*, can it? Am I going to go crazy now that I've seen it? What kind of a prank is this to play on a friend?"

Bert chose that moment to use a stack of books and papers as a ladder to hop to the top of my coffee table, spilling them over in an avalanche of disorganization. "Of course I can talk," he said in the most soothing tone I'd heard him use yet. "I wasn't always a frog. You're not crazy, and neither is Janie, although I'm still surprised she didn't completely flip out, like you're doing, when she saw me." He waddled closer to her.

"You can't be real," she whispered, even as she reached out a hand.

Quick as a shot, his tongue darted out and barely grazed the back of her hand, proving his existence. She snatched her hand back, clutching it to her chest as she scrambled back to the top of the couch. A look of shock spread across her face as she looked to me.

"Yes, he's the frog from the first day of class, though I didn't know it at the time." I crossed my arms, trying to look calm, even though my mind was still racing from all the revelations tonight. Bert was right. I had reacted, but why hadn't I freaked out like Mia? What was wrong with me?

Mia rubbed her eyes with the back of her unlicked hand, blinked at Bert, and rubbed her eyes again. He winked at her when she opened her eyes the second time. "You can't believe any of this is true, Janie," she said, not taking her eyes off the frog on the coffee table. "It just isn't possible. It's too crazy."

I understood Mia's reaction, but I'd had a little more time to grasp the idea that, while I might be crazy, the stuff happening in my life wasn't any less real to me. "Mia, the guy who brought the pie is named Aiden. He introduced me to some people who know a little bit more about what's going on, a group called F.A.B.L.E.S., the Foundation for Ancestry, Biography, Legends, Epics, and Stories. They've told me I might be in danger. I don't know if I believe them, but something's definitely going on. I had the Bremen Town Musicians in the parking lot giving an impromptu performance last night; the animals were making what could loosely be called music outside my window. I've been told the hair stunt from the other day was something called Rapunzel Syndrome, which is supposedly a side effect of a curse someone put on me. And I've been told Dad was also cursed, as opposed to the cancer I'd thought he died from."

"And you believe this?" she asked, even as she shrank back from Bert from her perch at the top of the couch. Bert was smiling at her, and I think it was freaking her out more than calming her down; frog smiling is just that creepy and weird. She kept edging away from him and from me. I wondered how long before she fell backwards onto the floor.

"It's getting hard to deny what I've seen with my own eyes. They cured the hair growth problem with chants and some kind of potion. Mia, you saw the hair growth, and you saw me the next day after I was cured. Can you think of any prank I could pull that let my hair grow like that? You helped me cut it. Was it fake? It didn't feel fake to me. Bert helped me solve the problem of the musical animals last night. Things have been a little on the strange side for the past week or so, to say the least, but I have no other explanation for any of it." I stood up from my chair and went into the kitchen to get a glass of water for her.

She called after me. "So is this why you've been acting so strange the last couple of days? You've always been a bit off, but this week's been too much, even for you."

"A bit off? Thanks, Mia. Just what I needed to hear from a friend these days." I got some ice out of the freezer.

She snorted. "You know what I mean."

"No, I don't," I replied, as I came back and handed her the water. Hey, I was trying to be a good host, and I figured she'd had a heck of a shock. I tried to swallow the annoyance at her insinuation that I was nuts, and instead ignored it. "What did you mean by that?"

Mia shook her head and took a sip of water before answering. "You've always refused to talk much about your childhood. You never wanted to talk about your Mom. Now you're telling me you've got gaps in your memory, and you didn't think you were losing your mind when a frog shows up and tells you that your Dad was killed with a curse?"

Well, I'd thought I was losing my mind, but I hadn't second-guessed it as much as I should have. What was wrong with me? "Mia, I don't remember being evasive about my childhood, but I don't have a lot of memories of Mom. Evangeline's just weird, and Dad was already sick when you and I became friends. Is it any wonder I didn't want to talk about my family life? And this week, I can tell you that I've been more worried about putting one foot in front of the other and not getting behind in class than I was about everything else going on. Call me stubborn but, after the first day, I was terrified I wouldn't be able to cut it at school."

She sighed. "Janie, you can always restart law school later if you need to. I wondered if you were jumping in too soon after your Dad died. Maybe you should take this year off."

"I can't." I sat down again, this time on the couch next to her. I curled my feet up underneath myself to sit Indian-style. "I spent my inheritance on tuition, I don't have a job, and I'd lose money I can't get back if I dropped out now. Besides, what would taking a year off do besides waste money and time?"

"You really think you can handle it all?"

I looked around at my apartment. I saw the piles of books and notes in the corner for school that I'd dumped when I got home that day. I took in the stacks of papers and journals from Dad covering the coffee table and the floor. Bert was quietly watching the interaction between us, waiting for a final response. "Yeah, I think I can. But I can only pull it off with help, which is why you're here. Will you help me?"

She sighed. "You promise I'm not losing my mind, and you won't get me behind in class?"

I nodded. It meant a lot to me that she was even considering it.

"Then I'm in." She picked up another photo album. "You're a good friend, and I've never known you to be a liar. Even if you *are* starting to lose it, you'll need someone to tell you when it goes too far. Besides, I've always wondered what happened when you were a kid. Just keep that green slimy thing away from me so I can at least pretend there's something normal about all this."

Bert huffed, rolling his eyes at her as he hopped off into the bedroom. I wondered what he'd have to say about all this later, but I didn't have the time or the energy to deal with drama from him right now; I had enough of my own. I didn't follow him.

Mia wasn't paying attention to my mental meanderings; she was staring after Bert as he flounced off, hopping with his nose up in the air as he went. "Janie, what is it you're looking for in all these papers? This isn't just a trip down memory lane."

"I'm looking for anything in Dad's papers that either rules out what Bert and Aiden have been saying, or confirms it. For some reason, I can't remember all that I should. I've spent so much time lately on crisis management instead of figuring out why things are happening. I don't know who or what to trust. Dad's journal talked about stuff he saw that made his friends check him into a mental hospital, but he might really have been crazy. I'm looking for something I can independently check; so I know Bert and Aiden aren't pulling some elaborate prank, or con artists taking advantage of a daughter who misses her dad."

She stared at me for a minute. After considering what I'd said, she nodded. "That sounds very practical. I think I've found it for you." She handed me a photograph, pointing to something in the picture as she handed it over. "This picture was taken here, in Dayton, in Carillon Park. If you go there, and stand where the camera would have been, you might be able to see whether this still exists. If it does, you've got your proof."

I took the picture from her. She was right.

CHAPTER SIXTEEN

Mia and I piled into my Buick and headed for Carillon Park. It contains buildings and exhibits and wooded walkways that celebrate Ohio's history from colonial times forward, such as the Wright brothers and aviation history. There is a separate open space with a giant freestanding bell tower in the park that hosts concerts and other community events.

The historical sections of the park were closing soon, so we didn't have time to enjoy all the different exhibits and buildings, but the rest of the park was open to the public until dark. We had plenty of time to walk around in order to find out where the photo she'd found had been taken. It didn't take long.

Mia stood in the place where I'd been standing in the picture, on the hill, not far from the carillon, and crouched down to approximately the height of an eight-year-old. I looked over her left shoulder, searching for the same clues I'd seen in the picture.

I saw it quickly, but if I hadn't been looking for it, I'd have missed it. The leaves were glistening; it would be easy to mistake their sparkling leaves for the evening sun reflecting off the brown and gold of fall leaves. We raced over to see what it was. In the tree, in the same place where I'd seen the glistening in the photograph, was a gold apple.

It wasn't a Golden Delicious apple, like I'd bought the other day at the grocery store. Instead, the limb of the tree dipped gracefully under the weight of its single gold apple. As we stood there watching, a gold bird flitted from limb to limb, as if gauging whether the apple was ripe enough to harvest.

I looked at Mia, whose mouth hung open watching the bird. "Mia, act at least a little cool. You look like you're mentally challenged or a tourist if you gawk at an apple tree in Ohio like that. People are staring." Johnny Appleseed planted trees across Ohio over two hundred years ago. Almost every Ohio school kid learns about Johnny

Appleseed. Some of the trees he planted were still standing. They were everywhere. If other locals saw her staring like that, they'd come over and make fun of the crazy person staring at an apple tree, or laugh at the out-of-towner making a fool of themselves. If the purpose of standing out here was to see if we could prove I wasn't crazy, having people think she'd lost her mind seemed counterproductive.

She blinked. "You're right. But don't you think we ought to try and see what the apple looks like? Or how heavy it is? What if it's solid gold all the way through? Wonder how much it's worth? How much would that cover in tuition and books and fees?"

I hadn't even thought of that. "Mia, it's not like it belongs to us."

"Janie, it's likely this thing's been here since you were eight. You're twenty-two now. How many people pass through here in a day? A week? A year? It's been fourteen years since someone caught that thing on film, and no one has ever taken it. I say finders, keepers."

Mia was mesmerized by the gold glinting in the evening sun. The bird hopped around the apple a few more times, and spread its wings, shooting down to a lower branch. I caught Mia's hands before she could reach for it. "Leave it alone, Mia. It doesn't belong to us." I held up the photograph again. "Look, we've proven that this picture is real. There really is an apple made of solid gold in the tree. We're not crazy. Bert's not some shared delusion, and neither is that picture you found. We got what we came for. Now let's get out of here before we get chased out."

She wasn't listening, and I caught her reaching for a low branch as if she was going to scale the tree.

"What the hell are you doing? That thing isn't ours!" I grabbed her by the back of her shirt and yanked her down.

Mia pulled away as I tried to keep her from climbing the tree. She kept fighting harder and harder as I pulled her back. She yanked my hair and scratched my cheek with her nails as I held on.

I must have been more of a tomboy than she was. Memories of scuffles I'd gotten into as a child came back in a flood, along with Evangeline's frosty disapproval, and my father's barely concealed grin of understanding. In a flash, I remembered how to hold her down by the hair on the top of her head, how to use an elbow to distract her—by shoving it directly into her stomach, of course—how to twist her arm behind her back, and how to hold her down and rub her face in the grass to get her attention.

When all of that didn't work, I slapped her across the face, hard, which only stunned her for a second. Then, in a stroke of desperation, I took off my necklace long enough to wrap the chain around both our wrists. If she was being held hostage by some magical compulsion, I hoped Aiden's charm would help break it. I wasn't sure what I would do if that didn't work.

Park employees in historical costumes were heading our way just as Mia stopped fighting me and let me pull her to her feet. I was careful to grab her hand with mine and wrap the necklace through our fingers. I didn't want to drop it.

"Is everything okay here, Miss?"

"I'm sorry, sir," I answered. "We were just trying out some wrestling moves. We're attempting to get the university to start a women's wrestling club, since there isn't a wrestling team for women in college." What else was I going to say? I was making it up as I went.

The male employee dressed up like Benjamin Franklin's sloppy younger brother didn't look convinced. Mia stood beside me, nodding mutely, with a dazed expression on her face. When he asked her, she parroted my explanation, and then held up our clasped hands to show him we weren't angry at each other. He looked at us and leered. God bless men with minds in the gutter, I guess. As we stepped away from him, he began to stare at the tree as well, distracted and staring straight ahead in a trance. The other two employees with him did the same.

Before we got more than a few steps away, the golden bird suddenly swooped out of the tree and landed on my shoulder, holding the stem of the apple in its beak. Without a sound, the bird dropped the apple into my outstretched hand and flew away again, leaving a golden feather behind to mark its presence. I stuffed the feather into my jacket pocket along with the apple.

It was time to get out of here before the museum employees came out of whatever spell they were under and began checking into my story about a wrestling club. *Which didn't exist to my knowledge.* I settled Mia into the passenger seat, untangled the necklace from our hands, then shut the door. I weighed the apple in my hand as I rushed to get into the driver's seat and get the heck out of there. It was heavy, as I'd suspected, but heavier than I'd thought.

I started the car and backed out of the parking space. When I finally got back on the highway, I looked over at Mia to see how she was handling it. She looked pale, but she turned and gave me a small smile. "I guess you're not crazy. And that means I'm not either."

"Yeah," I said. "I don't know what this apple means, yet. I don't know what the feather means, either. But I do know what it means to me."

She nodded.

I was at least a little bit relieved to find out I wasn't losing my mind, but I was rapidly becoming concerned for my own safety. If we weren't crazy, then Aiden and Bert weren't making things up, either. I was in danger, and my dad really had been murdered.

At that point, I couldn't do much more than wish they were wrong. I strongly suspected they weren't, and I didn't know what to do next.

CHAPTER SEVENTEEN

When we got back to my place that night, Mia didn't want to stick around long. She still looked shaken, and I couldn't really blame her. What could I say? I felt numb, worried about whether Dad had suffered, worried that it was too late for me to stop whatever was happening, and scared for my own safety. What had I missed in those last few months of Dad's life? Had I been able to do anything to save him, and failed because I didn't know what to look for?

Bert didn't have a lot of answers about the golden apple. He knew it was valuable, but he wasn't sure what to do with it. The feather was a different story. On the spine of the feather, there was an engraving, telling me to *"Beware of dangers closer than known"*. He'd never heard of such a thing before, and wanted me to talk with Aiden about it. I promised I would call Aiden later, but I wanted some time to process what I'd learned about my dad.

I spent the night wallowing in grief and fear and anger and loss. I didn't get much studying done, so it was a good thing there wasn't much scheduled in the way of classes on Fridays. I muddled through the day, hoping and praying nothing would happen during the two hours of class I couldn't seem to concentrate on. And then I realized I couldn't call Aiden that night: I'd promised Evangeline I'd help her at the Dayton Art Institute fundraiser she was hosting.

Before last night's adventure, I'd been looking forward to Evangeline's Friday night party, figuring it would be a pocket of normality in a week jam-packed with crazy. Even dealing with Evangeline's nagging and her condescending friends would be a nice break from the lunacy, stress, and drama of the last week.

I was wrong.

I pulled up that night in my Buick with Mia in the front seat, still a little shaken from the previous evening's weirdness, but she seemed better than she had looked when we started classes that morning. Bert had agreed to stay in the car, but I couldn't talk him into staying at home. He was convinced we might need his advice if things got strange. Bert hid under the seat as I parked the car and cracked the windows for him. Mia ignored his presence under the seat, almost as if she was trying to forget last night's revelations.

We didn't do much more than step foot out of the car in the parking lot before Evangeline was there to greet us. She was blocking our way into the building with her arms crossed over her chest, tapping her foot impatiently. As we walked up to her, she didn't waste a minute before she began the nagging routine. "Janie, I swear, I don't understand how you've been able to get through life without someone to make sure you get where you're going on time. You're always late. Haven't you ever learned that it's unprofessional? And didn't I tell you to buy a watch?"

What could I say? "Evangeline, I'm sorry. I thought you'd told me to be here at six."

She let out a long-suffering sigh. "The cocktail hour starts at six. That means you and your friends should already be passing out flyers and information sheets. You're lucky your other friends knew how to show up on time."

I figured that they'd actually shown up early, or she hadn't nagged them since she didn't know them, but I had no way to tell. Mia and I made our apologies and asked my stepmother where she wanted us to be. There really was no way to win this argument.

We headed toward the office that was serving as a temporary drop zone for the volunteers' personal effects to leave our jackets and purses. Evangeline pointed us toward the atrium doors, and provided us with stacks of programs and fundraising envelopes and other materials to give out as the guests arrived, with strict instructions to circulate with them later to make sure everyone got all the paperwork necessary to make a donation. "Because they can't donate if they don't have the right forms."

Once Evangeline left us alone, Mia turned to me. "She's pleasant," she said, the sarcasm dripping as we waited for the donation targets, I mean *guests*, to arrive.

I shrugged. I'd spent my life trying to avoid introducing my friends to Evangeline, because I was never sure how she'd treat them.

I'd always walked to Mia's house, or met her other places when we were in high school, and in college it was easy to avoid them coming in contact altogether; Dad's illness kept me from being too social.

"I'm used to it. Hey, why don't I stay here and you go check with the others to make sure she hasn't traumatized them too badly?"

She nodded and walked toward our friends, standing by the next set of doors. I settled myself into organizing our materials and taking a minute to familiarize myself with what was going on that evening.

From what I read, it was a formal sit-down dinner for the Friends of the Art Institute group Evangeline belonged to, and these people were paying one hundred dollars a head for chicken and rice with asparagus—we were handing out the menus as well. I couldn't believe they were paying that much for a meal I could probably throw together for less than five bucks a serving. I could also think of causes I'd be more likely to spend that kind of money on, like feeding hungry children or ensuring world peace. I'd never say that out loud to Evangeline; she spent hours working for the museum, and I had seen first-hand some of the exhibits she'd raised money for. They weren't always my cup of tea, but without her work, I doubted the museum would have had the variety of exhibits and programs I'd seen.

It looked like there was a short program in the auditorium after dinner, including a slide show of exhibits funded by tonight's fundraiser. I looked forward to that. Maybe it would give me something to talk to Evangeline about during our weekly brunches and enough information to ask her intelligent questions. It would also do a nice job of distracting me from the inner monologue blaming myself for not saving my father. I know, it was a little late for me to do anything about it, but I'm human. I couldn't help it.

Mia came back, and we made jokes about the overpriced food and the snooty guests until we got busier. My other friends didn't say anything about Evangeline, so she must not have been too horrible to them, or they were just being polite. We were overwhelmed for a while, giving out Evangeline's paperwork, being appropriately courteous and yet still meek enough to be part of the woodwork, which was where Evangeline preferred me. We finished with the first round of guests before we went looking for our overpriced chicken.

Evangeline pointed us in the direction of the caterers and told us we should stay out of sight while we ate. I figured the request was to ensure that she could avoid the appearance of hobnobbing with the working class in front of her hoity-toity friends. We agreed, but I think I surprised her when I said I actually wanted to see the slide show. She smiled at me. "I think that would be wonderful, dear. It's about time you showed an interest in art and culture beyond the modern day trash you insist on corrupting your ears with."

Even though it was on the tip of my tongue to argue that my music wasn't trash, I just nodded and smiled, grateful to make an exit while still in her good graces. No amount of arguing would make her suddenly appreciate Linkin Park, Otep, Joan Jett, or any of the other stuff I loved. Mia and I collected our plates and silverware and headed back to round up our friends.

Mike and Leann, the other two from our study group, had agreed to man the door for latecomers while Mia and I ate in the office. We planned to come back and relieve them as soon as we were done, so they could eat. I didn't want to stay late, and I was hoping I'd get to see Evangeline's slide show after my friends ate their dinner.

Evangeline had really packed them in. I'd counted two hundred copies of flyers and menus, and most of them had been taken by guests coming in. That many cars would mean an interminable wait to get out of the parking lot unless we could beat them out the door. If we'd all eaten, and all the brochures handed out before the final donation pitch, it was possible.

Just as I bit into the buttered roll that came with my dinner, I heard a loud banging noise. "What's that?" I asked, my mouth full of bread.

"What's what?" Mia asked, as she cut into her chicken.

"That noise."

"What are you talking about?"

I heard it again. "It sounds like it's coming from just down the hall, almost like someone's trying to break through a wall."

She gave me a funny look. Okay, so we had spent last night testing our own sanity, and here we were again. "You're nuts. There's nothing there." She went back to her dinner.

I was still wearing Aiden's charm necklace. I could always wrap it around her hand to get her to believe me if this was something magical, but I had to go look. I put down my silverware and napkin, and headed out into the hallway.

She shook her head, but she stood up and followed me.

I headed toward the sound, waiting for someone or something crazy to jump out in our faces. Instead, I heard a muffled grunt, a groan, and a curse as we came around the corner.

"What's going on here?" I asked, as I finally saw where the noise was coming from.

Seven short men stood in front of me. One held a sledgehammer, another had a screwdriver, others held crowbars and bolt cutters. One even had a welding torch. They all turned around and stopped trying to break down the wall and stared at me.

Now, when I say short, I don't mean they didn't hit my minimum height requirement for dating. I mean they came up to mid-thigh on me, and I'm only average height. I'd have thought dwarf, but I've never seen anyone diagnosed with dwarfism look as pinched-faced and green-tinged as these men did. And they had long white hair and beards. I had no idea what they were, but I couldn't let them break into the Art Institute.

Evangeline would never forgive me if other priceless treasures went missing and I could have done something to stop it.

"Who are you talking to?" Mia asked, wandering up behind me.

Oh crap. They must be magical. I could see them, but she couldn't. I guess that meant it was up to me to stop them. I just wasn't quite sure what I was going to do about it.

CHAPTER EIGHTEEN

The seven men dropped the tools they had been holding.

"*Mein Gott,*" one of them said, in a voice so deep and harsh he would have made a ninety-year-old chain smoker sound like a soprano. They took off running as fast as their short legs could take them, their strange pointed stocking caps trailing behind their heads like tails.

"Come on, Mia, we've got to catch them!" I called out, stretching into a run.

I heard a yawn behind me, but I didn't stop to look. I saw the men duck around a corner, and followed. I grabbed the corner of the wall with my hand, using my momentum to slingshot around it without slowing down. As I turned, I realized that Mia wasn't behind me, but I was distracted by the harsh deep chuckle in front of me.

Huh? The hallway was empty, despite the creepy laugh. I'd just seen them turn down this corridor. There weren't any doors they could have reached before I'd gotten around the corner; I hadn't been that far behind them. I mean, I'm not the best sprinter, but my legs were twice as long as theirs. They couldn't have gotten away.

I hurried down the hall to the single door. It was locked, with one of those electronic keypads protecting it. I hit one of the buttons to see if it was working. It beeped at me. I hadn't heard any beeps as I ran down the hallway, and as close as I'd thought I was, I couldn't believe they'd accessed security, opened the door, closed it behind them, then locked it again before I'd seen it. No way could they have moved that fast. Maybe they were around the corner?

I tiptoed to the end of the wall and peered around the next corner. No one was hiding from me. No one was there.

Somehow they'd disappeared.

I turned around. It was time for me to stop playing amateur detective hour and go find out where Mia was. I hoped she was okay. I didn't know if these men were dangerous or not. I retraced my steps, looking for Mia and keeping an eye out for the short men to show up again.

When I passed the hole in the wall, I glanced into it to make sure they hadn't somehow gotten back and hidden inside. There were several large crates with writing on them. I'd taken enough German classes in high school to recognize what the language looked like, but I didn't remember enough vocabulary words to figure out what they actually said. I wondered if the contents of the crates were part of Evangeline's exhibit for Oktoberfest. Given the earlier theft, it was very possible.

The boxes were close enough together that I didn't see how anyone, even men as small as the ones I'd seen, could have squeezed inside. I tried pushing on one of the boxes, but couldn't budge them no matter how hard I pushed. No way were they hiding inside. I wasn't sure what else I could do. There wasn't anyone else in the hall, and I still didn't know where Mia was. I left the hole the way it was and kept going, looking for where she might have gone.

"Mia? Where are you? This isn't funny. We've got to call the cops." I kept calling for her, hoping she'd jump out and tell me it was a joke, but she didn't. I'd be pissed if it was a joke, but the more I called for her and the more she didn't answer, the more worried I got.

I finally found her. In fact, found is a bit tame. I tripped right over her while I was looking the other way. I fell on the floor in a heap, bruising my hip as I landed.

"Mia, what do you think you're doing?" I asked, shoving her to get my feet loose.

No answer. And there was also no movement from my friend on the floor.

"Mia?" I asked, sliding over to shake her by the shoulder. I was rewarded with a resounding snore as I rolled her over so she'd be face-up.

I tried everything I could to wake her up. I called her name. I clapped and whistled and snapped my fingers less than an inch from her ear. I pinched her nose and twisted it sideways to get her attention, but all I got was a louder snore when I let go. "Mia?" I kept calling her name as I shook her by the shoulders, and finally gave in to the urge to slap her across the face.

She didn't budge, except for the movement of her chest moving slowly up and down in the rhythm of deep slumber.

I needed help. I didn't know what to do. There had to be someone out there who could help me. I wondered if there was a doctor among Evangeline's guests. If nothing else, I remembered seeing museum security on the edges of Evangeline's fundraiser. Maybe one of them could help me wake up Mia, or at least call for help.

I grabbed my friend's arm, and tried to drag her down the hallway. Tears pricked the inside of my eyelids, then leaked out to run down my cheeks. I kept wiping them away as I tried to get her down the hall. It got worse when I realized I wasn't strong enough to drag her far enough. I'd have to get help and come back.

I cried as I pulled her into the office where we'd started to eat our dinner, and looked around for anything I could use to wake her up with. I ended up throwing the contents of both of our water glasses on her face, but nothing worked. I didn't have a choice; Mia needed help now. There was something unnatural about how deeply she was asleep. I didn't know what was wrong with her, and I was no doctor.

I balled up my jacket, put it under her head, and spread her own jacket over her chest. The least I could do was make sure she was comfortable.

I closed the door behind me and took a deep breath. It was up to me to get help for my friend. It was up to me to report the break-in. I didn't even know if Mia had seen anything, so I was on my own. My eyes burned from the tears, and my hip throbbed from where I'd fallen when I'd tripped over her in the hallway.

I took off at a run, heading back to the party. Evangeline wouldn't thank me for an interruption, especially if the police showed up, but I was willing to put up with her complaints. Mia needed medical assistance, and I needed to get it quickly.

CHAPTER NINETEEN

There wasn't anyone in the halls. *That's odd,* I thought. At Evangeline's fundraisers, there were generally people bustling all over the place behind the scenes; caterers hurrying around with trays of food, volunteers ducking out to get a bite to eat, or guests sneaking outside for a smoke. None of that was happening. There were no security guards milling around, or museum staff giving directions and answering questions. And most amazing of all, at an event attended by more than two hundred people and a free open bar, no one was searching for a restroom.

I stopped and looked around, wondering where everyone had gone. A party of this size should've been making noise and a lot of it, such as clinking glasses and silverware, conversations between the guests, musicians playing a stuffy classical song Evangeline had selected, and there was also the presentation about the folklore exhibit she was hyping. Curious, I stuck my head into the Gothic Cloister where the dinner was actually held.

Evangeline's upper crust friends were collapsed in undignified heaps around the room. Two county commissioners were asleep on the floor beside the bar, and the bartender was face down in the ice and bottles, his arms splayed over the counter. The mayor was snoring with his nose in a salad, flecks of dressing festooning his hairline. Everywhere I looked I saw the same thing; guests, wait staff, museum security, and volunteers passed out as if they were puppets whose animating strings had been cut mid-scene.

I walked through the room to the doors on the other side, mentally cataloguing Evangeline's snobby friends in my head as I walked. The one person I didn't see was Evangeline herself. I looked for her, but I couldn't find her. Knowing my stepmother, she was probably in the kitchen prep area, collapsed while telling the caterers what they were doing wrong. I made the hard decision to keep going to the front and call for help, rather than take more time to look for her.

When I reached the doors on the other side, I found my friends Leann and Mike leaning against each other, blocking the doorway to the Gothic Cloister where they'd been posted, sound asleep on a pile of spilled pamphlets and menus. I swallowed the rising sense of panic in the back of my throat, and pulled them apart, checking for a pulse to make sure they were okay.

They were fine, their pulses strong and steady, but deep in sleep. It was like moving heavy human-sized rag dolls out of the way so they didn't block the entrance to the hall, and I couldn't move them very far. I *so* needed to start strength training. I pulled my cell phone out of my pocket and dialed 911 as I ran for the front door. I wanted to be at the door when the police and ambulances arrived.

"Hello, 911, what's your emergency?" said the bored voice on the other end of the phone.

"There's something wrong at the Art Institute. You need to send police and ambulances right away."

"Ma'am, I need you to tell me exactly what's going on. What's your name?"

I hit the entrance doors and got outside. "My name is Janie Grimm. My stepmother is Evangeline Kravits Grimm, the chairwoman of the Oktoberfest committee at the Art Institute. The committee was hosting a fundraiser tonight, and the mayor and the city commissioners along with a whole bunch of other people were here to raise money for the upcoming Oktoberfest exhibit."

"Ms. Grimm, why are you calling 911?" I could tell that the dispatcher seemed bored.

"I was one of the volunteers tonight. When I went back to one of the offices to eat my dinner, I heard a noise and went to see what it was. Someone was busting a hole in a wall to get into one of the storage areas. I think it had to do with the exhibit we were raising money for."

"I'm sending police units your way. Did you see where the suspects went?"

"No. I lost them. And then I got distracted by the fact that everyone in the museum, the donors, the presenters, the volunteers, and the wait staff, are all asleep."

"What do you mean *asleep*?" I could tell I had her attention now.

"I'm not a doctor; I'm a law student. They're collapsed, they're snoring, they're not responding, and I don't know what's the matter with them. We need ambulances out here to figure out what's wrong. My friend Mia is back in one of the offices. I can't find my stepmother. I need help, and I need it now." I was getting panicky, my voice rising as I talked faster and faster.

"Ma'am, I've got police and fire on the way, but I'm also trying to get them as much information as possible before they arrive."

I considered what she said, and heard the sirens in the distance, getting closer. From the front steps of the Art Institute, I could see I-75 in the distance, and the bubblegum lights of the police cars as they sped toward the exit that would bring them here. It made me feel better; I was outside, away from the creepy spread of bodies in the hall. The only things saving it from looking like some sort of mass slaughter or mass suicide was the lack of blood and the occasional snore or sleepy sigh. I hadn't realized how scared I was until the tightness in my chest disappeared while I sat on the steps outside.

The first police cars pulled up and stormed up the steps to me.

"Ma'am, are you all right? Are you the one who called 911? Is there anyone else inside that's awake?" The oldest of the first three officers on the scene asked me, as the other two bounded into the art institute with their hands rested on their service pistols.

"I don't think there's anyone else inside that's conscious. I didn't know what else to do." I hugged my knees to my chest.

"How is it that you aren't affected by what's going on inside? What can you tell me about it?" He asked me, concern on his face.

I didn't know. I told him that, and I wasn't sure he believed me, but I repeated my statement three times to him. It never changed. Finally, he tried to reach one of his fellow officers on the radio and got no reaction.

"Ma'am, I need to go check on them. Don't leave."

"I'm not going anywhere. My best friend's in there and I couldn't get her out. I couldn't find my stepmother. I'm not leaving until I know they're okay."

At that statement, he took off into the museum, calling the names of the other officers into his shoulder mike, and disappeared inside.

Other officers arrived. Ambulances arrived, and the EMT's ran inside. Fire trucks showed up, and the firefighters also went inside. I went to my car to get out of the way.

I'd forgotten Bert was still waiting in the car, as I'd asked him to do when we arrived. He hopped up on the dashboard of the car. I explained what had happened inside, and his eyes kept getting bigger and bigger as I explained.

"Janie, you need to get out of here."

"I can't. My stepmother's still in there and I don't know where she is. I don't like her, but I can't leave until I know she's safe. Mia's still inside, and I couldn't get her out."

His face fell. "We can't leave Mia."

"Exactly. Besides, I gave my name to the 911 dispatcher and to the police officer who talked to me on the steps. They're going to want to take a formal statement when they come out, and I'm sure I'd get in trouble if I left."

He looked out the front windshield and watched the front door. I followed his gaze. Nothing was coming back out. The police officers had left the lights on top of their cruisers on, illuminating the night sky in blue and red revolving stripes. We sat there in the car, the drivers' side door open where my feet were still on the ground.

"I've got a bad feeling about this," Bert said.

"I do, too."

There should have been officers coming out. There should have been EMTs carrying out prominent donors to the ambulances and trying to treat them for whatever it was that put them to sleep. There should have been shouts and voices. Nothing happened.

"Bert, we've got to do something."

"Yes, we do. Janie, you need to pull your legs inside the car and start the engine. Call Aiden and tell him there's an emergency. I believe this is magical. I don't think the police and firefighters and EMTs can do anything to help anybody."

I did what he told me to do, but I pulled the car closer to the entrance. I wanted a better view of what was going on than I was going to get from the back of the parking lot behind the building. We got as close as I could get without blocking the cruisers and the ambulances and the fire trucks, and I pulled out my cell phone to do as Bert had suggested. I thought he was right. I thought it was a magical attack on the fundraiser. I didn't know who the actual target was, and it was odd I hadn't been affected, especially with all the warnings from Aiden and Bert that I was in danger.

I was out of my league on this one. There was something big going on, and I had no idea how to handle it. I dialed Aiden's phone number, and waited for him to answer.

CHAPTER TWENTY

"Hello," Aiden's voice sounded distracted on the phone. "I'm sorry, did I interrupt something? This is Janie."

"Is something wrong?"

"Yes, there's something strange going on at my stepmother's fundraiser." I quickly filled him in on all the details I'd given the dispatcher and the police officers, and described what had happened when the police had gone inside. I finished with, "I don't know why I wasn't affected by what was going on, and I don't know what to do."

Aiden was quiet on the phone for a minute. "Janie, this is bigger than I've ever dealt with. I think you're right, I think it is magical. I'm going to call some of the council to get some advice, and then I'll come help you. Sit tight; I'll be there in fifteen minutes at the most."

"Thank you, Aiden. I don't know what else to do." I hung up the phone.

I didn't know what to think from Aiden's calm reaction. Had he expected something like this, or was he completely out of his depth? If it was the latter, was he going to be able to do something to help, or just hold my hand when they finally carried out my best friend and my stepmother? Would they ever wake up? Was it my fault? I shook my head before I started to cry again. It was out of my hands until Aiden could get here and I could see whether he had a plan to handle it or not.

I grilled Bert on safety precautions I could take if it was magical while we waited on our backup to appear.

"Being inside the car is a good start, Janie. And keeping the engine running means you have a fighting chance to get away if some big baddie comes after you. If the faerie courts are involved, they hate steel and iron. An older car like yours has a steel frame. Smaller pieces of metal don't do as much, especially if they are metal blends, but steel and iron burns them. It should offer some protection if that's what's going on, but there are other magical beings out there that it wouldn't have any impact on. I can't really say what it is. I don't know."

I didn't push him too hard, even though I didn't stop asking questions. He talked about goblins and red caps and witches and pixies and faeries and talking animals and curses, but he didn't relate any of them to what was going on. He looked scared, and I knew that I was. His chatter was all good information. I wished I could take notes, but I was too busy staring at the front of the museum waiting for some indication everything inside was okay.

Aiden was good to his word. He banged on the window of the car fourteen long minutes after I'd hung up the phone. I'd been watching the front entrance so intently I hadn't seen him drive up in the tiny compact car parked beside me. I screamed, and Bert jumped.

"I'm sorry to scare you like that," he said, unloading plastic grocery bags out of the back seat of his car. "The others will be here in a bit. They went to get more supplies. I'm not sure how much it's going to take."

I stepped out of my car to help him unload, and peeked inside the bags to see what he brought. He had bags full of Morton's table salt canisters, and boxes and bags of penny nails.

"I don't know why I didn't think of that," Bert exclaimed, hopping up and down on the front seat. "That's a great idea."

Three other cars pulled up, and I recognized the people who got out. I'd seen them in the hut the night Aiden had taken me to get my hair growth cured. I recognized them, but I hadn't really gotten a good look at them that night between the pain in my scalp, the dark hut, and the awful sludge they'd made me drink to fix the problem.

Aiden re-introduced Doris, the woman who'd made me a pie. I did remember her from that night. She looked like the grandmother I'd always wished I'd had, with iron-grey hair pulled back in a puffy bun on the back of her head. She wore a sweatshirt that said *World's Best Grandma*, so my assumption of grandmother must have been correct. I felt envious of the grandkids who might have given her such a sweatshirt; I had never met my own grandparents.

She came up to me and gave me a big hug. I was a little surprised, but returned it, and it felt just like a grandmother's hug should feel like—warm and comforting and safe and loving. If I didn't know better,

I'd have thought I already knew her, but I'd only met her the one time before.

I recognized an older man with a long gray ponytail, whom Aiden introduced as Harold, and a man with fuzzy Einstein-like hair and jowls as Stanley. I would not have pegged this group as magical protectors; I would have categorized them as a shuffleboard team at a seniors' center. I had to remind myself that Dumbledore hadn't been a spring chicken in the Harry Potter books and he'd been a badass. I liked them; they all seemed nice, and all asked how I was feeling. Maybe looks were deceiving. At least I hoped so. I wasn't looking forward to fighting magical badness with the Geritol set.

Harold shook my hand. "I was sorry to hear about your father, Ms. Grimm. I'm glad we might be able to do something to help you."

Doris elbowed him in the side. "I'm sure the girl's got more on her mind than her father right now, Harold. We've got a magical emergency on our hands. I'm sure we can talk more later, but right now she's got people she cares about inside. We've got to do something about this spell. I can feel it from here."

She could *feel* it? What did it feel like, and why couldn't I feel it? I didn't get a chance to ask her, because Stanley and Aiden began to pass around bags of salt and nails before heading toward the museum. Bert was begging to go with us, but Aiden told him to stay put and be our lookout.

"What am I supposed to do if something shows up? I can't reach the pedals!" he squawked, hopping up and down in frustration.

Stanley grinned at him. "Honk the horn."

"Oh," he said. "I guess I could do that." He positioned himself on the center of the steering wheel, poised for action.

As we walked away from the car, I plucked the fabric on Aiden's jacket. "Hey, Bert's not small for a frog, but that's an '80s model Buick. It takes some strength to honk that horn. Can he actually do it?"

Aiden sighed, but he kept walking. "Bert can't carry the bags. He has a hard time remembering he's not human anymore, even though it's been a few hundred years. He doesn't have the ability to help us with this. He's had a few bad patches over the past few years, where he gets really depressed and wants to end it all, but the magic that made him into a frog also made him immortal. He's full of information, and he's a good guy. I'm sure he'll find a way to get our attention if something comes; it keeps him from getting in the way and makes him feel useful."

"So what is it that we're doing with all of this stuff?" I asked.

He explained we were making a circle of salt and nails around the building to break the spell. "I believe we're looking at faerie magic, and they actually refer to iron as 'the bane' because it is so poisonous to them. It should break the spell. Salt contains magic; it's a purifying ingredient."

We'd walked right up to the building, and I saw Doris and Harold pouring salt in a thin line right beside the building with Stanley following, dropping nails in the line of salt. Aiden handed me a salt container and I followed their example.

I was surprised at how much salt it took to go around the entire building, and how many containers of nails we used. When we finally completed the circle of salt and nails I felt my ears pop louder and more intense than I'd ever felt before, ten times worse than if I'd been driving through the mountains or taking off in an airplane. I looked around, and the others were moving their jaws and cocking their head as if they'd felt the same thing. When I asked, Stanley explained it was similar to popping a bubble of magic. We stood in front of the entrance, waiting to see what would happen next. Nothing did.

"What are we waiting for?" I asked, ten minutes later, feeling like a complete fool. I didn't like the idea that I didn't know what was going on.

"Well, the circle we made should have woken everyone up, but we might have underestimated the strength of the magic inside. We may have contained it from spreading, but that doesn't mean it's broken the spell. That tells me there's something stronger at work than we've ever seen before, and I think we're going to have to go inside and see what we can do to wake everyone up." Aiden took a deep sigh, and squared his shoulders.

Doris, Stanley, and Harold stayed outside, saying they would try to slow things down if something came up to try to reinforce the spell we'd contained with our salt circle. Aiden and I headed up the steps.

Aiden slipped a chain around his own neck. It carried a heavy pendant with a large green jewel in the center that settled against the middle of his chest. "I assume you've been wearing your necklace tonight, Janie. That's why you weren't affected by the spell, but I can't promise how long it'll last. We might have ten minutes inside and we might have ten hours to get this done. I don't know. These are the strongest charms we have. That's the other reason that the others are outside; we don't have anything else as strong as these two immunity charms."

I nodded, taking a deep breath.

He kept going, taking my hand, and leading me through the front doors. "We've got to find a way to wake everyone up, and hopefully get them all to safety without getting in the way of whatever Big Nasty threw this spell."

Oh, goody. Operation Wake Sleeping Beauties Without Getting Our Faces Eaten Off sounded like such a great idea.

Aiden had a few containers of salt, and so did I. He explained the plan, which seemed simple. "We'll have to dissolve the salt in water, and sprinkle it on everyone inside to wake them up enough to herd them toward the door. The only catch is that we don't have water hoses or spray bottles, so I'm not sure exactly how we're going to pull this off." He suggested dissolving the salt in the water glasses in the hall and throwing it on each person. "And if you find yourself confronted by a magical baddie, pour salt in a quick circle around yourself and scatter nails on the salt line. If you can get that barrier between you and whatever faerie being means you harm, you should be safe enough until someone can get to you."

I started to laugh, but I stopped myself; he was serious.

Then he grabbed me, spun me around, and kissed me.

He said it was for luck.

I stood there in shock. My lips were still tingling and my mouth hung open. I hadn't expected that, but suddenly Aiden no longer looked like the dorky nuisance he'd been for the last week. Instead, he looked like an earnest, slightly embarrassed, and good-looking young man who blushed when I stared at him. There was a lock of red hair that fell over his forehead, and I had to fight the urge to brush it back from his face.

I had the sudden, insane thought that all I wanted was to grab and kiss him again. Or for him to do it to me. I'd take it either way.

I blinked hard; trying to force myself to remember we weren't in a place we could continue such a thing. No time for kissing now. I had a friend and a stepmother and her guests to save. I hurried past him, muttering something about bad timing, and tripped over one of the police officers who had passed out face down on the floor just inside the entrance. I tried to catch myself, but my hands were full of salt containers and nails. I twisted at the last minute and landed on the same hip I'd bruised when I'd fallen over Mia earlier.

The officer let out a snore, a sigh, and a snort before subsiding back into a quiet sleep. I rolled over onto my back, looking at the ceiling, mortified that the chaste kiss had shaken me badly enough to emulate Aiden's clumsiness. As I did so, a light bulb went off in my brain.

I had a plan.

CHAPTER TWENTY-ONE

"Aiden, do we have to mix the salt with the water to get it to work?" I asked, propping myself up on my elbows.

"What are you talking about?"

"If we sprinkled salt on all of them, and then got them wet, would it work to break the spell?"

He reached a hand down to help me up as I continued to stare at the fire suppression sprinkler system in the ceiling. When he continued to look puzzled, I pointed. He looked up and I saw his face light up.

"Not a bad idea, Janie. If we set off the fire alarm, the security system will come up, alerting the police and fire departments that we need more help, and the sprinkler systems will go off in the exhibit hall. If we set this off right, I think there are screens to protect those few paintings in this area that could be hit, and maybe we can wake everyone up enough to get them to safety. I don't see a downside to it."

"Let's do it," I said, as I sprinkled salt on the police officer's face.

We headed deeper into the museum, salting everyone we found, and when we went back for Mia, I showed Aiden the hole and the boxes inside. There were still no signs of the short greenish men I'd seen, but I couldn't help looking cautiously around corners whenever we turned in a different direction.

We tried to hurry since we had no idea how long we'd have with our immunity charms. We doubled back into the exhibit hall to make sure we'd gotten everyone, grabbing the salt shakers on the tables when we ran out of the salt we'd brought in. We'd seen and salted every face in the exhibit hall, in the makeshift caterers' kitchens, and in the bathrooms, but I still hadn't seen my stepmother.

"I can't leave until I find Evangeline." I knew we were on borrowed time. I had no idea just how much time I had left, and I was starting to get a headache. I didn't know whether that was from stress, or adrenaline, or from the charm around my neck beginning to wear off. We'd been inside for almost twenty minutes. There was no way to know for sure.

Aiden rubbed his temples at the same place where my headache had started in my own skull. "Janie, with all the salt in the room, and all of the water we're about to unleash, we can assume she'll get soaked in it too if she's on the floor somewhere. With all the salt we spread around, it should be enough to break the spell, and get her, too. Even if it doesn't, it should be enough for others to get in and look for her. Let's get everyone awake and the alarm set off, so the police can call for backup. They've got the training to look for people; we don't. I think we're running out of time."

I had to grudgingly admit he was right. We'd been all over the place, retracing my own steps all over the museum and hadn't seen her yet. Another lap might not find her, and might stop us before we could get the sprinkler system to go off. I nodded at him, and he climbed up on one of the tables, reaching a small Bic lighter toward the sprinkler above us.

Nothing happened.

"Isn't that how those work?" I asked. I didn't have a clue if it was, but it seemed a little silly. "Doesn't it go off when there's a fire?"

He shrugged, and then flinched when the lighter got hot enough to burn his hand. I spied a fire alarm on the wall, and told him to jump down.

"It can't be that easy, can it?" he asked.

I pulled down on the handle and alarms went off, shrieking and screaming at us as the sprinkler system kicked in. We both tried to get out of the room as fast as we could, but we were slipping and sliding on the wet marble floor.

We weren't fast enough. The water-tight shields slid in front of the paintings down the hall, slamming shut with a bang, and the sprinklers opened up, pouring water over our heads. I was wearing a white button up shirt. I crossed my arms over my chest, glad I'd worn a decent looking bra since my blouse was becoming translucent from all the water. The last thing I needed was a wet t-shirt show in front of Aiden. Much as I had been intrigued by that kiss, this wasn't how I wanted him to see me. Crossing my arms, however, meant my balance was affected.

The floor dipped and slid underneath us as we hurried toward the entrance doors. I felt my balance slip, and initially, I blamed the wet floor and the dress shoes Evangeline would have approved of but I hated as a matter of principle. A few steps later I skidded again, and I saw the ceiling shift above me as I went down. I landed on my back, knocking the wind out of myself as I hit the ground.

"Janie!" Aiden's voice cut through the fog. I struggled to sit up and ask what was wrong, but my mouth wasn't working right, like I'd stuffed it full of cotton candy and tried to talk through a mouthful of fluff.

I tried to tell him that I was fine, but I didn't get the whole sentence out. The last thing I remember seeing is Aiden's face as he tried to get my attention, and calling my name as he toppled over backwards in front of me. My vision went gray around the edges and I slowly blacked out in heavy, slumberous oblivion.

CHAPTER TWENTY-TWO

I came to as an EMT checked my pulse and a soaking wet Evangeline patted my hand. Aiden stood nearby, drenched from head to toe, with a worried look on his face.

"What's wrong?" I asked.

"You stopped breathing, dear." As usual, Evangeline's frosty voice annoyed me, despite her concern. The "dear" sounded out of place coming from her mouth. "We were worried you wouldn't wake up."

I squeezed her hand and grinned at her. She looked a little surprised, looking down at our hands. I guess I'd never been affectionate with her before. It wasn't like she inspired affection, but she was my stepmother, and I had been worried about her. "Obviously, I did wake up. I feel fine. Am I okay? Are you guys okay?"

Aiden nodded, and Evangeline stammered something about her dress being ruined. *Typical*, I thought, shoving aside the earlier charitable thought towards her. I guess life was back to normal now if my stepmother had found something to complain about.

I reached up to find my charm necklace missing. I looked over at Aiden and he patted his pocket. I was glad it was safe, seeing as it wasn't mine; I considered it a loaner from Aiden. I wondered, briefly, if I had stopped breathing because he'd taken it off, due to the magic, the stress, or a side effect of the necklace itself. I couldn't ask Aiden in front of everyone without looking like a certifiable lunatic. Why did I trust him so easily? And did he really kiss me? Why had he done that? Another question I couldn't ask in front of everyone else.

I turned toward Evangeline to take my mind off of it. Evangeline could always distract me from thoughts I didn't want to examine from sheer frustration alone.

It was the first time I'd ever seen Evangeline looking less than perfect, and even then she looked about as amazing as someone could be when they were soaking wet. Her hair was flat to her head with water, but it was usually shellacked back with enough hairspray to create an independent hole in the ozone layer, so there wasn't a huge difference. I saw a few small wrinkles that weren't carefully concealed by makeup any longer. Her mascara looked like it was about to run, but it hadn't created any black streaks yet. I had the uncharitable thought she finally looked older than she ever had. I still wouldn't describe her as mutton dressed as lamb, but she looked closer to her actual age than she normally did.

The EMT was still fussing over me, taking my pulse and my blood pressure. "You'll be fine, ma'am. Looks like there was a gas leak in the museum that made everyone pass out. I don't think they've figured out why the sprinkler system went off, but it's a good thing it did, as it woke people up so they could get out. The museum's gonna be closed for a while to deal with the leak and the water, but it looks like the art will be okay. No one seems to be suffering any ill effects from the gas; unless you're pregnant. I don't think you've inhaled too much."

I assured him I was fine, and he rolled up his blood pressure cuff and began unhooking his equipment, telling me I was free to go home, but to rest tomorrow if I could.

Was I pregnant? That was a laugh. I hadn't been on a date since before Dad had gotten sick, which meant Aiden's kiss was the most action I'd seen in almost a year. Was that why I'd reacted so strongly to it? I shook my head, changing the direction of my thoughts as I changed the topic. "I set off the fire alarms and the sprinkler system to make sure someone would respond. I wasn't sure what else to do to get help quickly, since the police who were already here had also passed out."

Evangeline looked like she'd sucked a sour lemon at the news I'd ruined her party. Aiden grinned, and said, "I was meeting Janie here. When she went back in, I followed. It's like she said. She had the idea to pull the fire alarm, and it looks like it was a good one."

The EMT waved over a plain-clothes detective and repeated what I'd said. The officer had me repeat it again, and Aiden backed me up. We kept the rest of the F.A.B.L.E.S. group out of it. I couldn't think of a good, non-magical explanation for them to be there, and I wanted the police to take me seriously about the attempted theft from the museum.

I saw Mia nearby, with an oxygen mask on her face while someone was taking her blood pressure. She seemed okay, but she looked tired and confused. I'd probably have a lot of explaining to do to her, later.

Evangeline waited until the police officers had taken my statement and Aiden's, and the EMTs finally walked away before she turned that frosty, disapproving look my way. She looked like an avenging sea goddess in her soaking wet cocktail dress, water dripping off the hem onto her gem-studded heels. "Whatever possessed you to think the police needed to be called? You could have ruined everything. The fundraiser is ruined. Artwork could have been destroyed with the water you dumped everywhere. And I'd hate to think what the mayor and the commissioners will say about what you've done. You know, you could even face criminal charges for pulling that fire alarm. You're not supposed to do that unless there's an actual fire. What would that do to your bar application? All that money you spent on tuition, flushed down the drain. Did you ever think of that?"

I sighed. Nothing would ever be right for her. No matter what I said or did, she'd find some way of making it a Bad Thing. I had the sudden, irrelevant thought that I could win a Nobel Prize and she'd spend the day telling me how I'd ruined it by wearing the wrong dress. There really wasn't anything I could do but let her quietly nag me. If I tried to explain again, it would just get worse. I understood she was upset. She had a right to be upset after all the work she'd done. But if she really thought I was trying to ruin all of her hard work, it wasn't unusual. She'd blamed me for trying to ruin her life for years.

Her rant was interrupted by a police officer in a white shirt who introduced himself as Sergeant Jones. "I understand when you called the police you also reported a theft in progress. What made you think someone was trying to steal something?"

"You mean something other than the men with tools busting a hole in the wall? And the boxes of artifacts on the other side of the hole?"

He chuckled. "Yeah, that's what I mean. And yes, that would be a classic sign of theft. Tell me what you saw. Can you describe the men?"

I did, leaving out the fact that they were green, extraordinarily short, had hoarse voices, and were wearing long stocking caps, which meant I didn't have a lot of description to give him. I explained to him what I'd seen after Mia and I had gone to eat dinner in the office finishing with the short version of how I'd pulled the fire alarm.

"Ma'am, let me be the first to thank you for your quick thought and action," the sergeant said. "I'm still not sure how you stayed awake so much longer than everyone else, but the EMTs said they didn't think the gas was evenly distributed throughout the hall, and you were moving around the museum more than anyone else. Besides which, we haven't found an actual leak. It could be something your burglars brought in themselves to distract the fundraiser."

I bit my lip to keep from asking why Mia had passed out if she had been with me the whole time, because the only explanation I could give was the necklace in Aiden's pocket. I remembered Evangeline's statement about charges. "Will I be charged with a crime for pulling the fire alarm? I didn't know what else to do."

He laughed at me. "Heavens, no, you won't be charged. If you hadn't pulled it, the thieves might have been successful. The museum representatives don't believe anything's missing. I think they'd throw a fit if we tried to charge you, and even if we did, you'd have a defense, since it was an actual emergency. Thank you," he said, as he shook my hand and tromped back to the front doors of the museum.

For some reason, the idea of me as a hero had Evangeline looking even more sour than before. I'd have thought she'd be happy I'd saved the artwork, thwarted would-be art thieves, and rescued her guests, but I guess it had ruined the fundraiser she'd worked so hard to put together. I doubted the museum raised much money tonight, other than for the cost of the overpriced dinners.

I did feel sorry for her, but could she ever think of anything but herself, and how to put me down? I wondered how she'd treated Dad when I wasn't around, and I hoped she hadn't been this self-centered around him, especially when he'd been dying.

It took several hours of giving statements to officers, repeating myself over and over again, and waiting for the EMTs to release Mia before we were allowed to leave and head home. Aiden hadn't wanted to let us go alone, but I convinced him I had to explain to Mia what had happened.

On a sudden wave of inspiration, I asked him if he had a truck I could use in the morning. He gave me a funny look, and said he knew someone with a truck who owed him a favor. I explained again that my father's trunks were at my stepmother's house and she'd wanted me to take them for a while.

"We'd talked about meeting for coffee tomorrow, but I think there are more important things to do. Now that I'm settled in at my apartment, I want to get those trunks out of there. Besides, there might be information in them that could help us figure out what's going on."

"Sure. What time do you want me there? How many are there to move?"

I told him there were three trunks in the attic, and we should start at ten in the morning. I promised to call him if I had any problems tonight, and shooed him away to herd Mia to the car.

Chapter Twenty-Three

Mia seemed confused and out of it as we got in my car, almost as if she'd fallen asleep on her feet as she'd waited for me to join her. It was three o'clock in the morning, so she had every right to be tired, but I'd seen her stay up later in college without looking this exhausted. "Mia, are you okay?"

"I just need to go home and sleep. What happened tonight? Did Mike and Leann get home okay?" She looked bewildered, but I hadn't seen Mike and Leann before they left so I had no idea if they all looked that worn out.

I told her I'd seen them leave an hour or so earlier. They'd been among the first people carried out since they'd been so close to the front doors. Mia had been at the back of the museum, so she'd been one of the last ones carried out. Most of the people who had been inside were being given clean bills of health, but I'd heard an EMT try to convince some of them to go to the hospital. It seemed everyone had just wanted to go home. I could relate.

"Janie, I don't like this. What's going on?" she asked, even as she yawned, her mouth opening wide enough to swallow her own head.

"I thought you heard the last statement I gave the officer." I said as I pulled the car out of the driveway to the museum. It felt good pulling away; I'd started to wonder if the night would ever end.

"I did, and I'm really tired, but I'm not so out of it to miss when you're hiding something. I know there's more you didn't tell the officer."

Crap. She did know me that well. "Well, the reason I didn't pass out like everyone else is because of my necklace. Aiden gave it to me."

"The Dork of Destruction is the one giving you jewelry? The necklace you showed us at the study group meeting? You did say you'd gotten it from a guy, but I never put the two together. Boy, I did miss something." She gave me a wan smile. "I did tell you Aiden was cute. Maybe you're working faster than I thought with him."

"It's not like that." I wondered if I should tell her about the kiss. "It's not a romantic gift; it's some kind of magical immunity charm." I finally pulled onto the highway to head toward Mia's apartment complex, and rolled down the window to get some fresh air into the car to keep us both awake until we got there.

She was quiet for a minute. "Was there something weird about the thieves you were describing to the detective? You hesitated a little bit every time you mentioned them."

I hoped the police didn't notice that one. "Yeah, they were little green men. They looked like dwarves or gnomes or something, with long white beards and long stocking caps on their heads. They looked like something . . ."

"Right out of a fairy tale, right?" she added. "This is happening again, isn't it, just like the long hair and the frog and everything else?"

I wasn't sure it had ever stopped. "You're right, Mia. I think this is all related, but what I don't know is whether it's all related to me. Aiden's helping me get those trunks out of Evangeline's attic tomorrow morning, so I'm hoping I'll find something in them to figure it all out."

She yawned again, stretching her jaw hard enough that it had to hurt. "We said we'd meet at three on Sunday, right?"

"Yeah, I'm planning for everyone to be there." I said, happy to be talking about something else.

She laid her head against the window. "I can't believe how tired I am. I was going to do some reading after I got home tonight."

"Mia, you're going to be lucky to stay awake long enough to change your clothes," I laughed. "We have a weekend to get things caught up. Go home and get some sleep." I pulled off the highway and turned down her street.

"Janie, I just don't get why all of this is happening. And why now? Why right when school's starting? Why you?"

"I wish I knew." I didn't have any answers for the same questions I was asking myself.

We rode in silence until I pulled into her complex, and she got out. "Janie, if you need anything, let me know. I don't know how to help you, but I'll do everything I can."

I nodded, thanking her for her offer. I wasn't sure what she could do either, but it did feel good that she'd said it. I waited until she let herself into her apartment before driving off; she was almost asleep on her feet and I wanted to make sure she'd gotten inside before she fell asleep again.

When I pulled away, Bert poked his head up on the back seat. It startled me. "Bert, I'd forgotten you were back there. I'm sorry."

"No worries. You needed to talk with Mia. I like listening to her talk. She's got a lot of common sense. You're not going to be able to keep things from her, are you?"

"No, I'm not. She knows me well enough to call me on it when I'm trying to avoid saying something." I kept driving till I pulled into my own apartment complex.

"That could put her in danger," he said.

I pulled into my parking spot. "You know what, Bert? I'm tired of being told I'm in danger; my family is in danger; my friends are in danger. Right now, I just want to go inside, get some sleep, get my dad's trunks, and get some studying done before I get distracted again."

He didn't say anything; he just let me hit my stride in my rant. Sometimes that really is the best thing to do. Bert had only been around me a few days, and he was showing some serious wisdom. Or, at least, he was learning how to deal with me through experience.

"You know what else?" I asked, continuing as I put the car in park. "I feel like the rug's been pulled out from under me. I don't know what to do. I wish everything could stop happening just long enough for me to find my footing."

Bert didn't say anything until I turned off the engine, crossed my arms over the steering wheel and laid my head down on the back of my wrists. Then, he spoke.

"Janie, I know you're feeling overwhelmed. I don't know what to tell you, except that you're not alone. I'm here. Aiden's here. Doris and Harold and Stanley and all the rest are here. Mia's standing by your side. And I haven't actually met your stepmother yet, but if she's got an ounce of brain in her head, she'll stand with you. My point is that no matter how nutty things get, you've got friends."

I turned my head to look at him, now perched on the front passenger seat Mia had vacated. "You're right, Bert. It doesn't fix the problem of how to figure it all out, but you're right. And it does help. Thank you."

"Can I stay with you at least until this is over?" he asked. "I promise I won't get in your way when you study, and I might be able to help you with some of the law school stuff if you're having problems. I might be able to help you if something weird happens."

He was right. He had helped me with the animals in the parking lot. He'd given me good advice tonight, even if that advice had consisted of "call Aiden". He had mentioned he knew a little something about contract law, and I still had no idea what the professor was talking about when he was describing what constituted offers to make a valid contract.

I wondered if Bert really had somewhere else to go. "Let's take this a little bit at a time, Bert. I didn't really plan to have a roommate, especially one that isn't contributing to the rent, but you're right. You did help out, and you could help out again. Let's see how it goes until Monday morning, and we'll take it from there."

He seemed so grateful that I smiled. I had a lot to get done in the morning, and a lot of reading to do over the weekend. If nothing else, I could ask him to be a lookout to watch the parking lot while I studied. If he did that, then maybe I could concentrate long enough to get caught up, spend some time figuring things out with Aiden, meet with the study group, get Dad's trunks, and maybe even get some sleep. Suddenly my pillow was calling me loud and clear. I was exhausted just thinking about all of it.

I walked into the apartment and locked the door before depositing Bert on the sofa. I dropped my things and collapsed on the bed as a wave of exhaustion hit me like a brick wall. I barely stayed awake long enough to set my alarm before collapsing, fully dressed, onto my bed in a deep dreamless sleep.

Chapter Twenty-Four

I woke up the next morning with a smile on my face. That doesn't normally happen before I've finished my first cup of coffee. I was still tired, but I'd slept in my own bed uninterrupted by rapid hair growth, animal musicians, Bert's singing or snoring, late night studying, or worrying about waking up early to get reading done before class. I could get used to this.

I showered and dressed before I got coffee. I expected Aiden to show up to help move my father's trunks out of my stepmother's attic, and wanted to be ready when he got there.

"Good morning, Bert," I said in a sing-song voice, grinning at him as I walked through the living room on my way to the kitchen. Hey, I might have woken up in a good mood, but that didn't mean caffeine wasn't required to get going for the day.

"What the hell happened to you?" he grumped.

I ignored him, smiling into my mug, and sitting down on the couch beside him.

"Seriously, Janie, you're creeping me out. I've stayed at your house, what, five days now? You never wake up in this good of a mood. Did something happen last night I didn't see? What happened? I've never seen you this smiley and happy when you wake up. Something magical must have gotten to you." Bert was awake, and out from under the afghan he'd used on the couch while he slept, hopping right for my lap.

I tried to put my mug down on the coffee table, hoping his sudden paranoia didn't turn into scalding coffee spilled in my lap. I was almost successful; some of it sloshed over the edge onto the back of my hand, but didn't spill anywhere else. I lifted my hand to my mouth to soothe the burned spot.

"Give me a break, Bert. It's Saturday. I don't have class. I'll have the time to do some catching up this weekend, and I can't get further behind for a couple of days. Evangeline's been bugging me to come get the trunks out of her attic for months, so she should be happy that I'm getting them. I got a good night's sleep. Add those things together and of course I'm in a good mood."

He harrumphed at me. "And Aiden's coming over."

"So what?" I asked, going back into the kitchen to rinse the spilled coffee off my hand and refill the mug.

"He tends to have that effect."

"What effect?"

He sighed. "Well, I've seen women get a crush on him pretty quick over the years, but I've never seen him know exactly what to do about it. He just gets embarrassed and runs away as fast as he can without being rude. Any other guy would be trying to turn on the charm, but Aiden's awkward around girls."

"What are you trying to tell me, Bert?"

"He doesn't know what to say around women, even if they really like him."

"Are you saying he's shy or are you saying he's not into women?" I asked, coming back into the living room.

"You like him, don't you?"

"I didn't say that." I stared into my coffee cup.

"You don't have to. It's written all over your face. And he's not gay; he's just shy and awkward and doesn't know how to respond."

What do I say to that? I just wanted to ask Aiden to teach me about magic, or at least how to protect myself from magic, not to whisk me off for a romantic tropical getaway. But that actually sounded like a great idea. Or could I ask Bert if he thought Aiden liked me? Oh my God, this was sounding like a junior high soap opera. I didn't have this much drama when I was actually in junior high school.

I ignored Bert, who, with his taunts and jokes, was sounding like a five year old, telling me that I *lurved* Aiden, and that we were sitting in a tree K-I-S-S-I-N-G. "Shut up, Bert," I said, when he got louder.

I was saved from further argument with my temporary roommate when the doorbell rang.

Aiden was punctual; he'd promised to be at my house at ten, and it was just a minute or two before that when he showed up on my doorstep. He handed me the necklace I'd been wearing the night before, the one he'd pocketed while I was being examined by the EMTs. Trying to avoid Bert further embarrassing me, I grabbed my purse, stuffing the necklace inside with my keys, and shut the door behind me, leaving the sputtering frog behind.

Aiden was there with an extended cab pick-up truck and two other guys, one with really short light hair and the other with dark hair, who were waiting inside. "Janie, this is Bobby and Jake. They're friends of mine and they're here to help us with the trunks."

I thanked both of them for their help, and they grinned, shaking my hand and teasing Aiden about something. It turned out Aiden had wrecked his car on the way to meet them, and they'd had to go pick him up. "It happens all the time with him," Bobby said. "We always plan to be earlier than he thinks we should be, and that way we can pick him up from whatever disaster he's in and still be on time."

I couldn't help laughing. They had his number. As we left the parking lot, with Aiden and me in the cramped back seat of the truck, the boys regaled me with tales of Aiden's catastrophes over the years they'd known each other.

"Then there was the time when he literally slipped on a banana peel in the produce department of the grocery store. The manager didn't believe him when he filled out the incident report form," Bobby said.

"Who could forget the time he caught the sleeve of his sweater on the door going into the school building? The principal actually called his mother to report him being truant to school, when he was there but couldn't get to the classroom because he was stuck. You know, Aiden, you could have simply taken off the sweater and you'd probably have been free," Jake laughed.

"Hey, I was new in school. Give me a break. I didn't know how much trouble I'd get in for leaving my sweater hanging on the door," Aiden laughed.

It seemed like they'd known each other for a long time. Was it just me, or was Aiden blushing while they recounted stories of his mishaps? Or was I reading a bit too much into Bert's teasing earlier?

It was a good thing he'd brought others along. I wasn't sure Aiden and I could get the trunks down the stairs and into the truck without a problem. I wasn't a total weakling, but Aiden's sure-fire klutziness would make the whole thing a comedy of errors. That was something I could do without at Evangeline's house-of-the-perfect-white-everything.

I'd figured going to her place at ten a.m. would be late enough that she'd be up and moving, and yet early enough that if she was hosting some big Saturday luncheon, we'd be able to get out before her guests arrived. Advance planning like this keeps me from dealing with more of Evangeline's disapproval than I had to. We'd never be buddies, but I'd settle for an unspoken truce rather than constant disdain.

In between tales of Aiden's past foibles, I gave them directions to my stepmother's house. Of course, *house* might have been the biggest understatement of the morning.

Evangeline's home was the largest on a block of large houses in Oakwood, one of the wealthier suburbs of Dayton. The housing regulations were very specific, their schools highly competitive, and I definitely hadn't fit in there when I'd been a kid.

It was a white monster of a house, with a rounded front porch, six bedrooms, four bathrooms, a butler's pantry, a gourmet kitchen, and a partridge in a pear tree. I had loved the nooks and crannies of the house, perfect for hiding places when the younger me had done something wrong, whether it was smearing chocolate on the walls in the butler's pantry, leaving a wet towel on the floor in the master bathroom, or forgetting to clean up after myself in the kitchen. Even so, the house would have been too small for me to live with Evangeline after college graduation without a constant nagging urge to punch her lights out for the small sniping comments she liked to drop in my general direction.

"Nice house," Bobby said, as we pulled up in the driveway.

"I bet cleaning is a bitch," Jake responded.

"It is," I said, trying not to elaborate. They certainly didn't need to hear that Evangeline's idea of punishment for a teenager who would rather have been anywhere but home had been to hand me a bucket and scrub brush and tell me to clean. And then she told me to re-do it when it didn't meet her exacting standards of cleanliness. And there was always something she hadn't wanted to complain about to the help but knew "I could help her get it just right."

We hopped out of the truck and walked up to the front door. I rang the doorbell.

A woman in a starched apron answered the door. I had no idea who the woman was since Evangeline couldn't seem to keep the same housekeeper for more than a few weeks. I had always wondered how people were dumb enough to keep applying when my stepmother was an exacting obsessive-compulsive clean freak who drove them nuts by nit-picking every little thing they did. A person would think word would get out that she was impossible to work for, but it never did. I didn't know how much she paid them, but no matter how much it was, it wasn't enough to put up with her insane requests delivered in her perfect, frosty voice.

The housekeeper led me to the back sitting room, and the boys followed a short distance behind me. I tried not to notice them looking around at the crown molding and the antiques and the artwork hanging on the walls, but I knew she kept her place looking like a showpiece from the early nineteenth century. It was something unique in a house, especially one that wasn't a museum charging admission for tourists to gawk at, but I was used to it. The only concessions to modern-day living that she allowed were in the kitchen, the bathroom, and the laundry room. She didn't even like having a television in the house. I'd had to escape to friends' houses to watch MTV as a kid. Since Dad had been a bigger reader than television-watcher I wasn't sure he minded, but I sure had.

Evangeline was sitting on the settee, sipping tea from a delicate china cup. I say settee, because this thing was way too prissy to be called a couch. "Oh, Janie, it's good to see you," she said, rising from her seat to air kiss my cheek. "I'm glad to see you're doing all right after last night's excitement."

"Are you okay?" I asked, sitting down on the settee next to her as she lowered herself back down. I was careful to tuck one foot behind the other in a ladylike fashion as I sat down, ripped jeans notwithstanding. She wasn't going to like my clothing choices no matter what I wore, and I wasn't trying to win a beauty contest or serve tea in a formal dining room today. I was here to move heavy trunks, but the least I could do was observe the etiquette of Evangeline's world for a civilized conversation, especially after the drama of last night.

"I'll be fine," she said, putting the china teacup back on the tray in front of her. "Last night just took a lot out of me." No digs, no insinuated slams, no comments on my *inappropriate attire*; I looked closer and saw that she was right. I could see a faint shadow under her eyes, and a few fine lines in her face. Was her Botox wearing off? Or maybe she was just more shaken than she'd let on last night. Even when Dad had been sick, I hadn't seen her look even slightly imperfect, but today it was like she was wearing an Evangeline mask instead of her own unnaturally calm face.

"Evangeline, we're just here to get those old trunks of Dad's out of your attic that you told me to take. We won't be here long. What's going to happen with the Oktoberfest exhibit?" I reached out and patted her hand, much as she would have done to me. It wasn't a natural move for me to make, but it was an acceptable form of condolence and commiseration in Evangeline's world. Hugging was way too intimate for her.

She seemed to pull herself straighter. "Well, there aren't any pieces missing, so I think they are planning to go ahead with the exhibit. Even though you ruined the fundraiser, and we didn't raise all the money they needed to pay for the security and the exhibit setup, you kept things from being stolen, so I guess it could be worse."

I had to remind myself she was upset, and she had done a lot of work for the fundraiser. Despite that, I couldn't help wondering what I was supposed to do last night that would have made her happy. If I'd done nothing to report the theft, there wouldn't have been pieces to put in the exhibit.

"I'm glad they're still able to go ahead with it. We'll just get those trunks out of the attic and get going, so you can rest. The museum's going to need you at full capacity to plan the exhibit, and it wouldn't do to let them down."

She clutched her hands in her lap. "The art preservation committee meeting for today was cancelled because no one feels up to it after last night, so I've got the day to rest. You kids go get what you need, and I'll see you for brunch tomorrow. We'll talk more then."

Crap. I'd hoped she'd be too wiped out for that agreed-upon weekly meeting, but I had made her a deal. I'd follow through with it. If nothing else, I'd make sure she was okay, and encourage her to cut it short tomorrow to get a bit more rest. Oh well.

We left her in the sitting room and headed to the stairway for the trek to the attic where Dad's things were stored. I pointed out the three steamer trunks that had been sitting here since he and I had moved into the house. I had them take a few boxes of my own childhood things as well; it just made sense to get it done while I had help with a truck today.

Bobby and Jake and Aiden didn't say much beyond asking which boxes to take. Even so, I caught them giving each other meaningful looks. I kept asking what was going on, but Aiden said we'd talk later. I let it go. We loaded up the last of it after I'd said a quick goodbye to my stepmother, who'd retired to her bedroom to rest.

We headed back to my place, and the boys all helped to carry my things inside. I offered to buy pizza for them, since they'd helped me move my things—I'd moved enough between dorm rooms and college apartments that I knew the currency of paying moving help; I might not have beer in my budget, but pizza was always cheap, hot, and adequate for volunteer movers. They turned me down, saying something about needing to get to work.

Aiden stuck around as they said their goodbyes. Once they had left, I asked, "How are you going to get home?"

"Well, my car's in the body shop and they picked me up there. I didn't want to make them late for work. I was hoping I could use your phone to call Doris for a ride."

"No problem; it's the least I can do after you and your friends helped me out today." Why did I suddenly feel so awkward with him in my living room? And where had Bert gotten off to? I tried to distract myself by offering Aiden something cold to drink.

He took a glass of water, and sat down on the couch. "I'm glad to help. Besides, there may be something in your dad's trunks that could tell us something. It's worth getting them so you can look."

I let him use the phone, and Bert popped his head out of the bathroom at about the same time. I needed to ask more about what had happened the night before, how to protect myself from magic, and what was going on with all those strange looks the guys were giving each other at my stepmother's house. I busied myself picking up the living room for the study group meeting the next day. How do you try to appear uninterested in someone else's phone conversation when there isn't enough room to get away from it in a small apartment? I had a million and one questions for him, and no idea how to start.

CHAPTER TWENTY-FIVE

"**D**oris should be here in about half-an-hour," Aiden announced, as he hung up my phone. He began talking with Bert about what had happened the night before.

I went into the bedroom with the cordless phone and called Mia. She seemed a little confused when she first answered. It was well past noon. I'd never known her to sleep late, but with all of the excitement the night before, and getting home as late as we did, I was only mildly surprised. She told me she'd talked to Mike and Leann by phone that morning, before going back to bed and sleeping until I called.

"Did they seem okay to you?" I wasn't quite sure what I was asking her to describe, but I trusted Mia's judgment.

"They seemed fine, just really tired. I am, too. I'm hoping a few extra hours of sleep is just the ticket to recover from whatever we were exposed to last night." I agreed. What else could I do? I promised myself I'd stop by Mia's place or call sometime today and check on her, and maybe call the other two later. I sat down on the bed, looking at the phone, and wondering what had gone wrong.

Aiden knocked on the bedroom doorframe, even though the door was open. I put down the phone and looked up at him.

"Are you okay?" he asked.

I gave him a weak smile. I explained about feeling guilty for dragging my friends into something that could hurt them, but if I tried to explain what really happened they'd probably think I'd lost my mind.

"Your friends will be fine after they get a little rest." Aiden leaned against the doorframe and crossed his arms in front of his chest. "Janie, I didn't ask about your friends. I asked about you. How are you holding up?"

"I don't know."

"I'm sure you'd like to take today off and get some sleep, but . . ."

"No, it's not that. I'd love to sleep the day away, but I know there's more I need to get done. I need to do more reading for school. I need to figure out how to spot magic before it affects me or the people around me. I need to know more about how to fight whatever it is that's causing my life to go haywire. I need to organize Dad's things and figure out what I'm keeping, what could go back to the department at the university he worked for, and what can go in storage. I miss him so badly it hurts."

"You haven't been talking about your dad much."

"I know. I've been trying not to." Oh, God, the waterworks were going to start. Again.

"Your dad was a good man. I know you miss him, and you're right to miss him. Don't shove it so deep that it makes it worse to deal with later." He reached out a hand to me.

I couldn't take it, or the comfort he offered. "I tried processing it. I tried mourning him. I don't get anything done if I think about it. I miss him so badly I can't even talk about it. Please, don't. I have to keep going, and sooner or later it'll get easier."

"Don't ignore it. Grief can make you do strange things if you don't deal with it. I know you feel overwhelmed right now. It would be unusual if you didn't feel that way, but Janie, you're smart. With everything going on, you've been in triage mode; dealing with the most pressing thing in front of you at the moment, and figuring you'll deal with the rest as you can. It's not a bad strategy, but it takes a toll. I know you can figure this out. Maybe having a free day is exactly what you need to get a handle on all of this."

It was the right thing to say and exactly what I needed to hear. I was beginning to feel like I was trying to put together a puzzle from the inside out, without the box cover as a guide, and with a few pieces missing. If I'd tried something like that as a teenager, I'd have given up, shoved the pieces to the floor, and faced Evangeline's wrath for making a mess. Dad would have laughed. My stomach clenched in sudden grief. I swallowed hard, trying to shut down the memory of him. I wouldn't be able to function if I let it go. It took a minute to stop, but I was able to hold back the tears and wall off the pain so Aiden wouldn't see me cry.

I stood up to head back to the living room. I'm not sure Aiden realized what I was doing, because he didn't step back to let me through the door.

"Oh, I'm sorry. Excuse me," he said, when he figured it out and tried to step back. I'd have been able to get through, except for the fact he fell backwards, hitting the door to the linen closet behind him with a crash.

Some things don't change. I kneeled down to help him up.

"I hate this," he said. "I hate always tripping and falling down, looking like a fool and never being able to have things that aren't broken or dropped. I don't even keep Kool-Aid in my refrigerator because I'm afraid I'll spill it and stain everything."

"Have you always been this accident-prone, Aiden?" Oh, good. A topic not involving Dad, or how behind I was, or how clueless I was about magic was exactly what I needed.

He stood up, and leaned against the wall. "I was pretty normal until I hit puberty. I think I was about twelve or thirteen when I realized it wasn't just growing pains. I stopped growing when I hit seventeen, and it's never gotten any better."

Just like everyone else on the planet I'd had klutz moments myself, and I always felt like an idiot when it happened. With the amount of disaster following him around, he probably felt like that all the time. "It doesn't make you a bad person, Aiden."

"I'm always afraid I'll get pulled over when I'm driving for one reason or another and they'll want me to walk a straight line to see if I'm drunk. I'll fail the test despite not having a drop to drink. I sometimes make choices about my social life because of it."

"What do you mean?"

"Well, I'd go to a museum as long as I wasn't walking through a pottery exhibit. I don't go to china shops. If a store looks like it has crowded aisles, I'll give it a pass." He grinned. "I don't take girls on the first date to an Italian restaurant, because I'm sure I'd end up with red sauce everywhere. I'll probably get fired soon from my job."

Now I really felt sorry for him. How could one person worry about such things all the time? "Why do you think you'll get fired?"

"I work in a restaurant, Janie. Do you have any idea how many dishes I've broken?"

Why had I forgotten he worked at the restaurant where I'd met Evangeline for brunch last weekend? Especially since he'd crashed an entire tray of dishes the last time? How does one forget that? I'm not normally that scattered.

Or am I? Mia had reminded me there were gaps in my memory about my childhood. Evangeline was always nagging me that I didn't get to meetings and appointments on time. Was it just chronic lateness or forgetfulness? What else was I missing? What had I forgotten?

I didn't get a chance to ask him anything else. Aiden gathered me close, and gave me a hug, thanking me for not making him feel like a social outcast just because he was a walking menace to breakables everywhere. I hugged him back, and he leaned down to put his chin on the top of my head—he was tall enough he had to slouch down to do it. We stood there a couple of minutes, soothing the weight of the emotional baggage we both seemed to be carrying around.

He straightened up and brushed a lock of hair off my forehead, before leaning in and tenderly kissing me. This time, there was no urgency about his kiss, no rushing off to break a magical spell or save people. Instead, it was just him and me, with all the time in the world to explore and relax, and savor the time we had to experience each other.

Aiden cupped my face in his hands, and I learned first-hand he definitely knew how to concentrate. The kiss deepened and he caught my lower lip gently between his teeth. I sucked in my breath, trying to steady myself from the wave of feeling crashing over me. It had been so long since I'd felt this way. I felt safe and secure in Aiden's embrace, as if the rest of the world had ceased to go crazy around me.

The mood was broken by a loud contented sigh coming from the living room. We broke apart. Aiden had a guilty look on his face that I was sure was echoed on mine; like two junior high kids, kissing under the bleachers at a football game and getting caught by one of our parents. Instead of parents, however, it was Bert.

"You guys make a cute couple."

Oh God. Had he been watching the entire thing? I was going to have to get a handle on the roommate situation, create some boundaries, that sort of thing. I'd had a friend who used to put a sock on the door when she didn't want a roommate intruding. I wasn't sure something like that would work with Bert. And I knew I'd never live this down with him.

We were saved from commenting by the doorbell. It was Doris, there to pick up Aiden.

Crap.

CHAPTER TWENTY-SIX

When I opened the door, Doris came in with a smile on her face. "Hey, kids, what's up? Janie, I was so worried about you when Aiden told me what happened after we left. I'm so happy you're okay, and that your stepmother and your friend got out safely."

Aiden came into the living room from the general direction of the bathroom. Her eyes narrowed a bit at us, as if she suspected we had been doing something wrong. It didn't help that Aiden was blushing and wouldn't look me in the eyes. I could tell she wasn't fooled.

Wait a minute. We were all adults. Why were we sneaking around like a kiss was something to hide?

I didn't have time to wonder about it; Doris gave me a big hug, distracting me from my thoughts. Her hug felt safe, but not the same kind of safe I had felt just moments before with Aiden. It was the safe hug of grandmotherly concern and caring, the kind of hug I hadn't gotten much of in my life. I almost didn't want to let her go.

I wasn't prepared for her reaction when she did let go.

"There's something odd about you today." She sniffed me. "Aiden, did you notice how she smells?"

He reddened. "I hadn't really thought about it."

She sniffed again. "It might be left over from last night's craziness, but I smell high court magic on her."

Aiden came over and sniffed me. I was horrified. Both of them had a somewhat disgusted, or was it scared, look on their faces. "How would I smell like magic? Why wouldn't I smell it myself? What does it smell like?" It had to be something I'd come into contact with last night. I knew there had been magic around then.

Doris wrinkled her nose at me, and Aiden did, too. That wasn't quite the reaction I wanted from anyone, especially someone I'd been lip-locked with in my hallway just a few minutes earlier. I knew I'd been moving heavy trunks and boxes just an hour or so ago, but I didn't think I smelled *that* bad. "If you can smell it, what does it smell like? I don't smell anything. From the look on your face, it's got to be as bad as old, dirty, sweat-socks."

Did they just come to my house and tell me I *smelled?* I wondered what my stepmother would do if someone said that to her. I had to suppress a giggle at the thought of Evangeline's cold outrage at such a breach of proper etiquette. I wondered what Evangeline and Doris would think of each other, as I looked at the sweatshirt Doris was wearing today. The front of her shirt had a picture of kittens playing with balls of yarn, with lettering that read, *Have a ball!* It marked her as someone more than slightly outside of my stepmother's acceptable social circle.

Doris and Aiden laughed together, distracting my mental wanderings. "We're not laughing at you. You don't stink. It isn't a bad smell. It is, however, distinctive, one we'd recognize anywhere because we know what it is. If you haven't learned how to distinguish it, it's not something you'd recognize as magic, and it smells different to everyone." Doris explained.

"What do you mean?"

"It's related to strong, pleasant memories and emotions; things that make you feel relaxed and off-guard. It's a prey-hunting mechanism that some of them use to find human targets. They lure you with scents you find comforting or appealing." She sat down on my couch, taking the opportunity to greet Bert, who was leering at me.

I ignored him. "What does it smell like to you?"

"Fresh-mown grass, overlaid with old-fashioned black licorice candy." Aiden smiled at me. "I remember playing baseball as a kid before I got clumsy, and we always had black licorice in the dugout to chew on during a game."

I saw Doris close her eyes, as if his memory was painful to her, before she responded. "For me it's vanilla, not just the extract you buy in the supermarket for baking, but the real thing, scraped fresh off a vanilla bean with a knife. If you can't tell, I enjoy baking."

Considering the pie I'd had earlier, I thought it went further than just enjoying baking. Eating baked goods Doris made was akin to a religious experience. The pie the other night had been superb. Out of a whole pie, I didn't have much left; Mia and I had eaten until we'd been stuffed and uncomfortable.

Bert hopped onto Doris's lap; content to let her scratch the top of his head and the area that used to be his nose while we talked, but that didn't stop him from joining in the conversation. "It's different for everyone. I don't really have a sense of smell, anymore. It's not the same as it was when I was a human. I can see when magic has altered reality, but I don't really smell it. Ooh, that feels good. I can't scratch my nose these days, either."

I had never really thought about it, but I could totally sympathize. I bet frogs didn't have fingernails, even if they could reach their noses.

"So, what you're all saying is that there's no one who can describe what it smells like to me? How am I supposed to know what I smell for?" I asked.

Doris laughed. "Well, she could join us for the potluck tonight. Maybe some of the other F.A.B.L.E.S. members have some ideas for how you can figure it out."

"I forgot that it was tonight." Aiden said. "Janie, you're free, right?"

"I guess."

"Well, then you should go with us. It's getting close to two o'clock now. If you come, you can meet some of the others, maybe get some questions answered, and see what we do. You'll get dinner. Besides, I'm betting there are several pies in the back of Doris's car for the potluck. I think dinner is at five. It's worth going for the pies alone, although the rest of the food is pretty incredible, too."

I agreed. Despite needing to spend time studying, I felt like I should figure things out first. Why not get dinner, talk to them, and maybe learn how to save my own life?

"Come to think of it, I smelled the same thing at your stepmother's house earlier today."

"Aiden, was that what you and Bobby and Jake were giving each other dirty looks about?" I asked.

"Yes, Janie, I'm sorry to ask this, but did your dad die at home, or was he in the hospital? I'm only asking because if he died at home, that might explain the smell of magic. How long ago did he die?"

I knew he was only asking to try to figure things out, but it still hurt. "It's been a bit over six months ago. We took him home when the doctors said there was no hope. Evangeline insisted on it." I had to give her credit for that one. I hadn't wanted him to die in a hospital, smelling of antiseptic and sick people. Much as her place had never really felt like home, it still wasn't the hospital, so I was okay with it and helped her convince the doctors he should go there.

"That must explain it. If he was dying of a curse, it would still leave a pretty significant smell signature. And if it was strong enough to kill someone, the scent would still be there for a while after he died." Aiden was quick to comment. I was glad. Maybe the discussion of Dad's death would stop.

Doris didn't look completely convinced, but after a quick look at both of us, she didn't ask anything else. Was it just me, or had Aiden shaken his head at her, discouraging her from asking more questions? Right now, I'd take it. My emotions were in turmoil, with the pain and the longing and the grief all rolled up into a great big ball of queasy stomach.

"Well, if we're heading to the meeting, we probably ought to get going. Aiden's right, I've got pies in the back of the car. If you want a ride, Janie, I'd be happy to take you as well."

Done.

CHAPTER TWENTY-SEVEN

We piled into Doris's Cadillac, and headed out, Bert hitching a ride in my purse again. I could smell the fruity scent of more than one pie in the back seat of her car. When asked, she told me she'd loaded up the pies because she didn't know how long she'd be gone when she left to pick up Aiden. Something told me she had some experience in picking him up after a car accident before.

They had an easy relationship. I could tell they really cared for one another, and that they had known each other for a long time. It seemed as though they were more than colleagues, but I didn't ask what the relationship was. I chickened out; I wasn't sure it was my business.

What I did ask was about magic. "When did you first learn about magic?"

Aiden answered first, turning his head back toward where I sat in the backseat to grin at me. "I was probably thirteen the first time I realized it was real. I'd gone out to mow the yard, and I saw a garden gnome."

"Something tells me you're not talking about the cheap cartoony plastic things like my neighbor collects. She's got ones wearing University of Michigan football uniforms and ones holding footballs and ones mooning people."

He laughed. "You're right, although this one was bad-tempered enough that mooning wasn't exactly out of the question. This one was the real thing."

Doris didn't say anything; she just kept driving. "Oh," I said, unable to come up with something more intelligent to say.

"He told me he knew my father and wanted to tell me something about myself."

"Sounds familiar," I shot back.

"It does, doesn't it? Well, I didn't believe him at first, much like you didn't believe me, but it didn't take long before I gave in and started trying to learn more about it."

I had a sudden, disturbing thought. "Are you saying that because magic has knocked on my door, so to speak, I have to give up everything I've been working for and drop out of law school and work for you doing research into magical creepy-crawlies for the rest of my life?"

They both laughed out loud. Doris stopped at a stoplight. "Oh, heavens, no, child. Harold and Stanley are our researchers, and Aiden's learning to take over from both of them. We're cutting down to one researcher. Our organization just doesn't have the budget to pay multiple researchers anymore. We don't have enough resources to do everything we'd like to do, and most of us do this in addition to having families, and jobs, and, well, lives. We wouldn't want you to give up your career, or your dreams. You've worked hard for them. We just want you to take magic seriously because it could kill you. We want you to be safe."

I must have made a funny face at her in the rear view mirror, because she rolled her eyes. "Yes, Janie, we have lives outside of magic. I'm a retired schoolteacher, and I have three children and six grandchildren. Someday my son might even give me a few more."

Aiden groaned. "Next thing you know, she'll whip out pictures of them."

"It's a good thing I'm driving, or he's right. I've always got pictures of them on me. My youngest grandchild just had his fourth birthday party. He's got a thing for Buzz Lightyear." She pulled into an empty parking lot next to a warehouse and shut off the engine. "He kept running around yelling, 'to infinity and beyond'. It was so cute. Now both of you need to get out and help me unload these pies before we do anything else."

What else could we do? We did what she asked. Aiden and I each grabbed for the pies, and helped her carry them in. It took multiple trips. How many people were going to be here if she'd baked a dozen pies? What was this gathering?

I didn't really notice anything inside until we'd brought in the last round of pies. From the outside, it was a nondescript abandoned warehouse just outside of downtown Dayton. It could have served one of a thousand different purposes in its heyday, but from the inside there was no question this place had been well taken care of. It was swept and clean, and looked well-used.

There was a basketball hoop at one side, with the markings of a full half-court on the cement floor in front of it. On my left, it looked like there were several cubicles, and possibly some cast-off office furniture inside. I saw enough wire running to the cubicles to realize there were probably computers and phones. To the right were long picnic tables, set up potluck-style, with plates and casserole dishes and Tupperware containers piled up on them. This was definitely a place where people gathered on a regular basis.

Other people came out of the cubicles when we showed up, and one of them gave Doris and Aiden a strange look. I translated it easily as *who is this person, and why is she here?*

One man came up to me and introduced himself as John. He asked me if there was anything he could do for me, and if there was anything he could help me with. In fact, he was a little pushy about it.

"Miss, do you want something to drink? Something to eat? Is there anything I can do to make you comfortable here? Is it too cold? Is it too hot? Can I get you a chair?" He stood right next to me, invading my personal space as I politely told him I was fine.

John's shoulders drooped in disappointment, and he shuffled away. Aiden looked at me thoughtfully. "I haven't seen John act like that in years. Next time he offers, it might be worth it to let him do something for you. He must recognize something noble about you, and like you for it. He's not a bad guy; he's just a little different."

"What?" I stopped walking and Aiden had to stop and turn around to face me to finish the conversation. "What are you talking about?"

"Well, we call him Trusty John. John's not someone who talks a lot, but if he finds someone he trusts, he's loyal and wants nothing more than to do everything he can to make you happy. He'd sacrifice himself for you if he could. Rumor has it he once sacrificed himself in order to save his master. His master had to kill his own children in order to save John."

"What an awful story." I crossed my arms over my chest, feeling goose bumps breaking out over my arms and running up to my neck.

"Well, it all worked out for the best. The sacrifice of the kids brought John back, and his resurrection also brought back the kids, so everyone was happy at the end of the day."

Aiden walked away from me, and I had to follow him, calling behind him, "If something happens to me, please don't sacrifice any kids, even if it could bring me back. That's just morbid and creepy."

He laughed at me. "Don't rule things out until you know what you're dealing with."

What the hell could he be talking about? I followed him to the opposite side of the large warehouse and waited as he opened a door. "Where are we going?" I asked, unable to see in the room because Aiden tripped over a crack in the concrete floor just as he opened the door, blocking my view.

He righted himself and gave me a wan smile, blushing. I had the sudden thought he must be completely embarrassed by his inability to do anything without hurting himself. If I was to read anything into the kiss earlier, it must mean he was mortified to have me see him foul up like that. "I'm showing you more about magic. Isn't that what you wanted?" He stepped sideways, and I finally saw what was inside the door.

It was a portal, much like the one he'd pulled me through to cure the Rapunzel Syndrome I'd dealt with earlier in the week. I hadn't noticed before, but the purple swirling air marking the portal made my stomach churn. I hoped I didn't have to drink anything foul this time, but I did need to follow him through the opening in order to find out what I needed to know. I reminded myself I'd be able to come back here later and eat some of Doris's pies.

At least I had something to look forward to.

CHAPTER TWENTY-EIGHT

I stepped through the portal, following Aiden, and suddenly I smelled musty pages and cheap peppermints.

My stomach clenched and my knees crumpled under me. I cried out, and Aiden grabbed my arm to keep me from collapsing. It was a smell I missed, the smell of warmth, of home, of comfort and love.

It was the smell of my father.

I'd forgotten how much that scent had comforted me when I was a kid after a hard day at school, after I'd fallen off my bike and skinned my knees, after I broke up with my high school boyfriend.

Aiden caught me, and hugged me, letting me cry it out. "I take it you've found the scent of magic?" he asked gently.

I couldn't answer him right away, burying my face in his shirt and trying not to smell it any more. No matter how I tried to block out the scent, I could still smell it. We were surrounded by it. I couldn't ignore it, or wish it away, or hide from it. I couldn't bury my feelings. I'd have to live with it, even though it left a gaping hole in my heart.

"Yeah, I think I've finally figured out what magic smells like to me." I lifted my face. The front of his shirt was wet with my tears, and no matter how much I apologized, he brushed it off like it wasn't a big deal. Knowing Aiden, tear drops on his shirt were probably the least destructive thing he'd seen all day.

"First of all, please don't be embarrassed. The smell is very personal to each one of us. There's always some deep emotion behind why we smell what we do. We all react to it, and I don't think anyone saw your reaction." He brushed my hair back, and kissed my forehead where my hair had fallen in my face.

It did make me feel better. I couldn't stop the smile. "Thank you."

"Do you mind me asking what you smelled?"

"I smell old books and peppermint. Dad always smelled like that, with all of his academic research. And he carried peppermints in his pockets all the time."

He took my hand. "No wonder you reacted as you did. Are you okay?"

I took a minute before I answered. There were so many emotions ping-ponging off each other that I couldn't have described how I was feeling. "I don't know. I keep thinking I'll be able to just move past it and then I get smacked in the face with the fact he's gone. My life's exploding all around me. I can't quite get a handle on everything if I'm dealing with Dad being gone, so I try to shove it deep down where I won't have to. I keep getting reminders that I won't ever go out for coffee and pie with him again, or talk about books, or walk around the park with him, and everything else seems stupid and simple and meaningless."

Aiden was a good listener. He stood there, holding my hand, and waited for me to finish. When I was done, he squeezed it. "I hate to push you, but can you do this today? Can you be on this side of the portal, knowing that you're likely to be reminded of your father the entire time you're here?"

Could I? I wasn't sure. All I knew was that I was rapidly becoming aware of a whole world existing within my own, which would continue to interrupt and endanger me if I didn't deal with it now. It didn't matter if I could do it. I had to. I believed what Aiden and Bert had been telling me; I was in danger. "I'll be fine. I can't put this off."

He nodded.

"Is it safe to leave the portal unguarded?" I asked.

"It's not unguarded. John's standing at the portal, on the reality side, making sure nothing goes in and nothing comes out."

"Aiden, how many portals are there? I mean, you pulled me through one at the drug store, and there's one here. Should we worry about there being more doorways that bad things can get through?"

He let go of my hand, and ran his own through his hair. "You've hit on the problem. We know of several of them, and we have people stationed where they can keep an eye on them and let us know if anything comes through, but it isn't like there's a master list we can download somewhere, like a Map of the Stars you can get in Hollywood. The only thing we can do is to keep looking for more of them and try to be vigilant about the ones we know about."

We walked down the same pathway I remembered from the night they cured my Rapunzel Syndrome. The path was still decorated by twinkling pixies waving and smiling and welcoming me back, lighting the way to the hut we'd been in. I was surprised when we turned away from the hut. For some reason, I'd figured we'd be meeting the others there.

I heard music, the volume growing as we approached. It sounded like a barbershop quartet singing in perfect pitch and harmony. I'm no musician, but it sounded really good. When we got closer, I realized it was actually four animals; the animals I'd caught serenading me in the middle of the night in my parking lot. "Aiden, are those . . .?"

"The Bremen Town Musicians, yes, they are. They're here to sing for us tonight. Aren't they fantastic? I mean, I wouldn't listen to this kind of music on my own, but they're pretty good, aren't they?"

I stopped for a moment to listen to the music. Aiden stopped beside me. "But they sucked when they were outside of my apartment the other night. How could someone as good as this suck that much, even on purpose?"

He smiled, and put his arm around my shoulders. It was comfortable, almost familiar. "Janie, magic isn't all bad. There are some things about it that are really cool, and some things that are fun and interesting and enjoyable. Think of it as a coin, with a good side and a bad side. Part of us bringing you here today is because you've only heard about the threat of the bad side. I want you to understand all of it."

"How does this help me protect myself?" I asked.

"It doesn't. It's good music that they can't make on the other side. The bigger picture is you wouldn't want to hurt the good things about magic to protect yourself from the bad things about it. You wouldn't burn down a day care to protect yourself from a trash fire, would you? It helps to know what your actions could affect before you hurt something you'd regret later."

He removed his arm from my shoulder and walked away.

"Do you think I'm irresponsible? Is that why you're saying this?" I asked, following him.

Aiden stopped, and shoved his hands into his pockets. "No, I'm saying it because you are the opposite of irresponsible. If you caused damage to something you could have avoided, you'd blame yourself for it. If I don't show you the kinds of things magic can do that are good, will you understand there's more at stake here than just what's in front of you? I don't want you blaming yourself for hurting something we should have shown you."

He had a point. I would feel that way. I felt a little small-minded for accusing him as I did, but I didn't know what to say. I shut up and followed him. We kept walking down the path and eventually stopped at a clearing in the woods. The others from the group were already there: Doris smiled at us when we came in, Stanley winked at me, and Harold shook hands with Aiden. There were three or four others there who I also recognized from the night of the Magical Hair Growth Cure. Bert was talking with a middle-aged woman I'd seen before. Apparently he'd hitched a ride with us, without my realizing it. Then again, they did know him, so he could have talked someone into bringing him through the portal with them.

"We're safe here. There's no possibility of magical eavesdropping in this clearing. We keep it cleared of magical interference, and we always have someone on guard patrol when we meet," he said. "We brought you here to talk to you where nothing could overhear us. Technically, even the warehouse isn't safe, although we do the best we can to make sure no one's listening in, but here we know we're okay."

Before I could ask about details or who would eavesdrop on a bunch of old people talking about crazy magic theories in the woods, Stanley stepped forward. "Ms. Janie, we think it's time we actually told you a little more about the Legacy."

I remembered Aiden mentioning something about it when he'd first introduced himself to me, in front of my dad's gravestone. Was it just a few days ago? It seemed like an eternity since then. "What is the Legacy?"

"Well, I guess the best way to start is to ask you what you know about your own family history," Harold said.

"Dad used to say that my great-great-great-grandfather was one of the Grimm Brothers, but I never knew if that was a tall tale told to amuse a cranky six-year-old or if it was actually true. Otherwise, he never really talked about his family. I don't think he knew much about them, but I've got an old family Bible that was his."

Doris came forward and clutched my hands in hers. "It's true. Go home and look it up in your Bible. Your great-great-great-grandfather was Wilhelm Grimm and your great-great-great-grandmother was his wife, Dorothea. She might even be listed as *Dortchen*; it was Fa family nickname for her."

I knew what I'd be doing the minute I got home that night. "Even if that's true, I don't really see why it matters. I mean, what happened more than a hundred and fifty years ago doesn't have anything to do with what's happening to me right now, does it?"

"It has everything to do with it." Stanley tried to take control of the conversation again. "Everything is related. Nothing is irrelevant. We're all here because something related to magic brought us to this moment, and now we're facing more magical danger, and it's someone's fault. Someone out there is planning all of this, and they're going to take over the world. I think George W. Bush is behind it. We need to go bind him and Dick Cheney and all his buddies. They're the ones that started this."

"All right, Oliver Stone. That's enough of your crazy conspiracy theories. Trust me; this is not some secret CIA plot." Aiden grinned at him, as if he was used to the allegations.

Stanley's jowls quivered. "Of course it is. How else do you explain what's happened to the economy and the fact it took us so long to find bin Ladin? They provided him a portal to escape, of course. And the economy's in the tank because of the secret government magical experiments to keep everything magic in the dark. It *has* to be the government. There's no other explanation for it."

Harold clapped a hand on his shoulder. "Stanley does have a point, in regards to what happened with your ancestors being related to what's going on now."

Stanley began to sit a little straighter with the validation.

"However," Harold continued. "It's not a government conspiracy. Let's all sit down."

Everyone lowered themselves to the ground. I was surprised at how easily some of them moved. No one seemed to be suffering from arthritis, or bad knees, or anything else, despite many of them being old enough to have joint pain. I couldn't blame their limber movements on extra glucosamine, or even Ben-Gay, which I would have smelled.

"It's not the CIA. It's all about what happened to your family. Stanley here knows there's not one shred of proof the Bush family has magical ability or connections to the faerie courts. And there's no indication the CIA is involved in magic. Here's what we do know," Harold explained. "Wilhelm Grimm and his wife had three children who survived past childhood. Through the years, their children married and had children who emigrated and moved. From wars and deaths and fevers and plagues and accidents, you are the last living direct descendant of the Grimm Brothers."

"Wait a minute," I said. "I thought you said 'Brothers'. As in, plural, right?"

"Jacob Grimm never married, and had no children that we've ever found. It's not like nineteenth century scholars saved DNA exemplars for us to use for comparisons. Even if we did, there's no information out there that even hints he has any descendants." Aiden explained.

I rolled my eyes at him. "Okay, so let's say my ancestor really was one of the Brothers Grimm. Are you telling me they're coming back to life or some such nonsense?"

Doris arranged her legs underneath herself, Indian-style on the ground. "No, Janie. We're telling you that you are the last remaining living bond to the biggest magical coup ever pulled off. Your life is important, not just because you're a good person with hopes and dreams and likes and dislikes and goals and motivations, but because your life also keeps the witch bound."

"Huh? Witch?" Okay, I'd so far accepted the craziness of the last week as a result of some goofy curse. I had to admit something was affecting me, and making my life a living hell. At the same time, the rational, analytical side of me was screaming that they'd somehow jumped from real life into the figment of some schizophrenic fiction writer's imagination.

"Yeah, witch. Wilhelm and Jacob were able to bind the witch's powers by pure human logic and making her play by the rules, but they had to tie the promise to something. It had to last beyond their own lifetimes; so they tied it to the lives of Wilhelm's children and their descendants. To be fair, I don't think he realized just what he'd be putting them through, but it's worked so far." Harold was picking at his fingernails while he talked, his head bent low enough that I could see the black cord he'd tied his grey ponytail back with.

I wondered what he meant by "putting them through." Did that mean other members of my family had died before their time, like my mom and my dad and my grandparents? Was that why I was the only one left? What was killing us all off?

CHAPTER TWENTY-NINE

Doris finally shut them all up and claimed the right to tell me the story of my family. Stanley pouted a bit, but in the end, settled back. It seemed to me it was a familiar tale to them, and made me wonder just how long they'd been watching my family. Despite my healthy skepticism, it was an interesting story.

According to Doris, my great-great-great-grandfather Wilhelm had met his wife Dorothea when he rescued her from a ravening beast holding her captive at her grandmother's house. She had been the little girl whose story had started their first written tale, *Little Red Riding Hood.*

"So, you're telling me the red hood my stepmother claimed was stolen from the art institute was a replica of my however-many-greats-grandmother's and that the story of the Big Bad Wolf who ate her grandmother was real?" I asked.

Harold piped up. "It's not a replica. It's probably the real deal. There's a Grimm Brothers Museum in Germany we sometimes partner with for research, and they were the ones who arranged for items to be displayed here. We objected, of course, but we don't always have a lot of pull when it comes to serious academic institutions. There's a bit of bias still; even your father wasn't immune to it. In fact, I've wondered at times whether he would still be alive if we'd had a reputation that lent itself to what might be considered *serious* research."

It was the *real* Red Riding Hood? And it had belonged to my multiple-greats grandmother? This was definitely interesting. But why would someone steal an old red cape? Other than pure curiosity, or what it might fetch on eBay, I couldn't imagine why someone would seriously want a piece of old worn out cloth. I couldn't bring myself to keep my mouth shut, so I asked the question out loud.

"Well," Doris said in response, "it is a collector's item. There are some eccentric collectors out there, but you're right. We can't prove it's real. It's not like there's some kind of certificate of authenticity that comes with it to prove what we're saying. Even so, there's some who believe the hood carries part of the protection of the Grimm bloodline."

Now I really wanted that hood and cape. I wanted it for myself, since it was a part of my family's history. I hoped the thieves had put it on eBay, but I wasn't going to be able to afford it if it was priced much higher than twenty dollars. Something told me it would go for much higher than that, but at least an eBay listing would give us something to go on. I'd have to check as soon as I got home.

The other F.A.B.L.E.S. members, or as I'd begun mentally referring to them, the Old Fart Council, were definitely comfortable on the grassy expanse of the clearing. Regardless of the ease with which they had settled on the ground, there were going to be bugs and we'd end up with grass stains. What if someone broke a hip trying to get up? How would we get them back through the portal and get them to medical attention? Aiden and I seemed to be the youngest and strongest of the group. Wouldn't that be a catastrophe, if he had to help carry someone to the portal with all of his motor control problems?

The more we sat there, and the more people moved around, I was somewhat relieved to see that no one seemed to be having any difficulty moving. Was it a side effect of the magic of the place? Doris smiled at me, as if she'd guessed the mental meanderings of my brain. I tried not to smirk when I smiled back at her.

She kept talking, telling me about how different family members had met with untimely deaths. "Well, your great-great-aunt Druscilla died when she pricked her finger on a rusted spinning wheel spindle. The records indicate symptoms that today would have been diagnosed as tetanus. We saw written records of facial spasms, fever, and severe muscle spasms. Today she'd have been treated with some antibiotic or curare, but she may have actually starved to death because she couldn't swallow."

Ew. So avoid rusty spinning wheels. Check.

Stanley puffed out his chest, and added his own contribution. "Then there was your cousin, although I'm not sure exactly what the relationship was. She was hospitalized quite a bit. They thought she was congenitally insane, but she put on an old pair of shoes and could not stop dancing. I'm sure she was put on just about every anti-psychotic under the sun, but nothing worked. I read her medical records. She dropped dead of pure exhaustion, but her feet continued to dance even after she collapsed. The medical staff thought it was muscle reflex."

Add cursed dancing shoes and mental institutions. Check.

"Another ancestor, your great-great-grandfather, was a victim of a horrible wagon accident; a wheel caught on a piece of metal sticking out of the ground, and fell apart. The wagon crushed him. His widow later learned the metal that caused the accident was an old iron stove, half buried in the roadway." That came from another member of the group, who looked like a soccer mom fifteen years my senior with her fresh-scrubbed face and *Go, Little Flyers Soccer* t-shirt.

I added riding in wagons with drivers who didn't watch the road to my mental list of things-I-shouldn't-do.

"Some of what you're telling me about corresponds to the things that are missing from the art exhibition Evangeline told me about last weekend. Even assuming they have some magical connection, as you seem to be insinuating, why would someone steal them?" I stretched my legs out in front of me. "Is there some reason why they would be valuable other than being cool bits of history? It just doesn't make sense."

Stanley joined in the conversation again, his jowls bobbing and swaying as he talked. He obviously needed to lose about eighty pounds, and yet he hadn't had any trouble lowering himself onto the grass. "Janie, there is more than one kind of witch, just like there's more than one kind of magic, more than one kind of person, and more than one kind of chili cheese dog. We have information that the witch who cursed your family is on the hunt for a specific item of historical Grimm significance which might be the Holder."

"Holder? What's that?"

Aiden stood up and walked over to where I was sitting. It wasn't far, but he sat down next to me and put his arm around my shoulder. "The Holder is a Grimm artifact. It carries with it the key to the binding. According to legend, if the Holder is in the possession of the youngest Grimm descendant, then it strengthens the binding on the witch. That descendant cannot be killed, or even harmed, by the witch."

"And what if the witch has it? I'm assuming that's the concern here."

"You're right, Janie. If the witch has the Holder, she can destroy all the descendents of the Grimm family and break the binding. If that happens, she gets back all of her powers and heaven knows what horrors she can visit on the world if she does."

"So, wait a minute. You're telling me not only is she gunning for me to get her powers back, but there's a thingamabob out there that makes it *easier* for her to kill me and destroy the world? Then why wouldn't we try to have those items locked up in a place where the witch couldn't get to them? I mean, wouldn't that be the best way to handle things?"

Aiden removed his arm from my shoulder and looked at the ground, picking at the grass in front of him. Doris blushed, and Harold, Stanley, and the others had all found something else to look at.

"What's going on here, guys?" I was suspicious.

No one said anything right away. Finally Harold piped up. "It's not like we know which piece is the Holder of the Legacy. How would we know which piece to hide?"

I looked at each one of them in turn. No one would look me in the eye. They'd done something. I was sure of it. What could they have done?

After several more uncomfortable moments of silence, I finally asked the question. Again. "What did you guys do?"

"We did what we needed to do. And we're not done doing it." Stanley crossed his arms over his chest, looking like a stubborn two-year-old in a sixty year old body. I swear his lower lip stuck out in a pout.

It took me a few minutes before I suddenly had an awful idea. "You guys didn't steal the artifacts from the Art Institute Oktoberfest exhibition, did you?"

There was only an uncomfortable silence that met my question, but I could see the guilt on everyone's faces. "You guys seriously pulled off an art heist?"

"It wasn't like we had a choice. We had to protect the items that might be the Holder. Most of the items in the exhibition are not ones that could hold the curse; many of them aren't even true Grimm artifacts, just replicas. Those aren't a worry. We took the ones that could be Holders, and we thought we got them all, but the attack on your stepmother's fundraiser might mean we missed one." Doris stood up in front of me, wringing her hands in worry. "We just don't know what we missed, and we won't get another chance at it. I'm sorry, Janie. I think we failed you, just like we failed your father. We had hoped we would just have to keep you safe until the exhibition ended, and then all the pieces that could be Holders would be back under lock and key in Germany." She began to cry, softly.

I sat there for a minute, stunned. Could what she was telling me be true? Had Evangeline unwittingly arranged for the display of the one item that could mean my death, and the death of every member of my family since the time Wilhelm and Jacob Grimm had bound the witch? Did I really believe one shred of what they were saying? And yet, how could I not believe them? They had come whenever I called for help. They hadn't asked for a single thing from me, other than to give them time, to hear them out, to believe in magic, to understand, and to see the big picture. And they'd given me a safe place to do it, here on the magical side, through a portal and in a safe clearing, away from prying eyes and ears.

I stared at them all, sitting in front of me, as if they'd run out of ideas. There had to be a better solution than just to bury the Holder in a safe place and hope no one found it. And I refused to live my life running and hiding. "Well, we still need to figure out which artifact is the Holder of the Legacy, for safety's sake, but don't we need to find out where the threat is coming from? Who is the witch, and how do we stop her?" I asked.

"We don't know. And even if we did know, what could we do? Most of us have no magical ability, just knowledge. How could we defeat the witch?" Harold asked.

Stanley began to call out reasons why we didn't have magic, including al-Qaeda, Homeland Security, and the Patriot Act. Everyone else rolled their eyes at him. We spent a couple of fruitless hours trying to come up with a way to find the witch, but didn't have a solution. Hopefully everything would look better after some pie.

CHAPTER THIRTY

We did go back to the warehouse, back through the portal where Trusty John had kept watch for us. The first order of business was to demolish the potluck dinner everyone had provided, including every single bite of Doris's pies. I was starving, and when I saw the clock on the wall, it was easy to see why; it was nearly six in the evening, and I hadn't eaten anything all day.

Trusty John seemed happy to see me, and was content to fetch me a plate of food, napkins, and drink refills while we sat there. As much as I felt bad, Aiden assured me no one thought I was being pretentious by letting him bring me things. "John's just happier when he's picked someone to wait on. And we all know you've been through a lot. Just relax and let him take care of you."

Even Bert seemed to be enjoying himself, gorging on pie and complaining because no one had brought any beer. He hadn't been able to use a fork, so the front of his face was smeared with sticky purple blackberry pie filling from putting his face straight into the slice. "Even Budweiser would have been better than nothing. Janie got it for me. What does a frog have to do to get a drink around here?" he mumbled, before diving back into the sweet, flaky pastry.

The conversation as we ate consisted mostly of the group's past adventures. They all talked about encounters with magic, and how they'd survived. "Then there was the time Doris killed a troll with a garden trowel," Harold said, teasing her.

"He was trying to eat my marigolds. I didn't want to replant them all, so I swung the trowel at him. I didn't even think I'd hit him, but I got him right in the leg with edge of the trowel. He got mad and charged at me, so I threw it at him and ran. That's what I had in my hand when he showed up. I didn't have time to look for some fancy weapon gizmo to use, but it hit him in the head and he died."

"She makes him sound like he wouldn't have eaten her face off if he'd had the chance. I just wonder who sent him," Stanley added, his mouth full of barbecued green beans.

"Don't forget the time Harold and Aiden had to fight off a whole flight of angry pixies," Doris added, changing the subject as she got up to slice another pie.

"Yeah, but you wouldn't have spotted them at all if you hadn't tripped and fallen right into their hive, Aiden," Bert teased.

Aiden looked at me and blushed. Bert winked at me. It didn't take a rocket scientist to figure out Bert was trying to see if he could embarrass Aiden in front of me, to test his reaction. I was pretty sure Aiden's reaction didn't have much of anything to do with me being there, and everything to do with tales of his clumsiness being exposed, since he'd told me how much he hated it. Or did it? I swallowed hard, and asked someone to pass me some more napkins, to break up the conversation.

After dinner, some of the group members made excuses and left, some to pick up kids, others to go to work, or to otherwise head back to normal day-to-day activities, promising to call if they thought of any ideas for how to find the witch. Harold and Stanley sat in a corner comparing arthritis remedies. They were moving more stiffly, as I'd expected them to, after we'd come back through the portal and sat down to dinner.

When I asked Aiden about it, he explained it was a side effect of the magical realm we'd been in. "Then why do they come back? If they feel so much better there, I'd think it would be a huge relief from the aches and pains they're complaining about."

"Because they have families, Janie. They have kids and grandkids and wives and husbands and significant others and siblings. Also, they know if they moved to the magical realm permanently, after a few years they would start to go insane. Being inside for a few hours, even a few days, isn't a big deal, and the side effects of being exposed to magic do wear off eventually. Being there long term eats away at your sanity. We try not to go into the magical realm unless there's some important reason to do so, like we did today to talk freely about magic, or when we fixed your hair. It wouldn't be good to be trapped there forever. You'd never die. You'd be insane for all of eternity."

I could live without that. I was glad we'd come back.

Aiden proudly showed off his sad little office cubicle in the corner, full of geeky computer parts, electronic gizmos, and wires. To me, it looked like a disaster waiting to happen, given his inability to walk and chew gum at the same time. Despite that, the expression on his face was so enraptured I'd have thought angels had descended from heaven to grant his every wish. I had no idea what half of it was or what it could do, but his enthusiasm was so infectious I couldn't help but smile.

By the time Aiden and Doris took me home, night had descended on Dayton, and I was getting tired. "Make sure you keep your eyes peeled, Janie." Doris warned. "We don't know what might happen next."

"Thanks, Doris, for the ride," I said, as I opened the car door.

"Be careful who you let in your apartment."

I stepped out of the car.

"Be suspicious of everyone," she warned.

I shut the door behind me, and walked up to my front door. She waited until I got my door unlocked before she pulled away. I turned to wave at her as I stood in the open doorway of my apartment.

Just as Doris's Cadillac pulled out of the apartment complex driveway, I saw a car turn on its headlights in the parking lot, shining them directly into my eyes. I still couldn't help but try to make it out, even as I was illuminated by twin beams of blinding light. I was a sitting duck if something attacked, but I had an overwhelming urge to go over and see who it was. I knew it was stupid. I knew I should go inside and lock the door, especially after what I had just heard tonight, but I couldn't help it.

I just wanted to know who the driver of that car was.

As the vehicle pulled away, I saw it was a white Escalade, which was totally out of place in the rental neighborhood I lived in. I couldn't imagine which of my neighbors might drive something like that. It was more of an economy car and pickup truck kind of neighborhood. And then I saw the vanity plate.

ART LVR. It was Evangeline's Escalade.

What was my stepmother doing in my parking lot? She'd been with me when I signed the paperwork for the lease, and she'd seen the floor plans for the layout of the apartment, but my place hadn't actually been ready at the time. She'd been upset that she couldn't get to see inside before the papers were signed, but the property manager hadn't budged, citing painters that hadn't finished their work, and promising new carpet before I moved in. Even with these promises she hadn't been happy, but she'd agreed the rent was reasonable, it wasn't a bad neighborhood, and it was quiet, my biggest requirement for an apartment I'd be doing a lot of studying in. And they'd followed through on the painting and the carpet.

Honestly, I'd have been happy in a smaller, cheaper apartment, but this was the best compromise we could come to. I liked the apartment and I hadn't wanted to look much longer with school starting so soon. Evangeline hadn't come to see my apartment since I'd moved in. I wondered why.

But if she wanted to see my place, she had my cell phone number. And it was a bit late for her. Even so, if she was in the neighborhood and saw me going inside, why didn't she stick around to say hello? Then again, I hadn't seen the face of whoever was behind the wheel of my stepmother's vehicle. It might not be her.

I went inside and helped Bert out of my purse. "Who's out there flashing their brights?" he asked, rubbing one eye with his front leg, as if it hurt to look at the light.

I didn't want to tell him. "I don't know."

He gave me a dirty look, as if he knew I was lying to him. Truth was, even though I'd recognized the Escalade, I didn't know who it was. For all I knew Evangeline's ride had been stolen by the nameless maid driven to Thelma-and-Louise heights of insanity by my stepmother's overwhelming anal-retentiveness.

Stranger things have happened. How else to explain the talking frog, the hair, the musicians, the magic portals, the curse, Aiden, or the golden bird and apple I'd seen just a few days ago? And that wasn't even considering the weird happenings last night at the art institute. A stolen car was something that happened in real life, to real people. It was more believable than the things I couldn't doubt anymore.

After locking the door and settling Bert on the couch, I picked up the phone and called Evangeline's house. The maid answered; I recognized her voice from the morning visit I'd made with Aiden. When I asked for my stepmother, she told me that Evangeline was resting and had asked not to be disturbed.

"Please disturb her."

"I'm sorry, Miss. She gave specific instructions."

We went round and round for a few minutes before I asked Evangeline's maid if the car was in the garage. "I haven't seen her go anywhere. She went into her room, and asked not to be disturbed. As far as I know the car hasn't moved," the maid told me. "Now, if you'll excuse me, I have to go scrub the fireplace."

Yikes. Evangeline had gotten even more obsessive-compulsive. Cleaning the fireplace? Wasn't it supposed to be dirty? And since when did she ever actually light a fire? I seemed to remember her saying she didn't like fires in the fireplace because it made the place smell like smoke.

I said my goodbyes and mentioned I'd talk to my stepmother in the morning at the weekly Sunday brunch meeting. I hung up the phone.

It didn't make sense.

Even though she didn't live far away, there was no way the driver could have gotten back to the house in time to pick up the phone. The only people with access to the Escalade were my stepmother and the maid, who would absolutely be fired if Evangeline found out she was driving around in the car without permission. I dialed my stepmother's cell phone, and, true to form, I got the predictable response; it went straight to voice mail. She always turned the phone off when she was "resting." Did she have a second maid I hadn't met? She never had before, but I had avoided her house as much as I could since Dad's funeral.

Bert interrupted my thoughts, neatly summarizing my worries. "Janie, I'm not trying to make you paranoid, but little things could tip us off about the identity of the witch. If we catch someone following you, or not acting normally, or otherwise trying to get close when they wouldn't do so in the regular course of your life, it could be some way of figuring out where the danger's coming from, so we can protect you."

Oops. He was still talking about my paying more attention to the strange car outside. Unless he'd gained some powers of ESP, he had no idea what I was thinking about, or who I was suspecting of being in the car. I really didn't like my stepmother, but could she really be out to kill me? Or was I suspecting her just because of the history between us?

I remembered her dramatics at Dad's funeral. She'd wept and wailed and cried as if her life was ending. No way could it be Evangeline. I couldn't call her a witch; I was more likely to use a word that rhymed and started with a B. I couldn't blame her just because I didn't like her.

Either way, I was safe for the night. I was at my own apartment. Bert was here to watch out for me. I asked him to stand lookout for a while so I could make a few phone calls.

I called Mia to check on her. I didn't feel comfortable leaving to go over to her place and see if she was okay. "Hey, Mia, how are you?" I asked when she answered the phone.

"I'm fine, just tired still. I talked to the guys in the study group, and they'd still like to meet tomorrow. Is it still okay to meet at your house?"

"Sure."

"Is three o'clock still okay?"

It was late enough that I'd make my brunch meeting with my stepmother with plenty of time to spare before they all showed up at my house. I didn't even have a good excuse for leaving early or cancelling. Rats.

Once I hung up with her, I tried Evangeline's cell phone again, and got no answer. It was time to buckle down and try to get some reading under my belt, especially in Contracts. I didn't understand the readings in that class, and the weekend was getting away from me. I had to take advantage of all the time not being taken up by my stepmother or my new magical friends, or I'd be so behind I'd never keep up.

CHAPTER THIRTY-ONE

I spent most of the evening feeling like a dunce, trying to figure out offer and acceptance; terms I would have thought were self-explanatory in English. I was rapidly learning that English and Legalese were two completely different languages.

Even Bert was getting impatient with me, and the fact it just wasn't sinking in.

"I just don't understand it!" I yelled, tossing a highlighter in his general direction when he acted disgusted with me one more time.

"Janie, it's not that hard once you wrap your head around it."

Was it homicide if the victim was a frog? Did it matter if he'd once been a human? Not a question I could answer–Criminal Law wasn't on the schedule until next semester. "Okay, I get that someone who says they'll pay twenty bucks for someone else to do the hokey pokey is an offer. But is it an acceptance when they say okay, or when they get up and start putting their right foot in?"

Bert considered for a minute. "Well, that depends on whether you're talking about a unilateral or bilateral contract."

I covered my face in my hands. Why couldn't there be a single right answer to a question? I could learn facts without a problem, but it seemed like there were no facts to learn here, just legal principles that never applied the same way to different questions. How was I ever going to learn all the exceptions and twists and rules? "What do you mean?" I asked.

"Well," Bert said, "if you assume the person making the offer intends to enter into a contract and makes the offer contingent on performance, then they accept by doing the dance, and the contract is formed when they dance. The dancing is the performance on the contract. One side is promising to pay. It's a unilateral contract; the dancer isn't entitled to anything until they perform on the contract, and the offer isn't good until they do it."

"Okay, I got that. I think," I said, staring at my textbook again.

"But if both parties make promises then it's a bilateral contract. For example, let's say the person offering money pays part of it up front and promises to pay the rest at a specific time when the dancer promises to do the dance, then both of them are making promises and the contract is formed at the time of the promises. They are each relying on each other's promises, even before anyone performs on the contract."

I could hear the words coming out of his mouth. I knew he was talking in English, but the words made no sense. "But I still don't understand. Is there even a right answer to this?"

"Yes, there is. You just don't have all of the information to give a specific answer to the question. You can't assume an answer in Contracts, just like you can't assume an answer in life until you have all the facts. You have to thoroughly understand how it could be either answer, or neither of them, so that you know what questions to ask to figure it out for yourself."

"Bert, I can't ask a question of a test booklet. How am I supposed to answer these things on the test? Despite your experience as a royal advisor, I'm sure you never had to take a law school test."

He sighed. "You're right. I never took a law school test. But that doesn't mean I'm wrong. Is the test going to be multiple-choice or essay or fill-in-the-blank or what?"

"The professor said essay."

"Then you'll probably have to write an essay explaining what questions you would ask and why they would be important. They likely won't give you a question that has an easy answer. They're going to want to see your analysis more than they'll want to know a specific answer, although they'll want to see that, too. They want to know how you got there, and that you'll know the right questions to ask a client when you practice law."

"But how can I ask the right questions if I don't know the answer?" I wailed.

We went round and round for two hours before I finally called it a night and headed for bed. The last two days had worn me out, and I wondered how much of my inability to understand, despite Bert's tutelage, was because of all the stress I'd been under, all the crazy events of the past week, and sheer exhaustion. It wasn't like I'd been sleeping well, with the hair growth and the humiliation and the musicians and everything else.

Two hours later, I sat upright in bed wide awake with an idea so scary, so upsetting, I wasn't sure it could be real. I stumbled into the bathroom and splashed some cold water on my face. When I looked in the mirror at my red, tired eyes, I realized I was still wearing Aiden's necklace. I must have forgotten to take it off before I went to bed.

I slapped around for the lights to the living room as I staggered out of the bathroom. "What the hell?" Bert mumbled. "I thought you were done studying for the night."

"Bert, is it possible for someone to be suffering from some kind of comprehension or memory blocker and not know it?"

He yawned, burrowing under the afghan he'd been using for the past few nights. "Just 'cause you don't understand Contracts doesn't mean you're under a spell. Lots of people don't understand at first, and some people never understand it. That doesn't mean they're all under a spell. You'll get it eventually. Now, can I go back to sleep?"

"That's not what I meant, Bert." I pulled back the afghan, making him wake up and answer me. "I mean, what if the answer to what's going on has been staring me in the face and I didn't recognize it because of some magical block on my memory? Is that possible? Is that why my memories of my childhood are so fuzzy? Why am I having trouble understanding things at school? Am I that obtuse, or has someone or something been messing with my brain?"

Bert's eyes became more alert as I ranted. Finally, he interrupted my diatribe. "Janie, I'm missing something here. What do you think is going on? Why do you think someone's been messing with you? Nothing has come in this apartment. I've been right here. You've got a decent threshold. Nothing happened here, tonight. You went to bed. I watched for a while before I went to sleep. Everything's fine."

I sat down on the side of the couch he wasn't lying down on. "Mia keeps telling me how I never talk about my childhood. My mother left me when I was eight years old, and I could never remember much about her. Suddenly, I remember that she loved pancakes, and my dad used to wake us up on Sunday mornings and make pancakes with faces on them. He used chocolate chips and whipped cream and M&Ms and syrup to make them smile for us. Why didn't I remember that until just now?"

He didn't have an answer for me.

"I've never really had many memories of life B.E."

"B.E.?" he asked.

"Before Evangeline. I always had trouble remembering small details, but now I remember she and Dad didn't date very long, or if they did, they kept it from me. I remember her giving me a really big lollipop the day I met her, and thinking she believed me to be a lot younger kid than I really was."

"How old were you?"

"I was ten. I remember taking the lollipop, but I gave it to the neighbor's three year old the next day. I'd have been happier with a book. I remember asking Dad what he thought was good about her because I didn't like her. Why didn't I remember any of this until now?"

Bert just stared at me, wide eyed.

I got up and started pacing as I talked. "She never had a single kind word for me. She's treated me badly all my life. She never even tried to care. In fact, I only ever saw her be nice to Dad when she wanted something, or if we were out in public. It has to be her. Dad didn't start getting sick until after he got re-married."

"What are you talking about?"

"It's Evangeline. She's the witch."

Bert didn't buy it. "Janie, I know you don't like your stepmother, but that doesn't mean she's the witch, and it doesn't mean you're under a spell. It could be nothing more than coincidences. And not understanding your schoolwork doesn't mean she's trying to kill you."

"She's weird. She's got this strange lotion thing where she's got to really cover up her hands with moisturizer before she touches hardly anything. You think that's to protect her hands from metal?"

"Hello, Earth-to-Janie? You're sitting in your apartment talking to a frog. How normal is that?"

He had a point. But I had one of my own. "Aiden smelled magic at her house today. Why would he smell magic there?"

"Janie, did your dad die in the hospital, or did he die at home? And was he in the hospital the whole time he was sick, or was he home?" Bert asked.

I swallowed hard, and leaned up against the wall next to the front door, sliding down to sit on the floor. "We wanted him home. We had Hospice care coming to the house to take care of him."

"If he'd been cursed repeatedly, over a number of years, the scent of magic would probably linger in the place where he died. That doesn't mean she did it. She might be evil in a real-life sense, but that doesn't mean she's out to get you in the way you're thinking."

Okay, so maybe I wasn't making a lot of sense. "Let's look at this logically, Bert. First of all, she's never been inside my apartment and I've never invited her here, but she was in the parking lot tonight, as if she was watching my apartment. There aren't any missed calls on my cell phone. Why would she have been sitting there without calling or without saying something to me? She had to see me at the door; her headlights just about blinded me."

"Did you actually see her behind the wheel?" he asked. "If you did, you need to call Aiden, and you need to stay home from that brunch tomorrow."

I had to admit I didn't see her behind the wheel. "But it was her car. No one else drives it that I know of, except the maid on an emergency errand. I called the house, and the maid was there. There's no way she could have gotten home fast enough to pick up the phone. It had to be Evangeline."

He didn't buy it.

"Second of all, Evangeline was in charge of the fundraiser where someone was trying to steal artifacts from the museum. What better way to coordinate an art heist than to be in charge of the event itself?"

"Or that's just a coincidence," Bert shot back.

"Third, she disappeared when I went looking for her in the museum before my charm necklace gave out. Why wouldn't I have found her among the bodies?"

He shrugged.

"And remember, most of the time, the bad guy in the Grimm

Brothers' tales was the evil stepmother. It almost seems like a clue from my ancestors."

"Pretty thin, Janie. I'm not sure you're right. I'm not saying you're wrong, but you need to talk to Aiden in the morning before you go to your brunch. Maybe you shouldn't go."

I stopped talking, and Bert stopped arguing. There wasn't a smoking gun, er, wand, painting my stepmother as the bad guy, but I knew it like I knew my eyes were blue, grass was green, and Bert liked beer. I just had to come up with a way to prove it.

My evil stepmother had killed my father. I tried to think this through, but ended up staring blankly at nothing in front of me.

Was there a support group for stepdaughters of the magically evil? If so, maybe I needed a lifetime membership.

CHAPTER THIRTY-TWO

I didn't sleep at all that night. Bert nodded off, but he still wasn't convinced Evangeline was evil. My sitting against the wall, staring at the baseboards, wasn't stimulating enough to keep him awake. Of course, Bert hadn't ruled out my stepmother being a witch, but I had no way of proving it, and he didn't seem eager to accuse someone without proof.

An hour or so later, I'd hauled myself up off the floor and went back to bed. It didn't work; I'd spent the night staring at the imperfections in my ceiling and wondering how I'd missed the truth staring me right in the face, rather than getting a good night's sleep.

How would I face my stepmother at brunch? I had to meet her by noon and would have to keep my suspicions to myself throughout the entire meal. What if I was wrong? Would I be in danger if I went? Or would the fact it was a public place induce my profile-conscious stepmother to curb her magically inclined homicidal impulses?

I did drift back off to sleep, but I didn't stay that way long. I tossed and turned for an hour trying to fall back asleep before I gave up. I still had to wait until a decent time to call Aiden and share my suspicions. I stayed in the bedroom so Bert could get a little more sleep.

"'Lo," he answered when I finally got him to pick up the phone.

I looked at the alarm clock. It was barely six-thirty in the morning, on a Sunday. Yikes. I must not have waited long enough for him to be awake and coherent.

"Aiden, it's Janie. I think I've figured out who the witch is. And I need your advice."

"Wha'?" Yup, still not awake.

"Aiden, I need you to wake up. It's Janie, and I know who killed my father."

I heard a loud thud. "Ow! Crap, that hurt. I'm awake. What did you say again?"

"Aiden, my stepmother is the fairy witch trying to kill me. It just makes sense."

He was quiet on the other end of the phone for a few minutes. I had to ask if he'd heard me again before he responded. For a moment, I'd wondered if he'd knocked himself out, but he asked me if I was sure, in a small, quiet voice.

"Well, it's not like I can prove it beyond a reasonable doubt if she was on trial for murder, but I'm convinced." I ran through my arguments, the same way I'd presented them to Bert the night before. In fact, speaking of my amphibian roommate, he was beginning to wake up and listen to the conversation. He didn't interrupt my recitation to Aiden, but he was definitely paying attention.

Aiden was quiet on the other end of the phone. "I agree that you might have a point, Janie. You make a good argument, but we can't assume anything at this point. I think we have to be careful from here on. You have to stay away from your stepmother, no questions asked, until we figure out what to do with this information."

"I can't." What if I was wrong? Would she stop paying my rent? Could I really cut her out of my life completely if she was innocent? Dad had asked me to check on her and take care of her. If I was wrong, was I betraying him?

"What do you mean?"

"I'm supposed to meet her for brunch today. Her condition for helping me with the rent was that I meet her weekly for brunch and keep her apprised of my progress. I promised I'd do it. I can't go back on that."

"Can't you make an excuse?" he asked.

"Not one she'll believe. I can't imagine her letting me out of it, especially since she stayed home yesterday, to rest up for it after Friday night."

There was a long, awkward silence on the other end of the phone. "Janie, you know you shouldn't meet your stepmother today. Please don't go. I'm not sure how to protect you if you're right. I don't want anything to happen to you."

That was sweet, but I needed to know for sure if Evangeline was the one who killed my father. "I can't live my life hiding from shadows.

I need to see if I can confirm what I'm thinking or not. I'll never figure it out if I don't take a risk. And if I'm wrong, Evangeline's the only family I have left. She might not be nice, but I can't ignore that."

"You know this is crazy, don't you?" he asked.

"Is it crazier than your friends looking for a Holder without knowing what it is?"

"Don't talk about that on the phone. In fact, don't talk about it except in the clearing. You just don't know who might be listening in. There's too much at stake."

I leaned back against the pillows on my bed as I talked with him. "I wasn't going to say anything else, but my point is still valid. If they can take a risk that big, why shouldn't I? Don't I have more at stake than anyone else? I'll wear the necklace." Never mind that I was still wearing it, and that I'd been wearing it all night. Worried I'd been wearing it too long, I took it off and set it on the bedside table. "We're meeting in a public place. It's the same restaurant we met at last week. Heck, you work there. Are you working today?"

"Yes. I need to leave in about an hour to be on time. Are you sure this is a good idea?"

I wasn't sure about good, but at least it was an idea. "You'll be there to help. Do you think Doris or some of the others would like to be there to help watch out for me? I know I'd feel better if they had my back."

"I'm sure someone can be there. What time are you supposed to meet Evangeline?"

I told him all the details and he promised to make sure we had a table in the center of the restaurant where it would be easy to keep an eye on me. We talked for a while about the meeting and he kept talking about things I could do to stay safe. He kept trying to talk me out of going, but I'd made up my mind. "Promise me you'll be careful. And that you'll wear your necklace. And take something with a high iron content you could use as a weapon, just in case."

I promised him I'd do all of the above. When I got off the phone, I looked at the doorway. Bert had hopped over and had listened to at least part of the conversation. "Is there any way I can talk you out of this meeting?"

"Not a chance. You coming with me?"

"I wouldn't miss it for the world."

There was still plenty of time before I had to show up; I had five hours to kill before I was to meet my stepmother at noon. I searched for another Evangeline-approved outfit, unlike the ratty sweatshirts and worn-in jeans I preferred to wear to class. I had to dig through my dresser and closet, discarding multiple outfits on the bed as I searched. I finally came up with a blouse, camisole, and slacks that didn't need excessive ironing that were appropriate for a meeting with my stepmother.

Aiden hadn't had to remind me to wear the necklace; I was convinced I wouldn't leave the apartment again without it. I ransacked my apartment looking for things I could use as a weapon as he had suggested.

I poured some salt into a sandwich baggie to put in my pocket. I found some cheap nails left over from hanging the few pieces of wall decoration I owned. I added those to the sandwich baggie of salt. What else should I take?

Bert wasn't much help; he kept asking if I was taking any crosses. "I'm not fighting vampires. I'm having brunch with my stepmother."

"How do you know she's not a vampire?"

"Well, let's start with the idea that I'm meeting her in broad daylight and she likes Italian food. If she was a vampire, sunshine and garlic would be out, wouldn't it?"

"You don't know what she is, do you? What if she's not the witch trying to kill you, but turns out to be another supernatural something-or-other?"

That was a terrifying thought. I didn't want to have to deal with more than one type of magical badness. To be safe, I got a rubber band and put a couple of toothpicks together in the form of a cross that wouldn't take up too much room in a pocket or purse. Better safe than sorry until I could prove different, right?

Aiden had told me to take something that could be used as a weapon. I agreed, but it wasn't like I was the next coming of Buffy the Vampire Slayer. I didn't have any training in how to use a weapon, or fighting techniques, or martial arts. It would have to be something simple. Even if I could figure something out, could I really use a weapon on my stepmother?

I laid out the possibilities on the scratched kitchen table. I found a pair of sharp metal scissors in my desk drawer and a long flathead screwdriver I'd bought when I moved in. Did I dare to take a large kitchen knife with me, or would I risk being stopped for carrying a concealed weapon?

Was this all I could come up with to fight the forces of darkness? I didn't feel like it was enough, but it was all I could come up with in my drab student apartment.

Wait a minute. Dad used to hunt. Aiden and his friends had helped me to move Dad's old trunks to my apartment. I wondered what he might have stashed away that could be of use without getting me arrested on the way to brunch. It was time to look inside and see what he'd saved for me.

CHAPTER THIRTY-THREE

B ert agreed that opening the trunks while I waited to meet my stepmother was a good idea. I'd stashed one in the living room and two in the bedroom. While my apartment wasn't exactly cram-packed with a lot of furniture, adding three iron trunks did make space feel tight. I wasn't sure what I'd do with them down the road, but they were Dad's. I would keep them, even if I had to stack them up in a corner.

All three were made of iron, and incredibly heavy. Although we'd tried to brush off the worst of it before bringing them into my apartment, there were some serious cobwebs on them. It looked like Evangeline hadn't touched them since my father had them moved into the attic.

Looking back, I realized she'd been insistent I come get them as soon as I was established on my own. I wondered if it was because they were made of iron. If she was a faerie witch, that would make a lot of sense. Of course, it wasn't proof either; there could be an innocent explanation. What if she'd wanted to get rid of her late husband's things so that she wasn't reminded of him?

But wouldn't she have wanted to hang onto the trunks as mementos, even if she didn't open them, if they'd belonged to the man she loved? Did she even love him? I didn't want to think about it. I mean, she wasn't the most expressive person in the world, so I had no idea what her feelings for Dad had been. I hated the idea he might not have been loved back in those last miserable years of his life, and I didn't want to think he'd spent his last days with a psycho magic killer-type.

I shoved that pain as deep as I could. It didn't matter; it still hurt, and it was hard not to think that I should have done something more to save him. I tried to divert myself by turning to the trunks. Maybe the contents would distract me from the twisting cramp in my stomach.

I opened one of the trunks in the bedroom first. Inside were more photo albums, with pictures of my mom and dad. Their wedding album was there, more of Dad's journals, my baby book, scrapbooks and boxes of photos all carefully packed and stacked inside. I skipped them for now; I was afraid if I spent too much time on memory lane, I wouldn't have my head on straight for meeting my stepmother. I could go through them later and try to remember details that weren't coming to mind after I'd figured this whole thing out. When I moved things around, I found there was also a heavy iron box at the bottom. I lifted it out, and opened it.

Inside the box was a small golden key, with a filigreed gold "G" on the handle. I picked it up out of the velvet cushioning it rested in, and held it in my hand. "I wonder what this fits," I asked Bert, who'd come into the room to watch me unpack the trunk. I was surprised how solid it felt in my hand, without being heavy in weight. It fit my hand, as if I'd held it before, but I didn't recognize it.

He didn't say anything at first, but looked closer. "I think it's really old, Janie, but I don't know what it's for. It must open something, but I don't see anything in this trunk it would fit. I'd hang onto it, if I were you. You never know when you might need it."

I tried asking him a few times if he knew anything about it, but he denied it every time. I couldn't come up with anything else but to do as he told me.

It was Dad's and he must have treasured it to have packed it away so carefully. I decided to put it in my front jeans pocket, where I'd feel it against my hip as I moved around today. Even if it was just a cool old key, it would be nice to have something of Dad's with me when I confronted Evangeline, a token of good luck while I tried to figure out what I was doing.

On another note, it didn't take long for me to decide the apple and feather I'd gotten from the bird in Carillon Park should be secured inside a trunk just in case someone magical searched my apartment. I put the feather and apple in the box that had held Dad's key, and wrapped it up for safekeeping, buried at the bottom of the trunk. No one would find it there; it would be safe until I could figure out what the apple was for. I wondered if it was the Holder. It could be, and, if so, I needed to keep it safe.

I packed up the photo albums and other memorabilia again, and secured the trunk before I tried the next one. I didn't want to make a mess with piles of stuff lying all over the place, especially since I had people coming over for study group later in the afternoon.

Oh, God. I should really cancel brunch with Evangeline.

I said as much to Bert, and he agreed, almost too quickly.

But what if I was wrong? What if I cancelled and it turned out my stepmother was just a mean lady who had never loved my father? Would she stop paying my rent? Could I really afford that? What should I do?

I shoved the questions aside for the moment, opening the second trunk. Inside, I found an old shotgun. I didn't know if it still worked, but even to my inexpert eyes, it needed cleaning. I wouldn't know the first thing about doing that, so I laid it off to one side. I'd have to see if I could find someone who knew how to do that later. There was also a bullet mold, crossbow and bolts, a long sword, a dagger with a large green jewel in the handle protected in a leather sheath, and several other sharp and pointy metal weapons I couldn't begin to name.

"What's that?" I asked Bert, pointing to a club with several pointy things sticking out of the business end of it.

"It looks like a morningstar," he responded, a look of disbelief on his face. "I haven't seen one of those in years."

I tried to pick it up without grabbing hold of the spikes, and couldn't lift it. It was too heavy to get a grip on it one handed. Instead, I reached for the narrower end and used two hands to pull it out of the trunk, the spiky end weighing it down as I lifted it. I almost dropped it, even though I thought I had a good grip on it. "Could this be any harder to pick up? How could someone use this as a weapon if it's this heavy?"

Bert laughed. "It's not that hard. You just swing the spiky end at the other guy, and it pretty much does what it's supposed to; leave holes and bruises on people."

Yikes. I wasn't quite sure I'd be able to handle that one. It was unevenly weighted, and awkward to handle. I put it down carefully, making sure not to damage the floor or the carpet. I did want to get my security deposit back eventually.

Okay, I could buy that Dad had a gun, and even the crossbow, since he did hunt at one time, but the other weapons just didn't make sense. Dad hunted deer and turkey, and even that was rare. He was the guy who wore tweed to work and talked about books no longer in print. He was more of a librarian than a master of combat. The idea he had any kind of martial training with esoteric weapons like these was just hard to swallow. He just wasn't the James Bond/Matrix kind of guy that would have his own armory of rare old weapons in the attic.

I took the dagger, and laid it on the table with other items I'd designated for potential self-defense. I was going to have to get my biggest purse to take enough weapons to feel comfortable. It didn't really match what I was wearing, but I was willing to withstand some fashion criticism from Evangeline in order to feel safer. I put the rest of the larger weapons back into the trunk and secured it.

Even with the purse change, I didn't like how slow I would be in getting to a weapon. I hid the dagger, in its sheath, in the back waistband of my slacks, and fastened a belt around my waist to hold it in place. I pulled my oversized blouse out over the dagger it to cover my butt and the handle sticking up. Was I being paranoid, or was I just being cautious?

A vicious cycle of bad thoughts ran like a hamster wheel in the back of my head, chanting, *she killed him, she killed him, she killed him, she killed him*. I kept trying to clear my head. I knew I couldn't have a normal conversation at the restaurant if that was the extent of my thoughts during brunch.

That was bad, but not as bad as the occasional interjection, *it's all my fault.*

Better to concentrate on what was in front of me instead.

Neither one of the trunks in the bedroom had a lock, but they did have a sliding bolt mechanism that held them closed. I was surprised at how simple it was, but now that I knew a bit more about magic and faeries, it made sense. It was a lock mechanism that had to be opened with one's hand and fingers; the knob was just too small to grasp in any other way, and it took enough finesse and force that using a tool just didn't seem possible. Someone with a sensitivity to iron wouldn't be able to do it.

I headed back out into the living room, looking for the third trunk. *She killed him.* I swallowed hard. When I opened the trunk, much like the other two, it was an easy lock to open, but completely made of iron.

Inside were several items, all securely packed. I had no idea what most of them were. It looked like there were old feather quills inside, dry and brittle with age, and stray sheets of parchment paper. Most of the trunk's storage space was taken up with clear vials of liquid. They reminded me of test tubes as I pulled them out of their packing, but I kept thinking that the test tubes I used in my high school chemistry class were longer and heavier; these seemed more likely to have been made from plastic instead of glass. They were capped by cork stoppers, and contained a light colored, somewhat viscous liquid. "Oh, my," Bert exclaimed. "That looks like iron gall ink. What a great idea."

"What's that?" I asked.

"Ink used to be made from a combination of iron sulfate and a few other compounds. If this is what I think it is, it could be used almost like acid if you threw it on a faerie being. It might not kill them, but it would be a nice distraction if you needed to get away."

"And what would happen if they got splashed with just a drop or two?" I had an idea.

"It would probably leave a mark, even up to a second degree burn, depending on the level of iron in the ink. It wouldn't hurt someone completely human, except maybe to stain a little bit, but with a faerie, it would itch and burn. And the color gets darker, almost a deep purplish-black as it's exposed to oxygen, so it would be a complete pain to have to wash off. I'd also prefer if you didn't splash me with that stuff."

Huh? "Why?" Was Bert actually working for the bad guy? Had he been feeding information about everyone to the witch, or was he what he had appeared to be? How did he know all of this?

"Relax. I'm human, or I was. Even so, it was faerie magic that cursed me and faerie magic that made me immortal. I'm just not sure what residual effect it would have, or what magic is still working on me. It's hard enough keeping amphibian skin moist; I'd rather not have a burn to deal with as well." He shrugged.

I felt silly for suspecting him. He'd been nothing but supportive and helpful, even if he had made me believe I'd lost my mind on several different occasions. "Sorry."

"Well, it's not like it's hard to figure out what you're thinking. I've been living here with you. It has been a long week."

Amen to that. I picked up some of the vials of liquid and stashed them in my pants pockets and purse. "It pays to be prepared," I said, as I looked at the clock and realized that I didn't have a whole lot more time to get to the restaurant. Bert had to be convinced to get into my purse with all the metal and ink tubes I'd put inside. I had to agree to put a hand towel over the weapons in the bottom of my purse so he wouldn't be standing on iron himself. I had to admit he was likely right; better safe than sorry if faerie magic had made him what he was.

It was time to go see if my stepmother was an evil witch. In the magical sense.

CHAPTER THIRTY-FOUR

I was right on time. In fact, I'd beaten Evangeline to the restaurant. Something was definitely odd. I got a table and waited for her, taking the opportunity to take out a tube of ink and dip the slightest corner of my napkin into the liquid. Aiden, who was working as usual, got me a glass of water, and promised to call me after I left to make sure I got home okay. I didn't get a chance to respond to him when another table called him away for drink refills.

When I realized I still had a moment or two, I did the same to my stepmother's napkin. I almost dropped the vial in my hurry to get the napkin touched to the ink, folded correctly, and get my rear end back in my seat before anyone noticed what I was doing.

I could feel the dagger in my waistband as I hurried to sit down before Evangeline got there. It was a nice reminder that I wasn't helpless. My hands were shaking, and butterflies were doing the Macarena in my belly.

I saw Aiden out of the corner of my eye, talking with another waiter. Harold sat two tables over from me, sipping a single cup of coffee and looking like a normal customer. Stanley, on the other hand, was dressed all in black, wearing black aviator sunglasses and a black Fedora hat. He was sitting at a booth with a direct line of vision to me, scribbling something in a notebook and darting suspicious glares over the top of a menu propped to stand upright on the table in front of him, shielding his notes from view. I had no idea what they were planning to do to help me, but I felt better just knowing they were there for me. I didn't wave to them, but I knew they understood why I was ignoring them.

In fact, Stanley was probably having the time of his life, rooting out evil government minions and conspiracies. I, however, felt like I was going to vomit from nerves.

Evangeline showed up, finally. She looked confused when she walked up to the table. "Did you really beat me here? What happened? Are you okay?"

I smiled at her. "I did. I just realized you were right, and I needed to watch the time a bit better." I didn't roll my eyes, I didn't snap at her, and I didn't get all defensive. Maybe it was a side effect of my shaky hands.

She sat down, not saying anything to me while she rearranged herself and called for a waiter, snapping her fingers. "This glass has spots, this plate is dirty, and there's some kind of stain on this napkin. Please get me a fresh one." She took out her ever-present hand cream and began to rub some of it into the back of her left hand.

My heart sank as Aiden arrived to take the items away. She ordered a cup of hot water with lemon, while I asked for some orange juice and coffee as her place setting was removed. I noticed she was wearing linen pants and a silk shirt; items that were dry clean only and probably cost her more than most of my closet put together. New clothes weren't exactly in my budget, but Kmart prices were a whole lot easier to squeeze in than the cost of replacing her clothing in case of an accidental stain. And I could actually wash mine at the Laundromat.

"My dear, I'm thinking law school is starting to have a very positive effect on you. I definitely approve. How are you doing for money?"

Right away, I had a bad feeling about taking any more money from her, despite the fact I felt broke, as usual. This student budget thing was just not fun, especially with the extra grocery runs this past week. Even so, I just couldn't shake the idea taking more money was a Bad Thing. "I'm fine right now, Evangeline, but thank you for asking. How are you doing after this weekend?"

She gave me a weak smile and said she was okay, meticulously rubbing more and more lotion into the back of her hand. It could take her forever to get both hands done, but it was something she did all the time.

"Are you guys going to reschedule the fundraiser? I was looking forward to the presentation." At least I had some topic of conversation to refer to.

Aiden came back with our drinks and fresh tableware for her. I ordered a Tuscan omelet with red potatoes and she ordered a small quiche. I had to stop myself from flinching at the prices, but our brunch meetings were on her. I caught Aiden's eye as he took our order, and I couldn't help myself wanting to walk away from the table with him. I tried not to look too long; I was afraid Evangeline would think something was up, but it made me feel better to know he was nearby.

"We won't reschedule the fundraiser, but the exhibits will go forward. Most of the guests have not asked for us to refund their money, so we still have enough to put on the exhibits we were using the event to fund. They won't be as big, but we'll still have them. And we'll have more security at our next event." She finally capped her hand cream and put it carefully back into her purse.

That opened a door for me to bring up some questions for her and see how she reacted. "You had museum security at the Art Institute Friday night. There were tons of people around. What more could you have done, even if you had more security there?"

She gave me an exasperated look. "Well, I could have asked the city to provide a police presence. The police chief said he would do it the next time we had a major event."

I sipped my coffee. "And how do you know police officers would have been able to keep the place safe? I mean, weren't the police officers who came after I called as knocked out as everybody else?" Except me, that is. And Aiden, right up until the end when both of us passed out like all the other guests. Of course, we didn't have enough magical immunity charms to hand around to keep everyone safe even if we could explain it to them. I hoped she didn't see the flaw in my argument.

"What are you trying to say, Janie?" She sipped her hot water and spread her napkin on her lap, rearranging things to her satisfaction, as usual, but not nearly as anal-retentive as last weekend's meeting. Aiden came by with a basket of bread.

"Even allowing for the men breaking into the museum, the fundraiser wouldn't have been ruined if people hadn't passed out. In fact, even if the police had been able to get there and investigate, they might not have interrupted anything until the end of the presentations and donations. Whatever put everyone to sleep kept the final fundraiser discussions and donations from happening. I know you get significant donations at the end, as people leave and turn in those envelopes." This wasn't the first one of Evangeline's fundraisers I'd worked at.

She set down her teacup, and gave me a hard look. I didn't normally criticize her decisions or question her, most of the time she was the one criticizing my life. "I didn't realize you were taking Museum Security 101 at that school of yours."

Aiden came back and delivered our plates. I really wanted to grab his hand and hold fast for some courage. Instead, I wiped my clammy hands on the napkin in my lap.

How could I explain it? How could I ask it? I gulped my coffee too fast and burned my tongue. "Evangeline, have you ever had something happen to you that had no reasonable explanation for why or how it happened?"

"I'm confused," she said, cutting into her quiche with her fork, taking a bite, and then setting her fork back down. Evangeline always ate like a bird, chewing every swallow with deliberate slowness. "What on earth are you talking about?"

I mentally gave Aiden tons more credit for sounding less crazy when he first told me about magic. And that was saying something, because I'd thought he was nuts. "Well, Evangeline, did you hear the EMTs talk about a gas leak?"

"Yes, I did. And that's a reasonable explanation for what happened, Janie."

Oh, dear. This wasn't going to be easy. "Well, what if someone told you that when you have a gas leak, the gas company normally gets called to check on the lines? No one from the gas company was there checking Friday night. Why is that?"

She wasn't looking me in the eye. Aiden was standing right there, pouring us more water, and he shook his head at me. In other words, I hadn't missed anything. The gas company wasn't there, but how could I prove that? I had to avoid mentioning Harold and Stanley and Doris, as well as Aiden. They were my witnesses, though they didn't really have a good reason to be there, despite the lame excuses Aiden had given the cops about looking for me. If I just came right out with my suspicions and I was wrong, would I be stuck having brunch with a very pissed off stepmother for the rest of the year? I turned my attention to my potatoes. Aiden came by and offered us another basket of bread and drink refills, which we didn't need.

I tried to give him a small smile, to reassure him. He had a worried look on his face every time I snuck a glance at him. He kept coming over to check on us until Evangeline finally snapped. "If you even hope to get a tip today, you will leave us alone to let us eat and talk. That is why people meet for meals, to enjoy each other's company. Right now I feel like I have talked to you more than my stepdaughter. Go away." There was a frosty tone in her voice, but she actually sounded angry. That wasn't going to help me get any answers.

Aiden left us alone, but I noticed he didn't go far. We ate in silence for a few minutes before I could come up with another way to attack the subject again, and this time, it was harder. "Evangeline, do you think about Dad?"

She smiled. "Of course I think about your father, Janie, I miss him. I just wish you had let me put up that cherub on his gravesite. It would have been so beautiful."

Gag me. "What if he didn't die of cancer?"

I watched for a reaction, but I didn't see one. She took another miniscule bite and put her fork back down on the table. "Of course he did. We went to all of those doctor's appointments, and his chemotherapy and radiation. You saw his hair fall out. He was so sick."

Was it the chemo and the radiation treatments that made his hair fall out or the curse that wore him down? Or had the doctors just misdiagnosed him and the treatments made it worse?

Despite the sentiment in her voice, there were no tears. If she did love him as much as she always said she did, why weren't there any tears? "Is there anything else of Dad's at the house?"

She went back to her quiche. "Well, I called Goodwill to take his clothing, and the university took the books and papers you didn't take. He didn't have much else."

He lived in that house for ten years, and didn't have anything else? Just three iron trunks, books, papers, and clothes? Heck, I owned more than that, and I'd lived in my place for just over a week. Was that it? And she'd gotten rid of everything he'd owned when he'd been gone less than six months? If she was really missing him, wouldn't she have held onto something of his?

And still, I saw no emotion on her face. For a woman who'd been married to him as long as she had been, I'd think there would have been more of a reaction to the disposal of her husband's things. It just didn't make sense with how hard she'd argued for the sentimental hearts and flowers and over-the-top gestures at Dad's funeral.

I was running out of ideas on how to find out the truth. She was just confusing me more.

Aiden came to the rescue. Or rather, his klutziness did. Despite Evangeline's outburst just a few minutes ago, he came up again with a hot water carafe and a coffee pot to refill our drinks, and spilled all over Evangeline's expensive dry-clean-only shirt. I hadn't told him about the ink. There was no way he could know about my napkin trick, but I wasn't about to let an opportunity to pass me by.

I grabbed my napkin and dabbed at her shirt and her hand, trying to wipe off the water and coffee. He apologized, bringing her more napkins and offering to pay for dry cleaning expenses. "I'm fine. Leave me alone," she said, even though I continued to try to help her. "I'm fine, Janie. Go sit down." She held her hand, as if it hurt.

I did what she asked, but I was pretty sure I'd gotten the back of her hand with the ink-stained corner of my napkin. She snapped her fingers for the manager, no doubt to get Aiden in trouble, and I saw it. Her fingers were red from the heat of the drinks that had been spilled on her, but there was a small, red, blistered burn on the back of her hand above where she'd been spilled on that hadn't been there before. It was exactly the spot I'd touched with the napkin. It had worked. Even when I'd put the ink in my pocket, a part of me hadn't believed it would work, but it had.

Oh, God. I was right. She was a faerie being. She was magical. And in all likelihood, she was the witch who had killed my father.

CHAPTER THIRTY-FIVE

She composed herself quickly, and I leaned back in my chair. My mind was racing and I couldn't come up with anything to say.

Evangeline babied her hand as we sat there, but she didn't say much about it. I tried not to look at the burn mark. It was fairly damning evidence against her, but I had to finish my meal and get home to talk to the others before I could do anything else. I just didn't know what the next step was. I needed a plan of attack. Or a plan of hiding. Or something.

She tore open a piece of bread, but I wasn't hungry any longer. I took another bite of my eggs, and I couldn't taste them.

"Why the sudden interest in your father, Janie? We haven't talked about him much since the funeral."

Much? Try not at all. "I miss him. Who can I talk to about him? Who knew him best, besides me? You were married to him. Even if we never see eye to eye about other things, we had him in common. Who else knew he carried peppermints in his pockets and kept a pipe on his desk even though he didn't smoke? Who else knew he always forgot to iron his shirt collars before he went to work?" Who killed him and played the grieving widow? Yikes. I needed to be careful of what I said.

She smiled, but it didn't reach her eyes. "I understand. I miss him, too. I just don't like talking about him, and I got rid of his things so I wasn't reminded of him."

Liar, I thought. She was making it up, and I knew it. For all of the words coming out of her mouth, her facial expression just didn't match up. How long would it take to finish this meal? Was there some excuse I could make?

There was. I hadn't cancelled my study group meeting. She'd understand having to prepare for guests. I took one last bite of my potatoes and explained.

"Of course you should go if you have guests coming, Janie. Don't forget to put out fresh towels in the bathroom, and have drinks and food for them. If you hurry, you might even have time to run by Dorothy Lane Market for some snacks. I know how much you like their Killer Brownies. That's my secret for last minute party planning; they sell trays that look like a caterer did them. Just be careful where you eat them; you wouldn't want brownie crumbs in your books."

Killer Brownies? More like killer stepmothers. Giving me hostess advice wasn't unusual for her. Letting me out of an obligation, even just a brunch that was in progress, was strange, but I took the opportunity to get out of the restaurant and run to my car. I dropped my purse on the front seat and started the car as fast as I could.

"Ouch! Janie, aren't you going to stick around and talk with Aiden and the guys? I'm sure they didn't hear much of the conversation. Are you okay?"

"He said he'd call me later," I said, as I whipped the steering wheel around and heard the tires squeal as I pulled out of the parking lot and drove toward the highway. I didn't even realize I was crying until the exit signs on the highway were blurred. Bert stuck his head up out of my purse, and kept asking if I was okay. I couldn't answer right away, but kept driving while I wiped the moisture off of my face and out of my eyes.

"Seriously, if you're not okay, you should pull off the road," he said, finally hopping out of the purse to sit on the passenger seat. "You're awfully close to that truck in front of us."

I had to hit the brakes to avoid running into the back of the truck.

I guess I wasn't okay. I drove the rest of the way home very carefully, signaling early, driving well under the speed limit, with my hands locked on the wheel so tightly at ten and two o'clock that my knuckles turned white. My heart pounded, and I tasted the sour-sick of too much adrenaline in the back of my throat.

When I got back to my apartment complex, I ran for the door, nearly forgetting Bert on the front seat as I did. "Hey, wait for me. I can't open the door," he yelled.

I doubled back after him, hurrying to get inside, and dropped him on the couch.

"Hey, easy there! I'm not the same as a Nerf ball, you know. I can get hurt."

I was rushing to get the door locks secured so nothing could follow me inside. Was it paranoid? Sure, but how else does one handle the knowledge that their stepmother was a psychotic faerie witch killer who murdered their father?

Wait a minute. I could prove she was a faerie. I couldn't prove she was the one cursing him, but it wasn't like I knew another faerie being capable of getting close enough to Dad in order to curse him to death.

She'd done it. And I'd been courteous in my father's last days, making sure to give them time on their own. I didn't like her, but my father had been so happy when they'd gotten married that I did try to be a respectful daughter and let them say their goodbyes privately. Now I wondered if there had been something she'd done during those times I'd made myself scarce, something to hurt him, or kill him faster. Had my staying away done him more harm? Was it my fault?

Bert watched me pacing back and forth in the living room, and I had to give him credit; he didn't interrupt my internal monologue until I stopped and sat down on the couch, slumping forward with my face in my hands.

"I'm sorry, Janie."

"For what?" I asked. "You didn't kill him. You've been trying to tell me what really happened. It's not your fault."

"No, but I didn't believe you last night when you suspected Evangeline. That was the first time I'd ever been around her. Faerie magic is just oozing off of her. She's probably got enough juice to wipe the entire city off the map in one go. In other words, it's not your fault, either. Don't blame yourself."

Despite the crying jag I desperately wanted to indulge in, he had my attention. "What do you mean? You can tell she's that powerful? I didn't even smell magic on her. How did you know how powerful she is?"

Bert snorted. "I'm not using my nose, silly. I told you I can't smell the way a human does anymore. Even so, I'd have to be blind not to see the amount of magic following her around like a cloud. I have never seen that much magic surrounding someone, well, ever."

"Why can't I see it?"

"It's not like you have practice doing that, now do you? I think you were probably too preoccupied today with what you planned to ask that you wouldn't have noticed anything else around you. Besides, I've had a couple hundred years to compensate for the fact I don't smell magic the way I used to. You've had a week to figure this out. Cut yourself a break."

I needed to call Aiden, but when I dialed his cell phone number there was no answer. I didn't have a number for Harold or Stanley or Doris. Bert didn't know how to reach them either.

I sat down on the couch, trying to decide what to do. I kept calling Aiden's cell phone, but his voicemail kept picking up. I decided to cancel the study group meeting, and tried to call Mia, but I didn't get an answer from her either.

I didn't have the time to be at home with my study group today. I needed to go confront my stepmother in private now that I knew the truth. I double-checked the locks on the trunks, and the vials of ink and other supplies in my pockets. The key was still there, as well, and I had the dagger in the back of my jeans. I wasn't sure what else I could hide on my body. I wasn't sure I'd survive, but I had to confront her. I had to know the truth.

"What are you doing?" Bert asked.

"I'm getting ready to go confront Evangeline at home."

"You can't do that. It's not safe."

We argued, but never came to a conclusion. The only thing that stopped us was the doorbell. It was Mia, come early to the study group meeting. She was white as a sheet, and still looked tired, but she smiled at me when she came in the door.

"Mia, I should cancel the meeting."

"It's too late; everyone's probably on their way already."

I'd just have to make some excuse. There was no way I'd be able to concentrate today enough for the meeting to be worth anything. I ran into the bathroom and splashed cold water on my face. My eyes were still puffy and red, but the cold water helped calm it down enough to look somewhat normal.

I came back out of the bathroom to try to explain it to Mia, and the doorbell rang again. It was Leann and Mike, carrying bags of chips and take out Chinese food.

"We figured that if you were still ready to host us after everything you'd been through this weekend the least we could do was provide dinner," Leann said.

Mike just grinned at me as he carried bags past me into the kitchen.

It took me a minute to realize they weren't mind-readers or psychics or magical; they'd been at the museum Friday night, and probably thought I was upset from that if they saw something wrong on my face.

"Guys, I'm not sure I can do this." I felt bad at turning them away, but how could I sit here and study if I knew that my father's killer was on the loose?

They tried to convince me we still needed to study, or at least try. I kept trying to tell them what was going on, without sounding like I'd lost my mind. The whole apartment began to smell of Kung Pao chicken and Moo Shu pork as I kept on saying I was unable to study today. Even though I was pushing them away, I couldn't believe how much better I felt with friends sitting around my living room, and Chinese food scenting the air.

We hadn't been talking long when the doorbell rang again. It was the last member of our group, David. I realized I was going to have to explain all over again about being unable to work today. I'd probably have to explain magic to pull it off, just like with Mia. I wondered what their reaction to Bert would be. I gave up, and answered the door. "Hi, David. Come on in."

As I stepped aside to let him into my living room, I smelled it. It was that scent of old books and cheap peppermints; the scent of my father.

And, as I'd come to realize, the scent of magic.

CHAPTER THIRTY-SIX

I was in trouble.

I tried to slam the door on David, before he could get all the way in the house. He grabbed the door, preventing me from closing it all the way.

"What do you think you're doing?" Mia cried out, snatching at my arm, as she tried to keep me from slamming the door on his hand. I shoved her away, but still couldn't get it shut. I heard him cry out as the door mashed his fingers, but he didn't let go.

I kept pushing, using my legs as leverage. "Someone get up here and help me."

Mike tried to grab me around the waist, pulling me away from the door. Leann tried to grab the door, calling out, "Let him in. He's here for the meeting. Why are you acting this way?"

I couldn't do it. "He's here to hurt us. Someone help me get this door shut," I called, over David wailing about his fingers on the other side of the door. I heard the thuds of his foot kicking the door, trying to get in, and his demands for me to get out of the way.

Mike continued to try to drag me from the door, and I fought with all my strength, kicking and twisting to stay where I was; blocking the door to keep David from coming into my apartment. "Mia, don't let him in!" I called, as I began to lose the fight against Mike. "Don't let Mike open the door! David's magical and he's here to hurt us!"

I didn't really have much of a chance against Mike; I remembered him telling us that he'd been a police officer before he started law school. Even with an injury that had taken him off active duty, he had training in dragging people away from things they were trying to block. I didn't.

Mia stopped grabbing at me and stood still, her mouth open as she stared at me. Despite my struggles against Mike, I saw the light dawn on her face. She tried to step in, to grab the door before David could get inside, but she wasn't quick enough. Mike had pulled me far enough away from the door for Leann to yank it open and let him in.

"What the hell do you think you're doing? You invited me. Why did you ask me here and then try to slam the door in my face? What did I ever do to you?" David asked me, his face red and pinched. He dropped his books inside, and sucked on the fingers I'd smashed with the door.

I stopped fighting with Mike, and looked at David standing in the middle of the living room. I had to ask Mike twice to let go of me before he made me promise to behave. Even then, he stood behind me. He was close enough that I knew he'd grab me again before I could do much of anything to physically stop David. I wasn't sure what else to do, but I knew I didn't have the training to be able to fight off an experienced police officer and go after a magical David at the same time. I needed a better plan.

So I knew he was magical. Did that mean he was dangerous? I didn't trust anything at the moment. I'd only stopped fighting to get Mike to let me go. I needed more information. "Why do you smell like magic?" I asked. I didn't really care most of them wouldn't know what that meant.

They didn't. Everyone but Mia began shouting, questioning my sanity, wondering what was wrong with me, or otherwise saying I'd cracked.

Over the din, David said, "I'm not sure I know what you're talking about. You've been studying too hard. Hey, I missed the conversation at the last meeting. Did you guys finish up with foreseeable damages last time? I hope not. I really need help with it."

For someone whose hand had been smashed in the door, he wasn't acting right. He should have been more upset with me, or more hurt, or at least acted like he was still injured. He should have been bitching about me trying to cause a scene, being indignant, or wanting to press charges on me for hurting him. He should have stormed off. Instead, he was asking about our study meetings as if nothing else was going on.

Mia's eyes were wide as she took it all in. The others kept asking if I was okay. I waited until they stopped talking, but I ignored their questions. "I'm not letting this go, David. You smell like magic. In fact, you reek of it. I'm sure there are people who would take offense to you being in their house for that alone."

Something was definitely off about him. I remembered thinking the same thing at our last meeting, when he'd bolted almost before we'd started. Why hadn't that thrown up any red flags? Why had I invited everyone over to my place when Doris and all the others warned me to be careful? It was stupid. And I hadn't thought about it. That wasn't like me, but if my own memory hadn't been too great over the past years, was it any wonder I hadn't connected such an obvious problem? No time to worry about it now, when I had the current problem of how to get him to leave without causing any harm.

He didn't answer me right away, and I took the opportunity to look him over carefully. His shoulder length hair was blond and one length, hanging over his ears. Magic rolled off of him in waves, like an old lady who wore too much perfume, and I couldn't tell immediately what it was that bugged me about it, but I knew that something was off. And then I saw it.

His ears were pointed.

Not enough to really notice right away. Not enough to stand out to a casual on-looker. I don't think I'd looked closely at him in the past week to notice much before, but now that I was looking, it was almost stare-you-in-the-face obvious.

"You're right, Janie."

The others stopped their fussing at his admission. Mia edged closer to me. I kept trying to push her out of the way, but she nudged me, standing to partially block me from David. I shoved her out of the way, and stepped in front of her. "Mia, I'm fine. What do you mean, David?"

"I mean that, yes, I've used magic today."

I heard Mike snorting in the background. "This is some kind of joke, right?" he asked. Leann laughed out loud.

"No joke. I was using magic earlier today. I didn't know you could smell magic. Are you telling me that you can use magic?" David asked.

I didn't want to answer him. If I said I wasn't able to use magic, did that paint a target on my head? "How did you use magic today, David?"

He glared at me. "I'm not sure that's any of your business."

"You're in my house. I have the right to know if you're a danger to me or to my guests. That makes it my business." As I spoke, I was taking a mental inventory of the items in my pockets, in my purse, and the remnants of my earlier search for weapons, still lying on the kitchen table. Could I reach something in time to protect myself? I wasn't sure.

The others didn't say much; they watched the entire exchange with open-mouthed looks of disbelief. Mia looked less shocked, but definitely scared. I didn't blame her. I was pretty terrified myself.

"If you must know, I cast a protective circle and magic resistance spell before I came here. I saw your hair on Tuesday. I know what that kind of hair growth means. You're into magic, big-time, aren't you, Janie? I had to do something to protect myself. You wouldn't begrudge me the feeling of safety, would you?"

I didn't believe him. I wasn't sure if Rapunzel Syndrome would show up in someone using magic, but Aiden and the others said it was a side effect of being cursed. They never said it could be anything else. I had no reason to think that using magic would cause hair growth.

"I'm not dangerous to you, David." *Unless you try to hurt me.* Maybe I wouldn't be all that good at fighting, but I was determined to try. "I've got things happening in my life that involve threats to hurt me. That's why I asked why you smelled like magic."

Mike and Leann were starting to yell again, asking if we were crazy. We ignored them.

"Don't we all have a right to know if coming to your house is dangerous?" David asked. "Your caution may be well placed, and it may be justified, but don't your guests have the right to know what they might be in for if they come to your house"

How did this become my fault? I crossed my arms in front of my chest.

He continued. "If you're going to invite someone in, you should have checked for magic before the invitation is extended. Otherwise, a threshold really doesn't mean much, does it?"

He was right. I should have tried to see if I smelled something first. I hadn't. "That doesn't change the fact I'm going to have to ask you to leave for my own safety and that of my guests." The others protested, but I ignored them. Honestly, couldn't they see I was trying to protect them?

He nodded at me. I thought it meant he was going to grab his things and leave. What a relief.

I was wrong.

David twisted his upper body away, as if he was about to throw me a Frisbee, but what he threw was a lot less fun. He threw a bolt of pure energy in a shockwave around himself, knocking all of us off of our feet. I flew backwards against the wall, and landed with a thud.

My back had hit the wall hard enough I knew I'd be bruised in the morning, especially where the dagger was hidden at my back. Before I could react to it, he grabbed my shirt and dragged me to my feet. Scrambling, I tried to get away, and only succeeded in grabbing my purse off the floor. It was one of those large purses with a long strap I could secure over my head and across my body, and I looped it over my head before resuming the fight. I'd packed it earlier with weapons for my protection, and I hoped I'd be able to use it now if need be.

David dragged me to the door, untangling me from the others. Mike reached up to stop him, but I heard a loud boom, knocking Mike and all the others back to the floor, unconscious, as I fought to get free. As I was yanked out my front door, my cell phone fell out of my purse and hit the floor. It began ringing. It had to be Aiden, calling to check on me as promised. I knew I couldn't reach it and had to keep fighting with teeth and fingernails and flailing limbs.

I was a twisting, squirming, uncooperative hostage all the way across the parking lot, but he never let go. No one came out of my apartment. I had to hope they would all be okay, and that they would be able wake up, answer the phone, and tell Aiden what had happened so he could come looking for me.

David had a strong grip on my upper arm as he shoved me into the trunk of his car, but he had to settle a hand on my chest, holding me down to keep me in the trunk to close the lid. The dagger in my waistband was going to leave a heck of bruise, and moving around wouldn't help, but I couldn't let him shut me inside. I kicked the lid every time he tried to slam it down.

"Rape!" I yelled. "Fire! Police! Terrorist!" Anything that could draw the attention of a person with a phone who could call the police came out of my mouth. I still didn't see anyone outside. I wondered if his spell knocking out my study group had worked on everyone in my apartment complex, because I couldn't come up with any other explanation.

I screamed even louder when I saw a syringe in his hand. I fought and kicked harder as he jabbed the needle into my thigh. I felt a sharp sting and a burning sensation in my leg. Whatever he had injected me with worked quickly; my arms and legs felt heavy and hard to move, and yelling took more energy than it should have.

It didn't take but a few seconds for my tongue to go numb, and my mouth wouldn't form words. The world went dark as the trunk lid came down.

CHAPTER THIRTY-SEVEN

I have no idea how long I was out. All I knew was that I woke up some time later in a dark room, and no clue where I was. I couldn't use my arms or my legs; something kept them from moving. I was sitting in a hard metal chair of some kind, and there was a rag in my mouth that kept me from calling out for help. The scent of magic was overpowering.

"Janie." I heard a whisper, in a voice I recognized. It was Bert. I felt better just knowing he was there, even though I didn't really know where *there* was.

"Mmphrmm," I said, really unable to say much more with the cloth in my mouth. I wanted to tell him I was okay, but I couldn't do anything but mutter.

"Janie, you have to wake up. You're in danger. I don't know what they're going to do to you. Can you get free? I can't see you."

I tried to get my arm loose, but it wouldn't move no matter how much I pulled. What was holding me in the chair? My head hurt. What had David injected me with? Were the others okay? Was it Aiden who had called my cell phone, and would he figure out where I was?

The thought of Aiden and the others had me scared. I wanted them to try and save me, but what, or who, was holding me? If it was something magical and dangerous, were they up to the task? All I knew was I needed to do whatever I could to get out of there.

I was able to spit out the cloth in my mouth after several minutes of working my jaw and moving my tongue and wiggling my chin. "Bert, is that you?" Yeah, I had recognized his voice, but I had to be sure.

"Yeah, it's me. Are you okay?"

"I think so. Where are we?"

"I didn't see what building we're in, if that's what you're asking, but I keep hearing voices upstairs, and people moving around. I don't recognize where we are."

"What happened?"

I heard a soft chuckle, and the faint sound he made when he hopped up onto a bare surface, his small feet landing with a soft clap. "When your friends showed up, I ducked back into your purse. I figured none of them would get into your purse, so that would be the safest place to hide. Why'd you grab it, anyway?"

"I knew I had weapons in there."

"Well, you probably don't have many left. I ducked out of the bag the minute they carried you in, and someone went through it." He hopped down from wherever he was, and eventually, I felt something bump against my leg. "Sorry. I think I found you."

"Guess that means you can't see any better than I can?" He agreed.

I began to realize I wasn't held down by magic; I could move my hands and twitch my arms, pulling against whatever held me to the chair. It even gave a little, though not enough to do much about being tied up. It had to be some kind of rope. That was a good thing. "Bert, there was a dagger in my pants. Do you think you can get it and help me saw through these ropes?" I hoped it was still there, but I couldn't feel it. I could only feel the beginning of a bruise where it had been, but I hoped that was leftover from whatever they'd doped me up with.

"Nope. They found it when they brought you in here. And even if they hadn't, I'm not sure I could use it. I have trouble lifting the television remote, remember?"

That was true. "Is there anything left?"

"I think there's still a screwdriver in here."

"Can you slip it in my back pocket?" I asked him. At least I'd have a weapon on me.

"I can try." He bumbled around a bit, and a few minutes passed before I felt him hop up in my lap. I slid forward in my seat to let him reach around to access my back pocket.

He was right; he wasn't very strong at all. It took several tries for him to actually get the thing lodged deep enough in my pocket to be sure it wouldn't slide out. By the time he was done, he was out of breath.

"Are you okay?" I asked.

Bert was huffing and puffing. "I'll be fine. I feel better now that you have a weapon."

"Did you touch the metal?"

"No. I was careful only to touch the plastic handle. I'm fine." He hopped off my lap, and disappeared somewhere into the dark. I hoped he was all right.

Having anything I could use as a weapon did make me feel better, but did I really expect to fight my way free with a screwdriver? That was laughable. What did I have? Nothing that could get me free of these ropes, just a screwdriver and a couple of vials of ink still in the front pockets of my jeans, along with a golden key I didn't know what to do with.

I felt like a failure. I'd failed my father. I'd let Aiden and the F.A.B.L.E.S. guys down. I couldn't even save myself. I felt the tears start, and I couldn't hold them back this time.

It wasn't pretty. I cried until I felt my nose run, and still couldn't stop. Bert kept trying to calm me down, but it didn't work. Everything I'd been bottling up for the past week came crashing out in a wave of despair and anguish I hadn't let myself feel since before Dad died.

I'd cried over Dad before, but I'd never really let myself cry it all out. It was as if the crying fits I'd had before had been just enough to keep the pot from boiling over. This time, I couldn't stop.

I stopped hearing Bert, and could only hear the roar of my inner demons unleashing hell in my brain. I never noticed when Bert stopped talking. Even the light coming on and the phone ringing didn't catch my attention right away.

When it did, I finally realized I could see where I was. And I recognized it.

There were state-of-the-art laundry machines just a couple of yards from where I sat, and an ironing board and iron stored neatly on a rack right beside them. There were random boxes stacked up in one corner, along with some plastic tubs labeled *Christmas Decorations*, *Wrapping Paper*, and *Craft Supplies*. In my own handwriting.

I was in the basement of Evangeline's house.

And off to my left, underneath the steps, I could see a faint, swirling, purple area, the beginnings of a portal to the magical realm.

Evangeline's voice floated down the stairs. "I just have to deal with some items in the basement, and then we'll be able to make plans for the next fundraiser. I'll have to see what caterers are available before we can schedule anything, but I'll get back to you as soon as I hear. Yes, I had brunch with my stepdaughter today. I know she blames herself for the problems with the fundraiser. She probably saved everyone there, but she's been very distraught lately. I wonder if she's bitten off more than she can chew, with law school and everything. Can you get me the names of some good psychologists? I'm afraid she may need some counseling, with the loss of her father, and all the stress she's been under. That, and I think I'll need the name of a good dermatologist. My hands are so sensitive I think I should get something stronger than my normal moisturizer. Thank you. I'll call you later. Bye."

I heard the click of a phone being hung up, and the sound of her feet hitting the top of the stairs.

I hadn't been wrong after all. She was the one who had killed my father.

And I was in big trouble.

CHAPTER THIRTY-EIGHT

Her heels clattered on the wooden steps as she made her way down the stairs toward me. Each clack of her stilettos echoed the drumbeat of my heart, which threatened to burst out of my throat. What would she do to me, helpless, in her basement, with no witnesses except Bert?

I glanced around, making sure he was hidden. Either he had crawled back into my purse where it had been thrown partially underneath the stairs, or he'd found another hiding spot, because I didn't see him anywhere.

"Oh, good. You're awake," she said as she came to the bottom of the steps.

"You'll never get away with this. What do you think you're doing?" I asked, trying for a bravado I wasn't sure succeeded. Hey, if I was going to die, I didn't want to look like a scared rabbit in the basement. I might feel like one, but for some reason it was important to me to prove I wasn't afraid of her, even though I was.

"Well, I'm trying to get this binding lifted, and you are standing in the way. I have tried being nice. I've tried resorting to theft. I've even tried magic, but nothing has worked. I thought I had gotten it done, but your father got in the way, and now you're in the way, Janie." Evangeline crossed her arms over her chest, and drummed her fingers against her upper arms.

It was a gesture I'd seen plenty of times in the past, but where I'd blown it off before, I was definitely terrified now. It was her you're-pissing-me-off gesture. I gulped, trying not to make it look too obvious. "So what are you going to do to me, Evangeline?"

"I'm still deciding, but you're not going anywhere until I do. Of course, if you just gave me the Holder that would make it easier for me to decide what to do."

I didn't say anything. Considering I didn't know what it was, I couldn't exactly answer where it was.

"I'm not kidding, Janie," she continued. "I know your friends in that silly group with the stupid name have told you where it is. Tell me, and I'll untie you."

Not hardly. Hadn't they told me if she got the Holder, she could kill me? I wasn't falling for that one. I just stared at her. Besides which, they didn't know where it was, or what it was, either, so there was no way they could have told me.

"Tell me where it is, or I'll start killing your friends."

"I don't have many friends, Evangeline. You saw to that."

I could see frustration on her face. "I'll start with the friends you brought to the Art Institute for the fundraiser. Then I'll move on to that stupid group of old people. Really, Janie? Putting your trust in a bunch of people who probably have to use Metamucil and need LifeAlert necklaces? What are they going to do, hit me with their walkers? You've got to learn to pick better allies. Those people won't be worth anything in a fight."

Oh, God. She was going to hurt Mia, Leann, and Mike. She was going to target Doris, Stanley, Harold, and the rest of them. She hadn't mentioned Aiden yet, but if she hadn't found out about him, she would soon. How could I protect him? Oops. I meant them.

"Ah, hit a nerve, haven't I?" she asked. "So who is it that puts that look on your face? You've thought of someone specific, haven't you? Is there someone special you want to protect? Who might that be?"

I figured I'd regret it later, but I was afraid if I said anything to her targeted question, she'd be able to figure it out. Besides, I'd wanted to do this to her for years. I stuck out my tongue and blew her a giant raspberry. I'd have flipped her off if I could raise my arm. I took comfort in the fact I'd caused her to have issues with her hand. I wondered if she was using so much hand cream so she could use actual silverware, among other things. It made sense.

"Going to play it like that, are you?" She reached out and slapped me.

That was a surprise. Evangeline had slapped me once before, when I was younger, before Dad put a stop to her disciplining me physically. It was the only time she'd done it, and the only time I remembered seeing him stand up to her. I still remembered how much it stung.

This time, it didn't sting at all. In fact, other than the recoil of my head snapping back, I hadn't felt a thing. I'd noticed she'd hit me, but the slap hadn't hurt at all. Before I could think much about it, she slapped me again, harder. Nothing.

"Who is it? Who is so special to you? I can see it on your face. There's someone. You can't be dating anyone, unless the relationship is fairly new, and I'd know, wouldn't I? Of course, David did say something about you getting jewelry from someone. Is that who it is?"

Did she honestly think I'd tell her? I hadn't told her about my first kiss in junior high, or my first date; I'd snuck out of the house and told Dad later. About the date, that is, not the kiss. I wondered if I kept my mouth shut long enough, whether she'd spill her evil plot. Hey, it worked in the Austin Powers movies.

"Well, I'll be asking around. I'm going to figure out who it is you're so keen to protect. Meanwhile, you'll have to wonder if I've decided to start hurting the friends I do know about. Think about it, Janie. All you have to do is give me the Holder, and your friends will be safe."

But I wouldn't be. I wasn't sure whether it was better that I couldn't give the Holder to her, which kept her from killing me, or if it would be better to be able to tell her and protect my friends. And even if I could, a more powerful Evangeline was not high on my to-be-trusted list.

She hit me again. "Give me the Holder, and all this will stop."

Again, the slap didn't hurt. And it kept on not hurting as she hit me over and over again. I kept feeling the impact, even grunting as she rocked my head back and forth. I was going to end up with a terrific headache from the motions and gyrations my neck was going through. We kept going in the same dance; her hitting me, me rocking back, and her demanding answers to questions I was unable to answer.

Only the sound of the phone ringing brought her to a stop. "Janie, all you have to do is tell me the truth. Be creative when you think about what I might do to your friends, because I will be. I'll be extra thoughtful about what I can do to this person who is so special to you.

You have the power to stop it. You just have to give me the Holder."
She left me and stormed up the stairs to the furious ringing of the
phone, shutting off the lights at the top as she went.

CHAPTER THIRTY-NINE

I was sitting in the dark again. Bert's voice was the only consolation I had.

I was glad to have it.

"Janie, are you okay?" he asked.

I took a quick mental inventory. My neck hurt from the angle my head had hung at before I'd woken up, and from the force at which I'd been hit, but my face felt fine. I didn't seem to be suffering any after-effects from whatever I'd been injected with. I couldn't stand up to be sure, but I could feel the ropes biting into my legs where they held them to the legs of the chair; I had plenty of feeling there.

"I'm fine, Bert. And I know where we are. We're in my stepmother's basement. It looks like I was right."

He paused before he said "You can say I told you so if it makes you feel better."

I smiled. He couldn't see me do it, but it was an involuntary reaction to the dismay in his voice. "Bert, we need to get out of here."

He came back to me from his hiding place, somehow dragging my purse behind him. I could hear it scraping on the cement floor of the basement as he did so. "There's got to be something in here that'll help." He dug around in my purse for a while, but other than an old pair of broken nail clippers, he was unable to come up with anything good.

Near the washing machine, the dark air began to swirl faster. The faint beginnings of the portal I'd seen earlier were opening up, the air taking on a darker purple haze even in the absence of light in the basement. "Bert, I need you to hide. If I'm taken through that portal, and someone comes to find me, I'll need you to be nearby to let them know where I am. If it is Evangeline who takes me through the portal, it'll be your job to try to sneak upstairs and get to the phone to call Aiden for help. She's got a cordless phone in the hallway. If you bump the table just right, you should be able to knock the handset off and it has a speakerphone button."

"Janie, you can't give up."

"I'm not. We've tried to get me free, and it hasn't worked. She's going to come back down here as soon as she's off the phone. Drag my purse back over to where it was, that way you have a hiding place when they come down again." I could still feel the vials of ink, the screwdriver, and the key in my pockets and wondered if that was enough.

After a bit more argument, he finally did as I asked.

I knew it wouldn't be long before she came back down the steps. The swirling purple air kept getting stronger and more visible, and I wondered who had opened it. It sure hadn't been me; I'd never opened one. I'd never seen Bert open one. It had to be either Evangeline or David.

It wasn't long before the lights came back on. No sooner did Bert get himself situated in hiding, my stepmother come clacking back down the steps. What I hadn't expected was David standing right behind her.

"Janie, I guess I should have introduced you to my son, but you know him, don't you? He's in your study group. Did you even think to invite him to the fundraiser?"

"I did invite him, Evangeline. He turned me down. He made an excuse about needing childcare. Does he even have a kid? Or was that another lie?"

She turned to David and struck him across the face. "How dare you! I could have used your help at the museum to search for the Holder, even after the police left. Why in the world did you think it was okay to stay away?"

He looked at the ground. "I didn't think you had plans to do anything that night, Mother. I told you I was dating a woman with a kid, and she really did need a babysitter. It sounded like a good alibi if something happened at the museum to throw off the scent if she suspected me. I told you I recognized the necklace she was wearing that day."

He was talking about the necklace Aiden had given me, the one that had kept me from passing out in the museum.

"What were you trying to do in the museum?" I asked.

Evangeline's face was red and angry, and my question interrupted another slap heading toward David's face. I'd never seen her that way. "What do you think we were trying to do? We were trying to find the Holder of the Legacy. Your friends sacked the museum's storage facility a week ago, and I can't find it. I need the Holder. And you're going to give it to me."

Oops. Didn't need to go back to that circular argument. I was saved from repeating my earlier statements by David, who started begging for forgiveness from his mother. She comforted him, but it didn't last long. Jeesh. Talk about a momma's boy. He was crying and telling her how much he loved her even as she told him he was worthless. Obviously this twisted dynamic was one that had been going on for years.

They began to bicker back and forth about how each one of them had screwed up. I began to laugh, and I couldn't stop. They were gambling everything on the premise that I knew where this item was, but I still didn't have a clue. Doris, Stanley, Harold, and all the others were sure they'd screwed up because they couldn't find it. I was going to die at Evangeline's—or more likely David's—hands, or go crazy at some point in a magical realm, and it was all for naught because I couldn't tell them what they were looking for even if I'd wanted to.

I was rapidly becoming convinced that the universe hated me.

The longer I stalled them from dragging me through that portal, the more likely I'd be sane when someone finally did show up to rescue me.

"Evangeline." I said, interrupting their squabble. "You've made some big assumptions in your argument. I don't know what the Holder is. Neither do the F.A.B.L.E.S. members. That's why they stole as much as they did; they didn't know what they were looking for. You could torture me all day and I wouldn't be able to answer your questions. If you told me what it is, then I might be able to tell you where it is." My plan was to keep her talking as long as I could.

She leaned in closer to me, placing her hands on my forearms. I noticed the palms of her hands were cold and clammy on my bare arms. Her face was only an inch from mine, and I could smell the delicate scent of Earl Grey tea with honey and lemon on her breath, a drink she always asked for if she was upset.

"And would you tell me where it was if you knew?"

If she didn't have the Holder, she wouldn't be able to kill me. It had taken her years to kill my father, building up that curse in his body until it looked like cancer. Or did she have David do it? And if she couldn't hurt me earlier, then she'd have to do something else to get me to talk. And the only thing she could do to me was hold me in the magical realm until I went insane enough, in her mind, to tell her what she wanted to know.

On the other hand, I had no intention of telling her where it was, even if I could figure it out. I didn't feel compelled to tell her the truth, but I didn't want to make a promise I knew I'd break. Hadn't Aiden warned me about that?

"No, Evangeline," I said. "I still wouldn't tell you."

CHAPTER FORTY

"**D**id you search her, David?" Evangeline asked.

"Yes," he answered. "She had a metal dagger at her waist in a sheath. I took it away and disposed of it."

"Anything else?"

"She has a key in her pocket, but it didn't burn my hand when I touched it and it doesn't have sharp edges. She's got some ink, probably from school."

She nodded, seemingly satisfied I wasn't some kind of female Houdini or Batgirl or G.I. Jane, with weapons and escape tools hidden all over me.

"Janie, what's the key for?"

"I don't know."

"What does it unlock?" David asked.

"I honestly don't know. I found it a while ago, and put it in the pocket of these pants, meaning to try to see if it went to anything. I must have forgotten to take it out when I did laundry." A little white lie, but I hoped I could keep a good enough poker face for them to buy it. I didn't know what the key was, but it was Dad's. I didn't want to give it up.

My stepmother wasn't very gentle as she freed my legs from the chair. I struggled to get free as she worked on my arms, but she held a vise-grip on my wrist as she did so.

I kept tugging and wriggling, trying to get loose, but David was right behind her to make sure I didn't get away. They didn't search me again. That meant I still had the screwdriver Bert had slipped into my back pocket. I'd have to pick the right time to use it. It was really the only weapon I had, beside the ink. And was David so old he thought the ink was from school? He had to be a couple of hundred years older than he looked to consider it usable. I wondered if he'd spent much of that time in the real world, or in the magical realm. If the latter, his assumption made a lot of sense.

They dragged me through the portal, but I put up as good a fight as I could. David finally drew back to hit me. I felt the warm wetness of blood where he'd split my lip and bloodied my nose; he'd hurt me. My face ached where he'd hit me, and it stunned me just long enough for them to pull my feet through the portal and shut it behind them, my stepmother praising David for drawing blood.

Why did it hurt when David hit me, but not when Evangeline did? All I knew was that I really didn't want him to hit me again. I couldn't care less whether she did or not, as long as she wasn't playing whiplash with my neck.

In my fight not to get yanked through the portal, I'd forgotten how much the scent of magic reminded me of Dad. Instead of the meltdown I'd had the last time, however, it was comforting. It was like Dad's arms wrapped around me, encouraging me not to give up. Instead of giving in to tears, the peppermint and old book smell was strengthening my resolve to fight my stepmother.

"Let go of me," I said, pulling against Evangeline's grip on my wrist and David's grasp on the opposite arm.

"You going to cooperate?" he asked. Evangeline snorted.

"Of course not, but I'm not going to be able to walk if you're hanging onto me that tight."

"Nice try," she said, grabbing my arm tighter.

I tripped over their feet a few times, exaggerating it on purpose to get them to let go. I was going to have bruises, at least from David's hand clamped like a vice on my upper arm. It didn't work.

I gradually became aware of my surroundings despite my continued struggles to get away. They were dragging me down a dirt path edged by stark white pebbles. I had no idea what time it was in the real world, but here it was night, with the moon shining brightly enough to illuminate the pebbles well. I had an idea.

I stopped struggling for a few minutes, just long enough for their grip to ease up, before announcing, "Evangeline, I gotta tie my shoe," and bending down before they could question it. They let go. I was surprised, but I knew I wouldn't get far if I made a break for it. I had no idea how to open a portal to get back home. I had an ulterior motive; I palmed as many of the white pebbles at the edge of the path as I could grab before I stood back up.

My stepmother was not happy. I could tell from the heavy sighing and the way she had her arms crossed over her chest in a classic I'm-pissed-but-too-classy-to-say-it pose, as I stood back up. We began walking again, and I tried to drop a white pebble in the middle of the path every once in a while. My hope was that Bert would be able to call Aiden and point him through the portal, and my pebbles would mean he could find wherever they were going to take me.

David kept trying to hurry me up, but I kept slowing down, over-exaggerating my reluctance as a diversion from my pebble trick. We walked for quite a while, and I began rationing the pebbles left in my hand as we went, worried I'd run out too soon.

My concentration was completely on leaving a trail for Aiden; I wasn't watching where we were headed until the sweet scent of the building we were walking toward finally overpowered the magical smell of books and peppermint. When I caught the scent, I had only one pebble in my hand, and looked up.

"You have *got* to be kidding me," I said, stopping in my tracks when I saw that the house was made of gingerbread. There were giant lollipops lining the walkway up to the house. The walls were solid sheets of gingerbread and the windows looked opaque, with the sheen of cooked sugar candy. The roof shingles looked like huge chunks of chocolate, formed into stubby planks and overlapping each other, and there were thick licorice whips forming the corners of the house. The whole thing was held together with tons of icing. I dropped my last pebble. If Aiden couldn't figure it out from there, I had no hope of rescue. The path didn't lead anywhere else.

Evangeline and David continued to drag me toward the candy construction. I stopped struggling quite as much, because I was still staring at the gingerbread house. They took me inside, and it was dark. I had the irrelevant thought that there probably weren't electric lights; it wouldn't be a good idea inside highly flammable candy walls. I wondered if they'd used cotton candy for insulation. Did they have an ant problem with so much sugar around?

David closed the door behind us, and Evangeline muttered under her breath. Lights came on with a soft, humming glow. I wondered where they came from.

The inside of the house didn't even come close to matching the outside. I'd expected the furnishings and décor to be made of sugar and icing and chocolate as well, but instead they were normal, made of wood and fabric and sophisticated enough for me to know Evangeline had a hand in the decoration. It matched her taste perfectly.

Except for the large, human-sized wicker birdcage in the corner, that is.

They herded me toward it, and I began fighting again, in earnest. I did not want to be locked up in a cage inside the magical realm. My fight to stay free, however, was as successful as my attempts to stay out of the portal and to get away on the walk to the gingerbread house. In other words, it wasn't. The good news was that my hands and feet were no longer tied or held by someone else, so I could move around easier, but I was still in a cage.

I wondered if I could chew my way out of it. I tested the wicker of the bars. There was no way I'd get it done this century and still have teeth left to eat with. The wicker of the cage seemed to be shellacked with some kind of polyurethane, making it as hard and unyielding as metal. If Aiden was right about the magical world eventually eroding one's sanity, I'd be insane long before I could get free.

David was standing right outside of the cage as Evangeline walked away. Another man, with wavy red hair barely brushing his shoulders, walked past, saying hello to David, but didn't stick around. The red-haired man looked oddly familiar even though I'd never seen him before. His clothing was striking; if I didn't know better, I'd say he was dressed as a gentleman from a Victorian-era movie with his well-tailored vest and overcoat. When he walked away, I turned my attention back to David.

I wondered if I could get him to drop a few hints about what was going on. "How can you lock me up like this? I thought we were friends."

"We were in the same study group for a week. That doesn't mean we were friends."

Fair enough, I thought. *It'd been worth a try.* "What's going to happen to me?"

"It's not for me to decide. You should've given her the Holder when she asked for it. She wouldn't have hit you or dragged you here if you'd have given it to her."

"How do I give her something if I don't know what it is?"

He turned to face me. "You really don't know?"

I crossed my arms over my chest in an imitation of Evangeline's you've-gone-too-far stance. "I don't. So why don't you tell me about it, so I can figure out if I know where it is."

David gave me an evil, leering chuckle. "You've told us that you wouldn't give it to us if you had it. I think you're fishing to find out what we know. The Grimms buried the information about the Holder so deep that people outside of the family have trouble researching where to find it. How do I know you're not playing some kind of game? I don't care what it is. I just want you to turn it over. I think you know exactly where that thing is, so if you don't mind, either tell me what you know or shut the hell up. I'm not letting you out of there."

Oh. My. God. I suddenly knew exactly what it was they were looking for. I hadn't thought it important. I sat down, cross-legged, staring at the floor. I didn't dare let David see whatever expression was crossing my face as my mind sped along, filling in clues and holes and gaps in my memory that hadn't made sense before.

It had been right there in my pocket all along. It had to be the key my father had carefully packed away, nestled in its velvet cloth, buried in an iron chest my stepmother would never open. Why hide clues to it if you already were in possession of it? Dad had buried it in the trunk. By all appearances, he'd been very deliberate about the trunks. And he'd repeated several times I should get the trunks if he died. He'd told Aiden about them. It was even in his will. I wondered if he'd suspected Evangeline of something, of being magical, of being faerie, or of trying to kill him. Of course, Evangeline had wanted those iron trunks out of her house if she couldn't touch them, but she obviously believed, and she was right, that the Holder had been hidden in the trunks.

But my father had not been the youngest member of the Grimm family when he'd been married to Evangeline; I had been. The key hadn't been in my possession, so her slaps and cruelty could hurt when

I was a kid. She'd been able to magically stunt my memory and my understanding of what was going on.

Evangeline's curse, hurting my father and eventually killing him, was possible because I was the only one who could be protected by the Holder. Until it came into my possession, I could be hurt. I no longer had the dagger I'd started out with. I'd bought the screwdriver Bert had shoved into my pocket earlier at Home Depot not too long ago. There was no way the ink could be the Holder; there were just too many vials of it in Dad's trunks, and the F.A.B.L.E.S. group weren't talking about multiple Holders, they always referred to it as a singular thing. Aiden's necklace had come from the F.A.B.L.E.S. guys; they knew what it was, but were still looking for the Holder. It had to be the key; it was the only other thing in my pocket.

So why had David not realized what it was when he'd searched me? I hadn't heard Doris or Harold or Stanley or Aiden, or any of the others for that matter, ever talk about the Holder binding *anyone* but the witch. If it could only affect Evangeline, it wouldn't have done a darned thing to David. He wasn't bound by it; his mother was.

I fought to control the expression on my face before I looked up to ask a question. I had to keep playing the ignorant girl David had accused me of imitating, while simultaneously doing anything and everything I could to keep the key in my pocket and hidden.

"Why is my stepmother so convinced she needs the Holder? What does it do?"

He didn't look at me. "I'm sure your friends told you the legend of the Holder. If she gets it, she can be restored to her full powers, take the throne of all Faerie back, and destroy the Pestilence that bound her. She's my mother, and she wants it, so I'm going to see that she gets what she wants. Your meddling human friends and the half-breed will be at an end."

I swallowed hard. They meant to kill my friends. But who was the half-breed, and what did he mean by that?

CHAPTER FORTY-ONE

Others began to arrive in the house shortly after my conversation with David.

I stood up and watched as they appeared wearing fine clothes from another century, with corsets and stays and floor length gowns on the women, doublets and tights and pointy-toed shoes on the men. I wanted to laugh at their overly elaborate costumes as they walked into the ridiculous house made of sugar, but their grim expressions wiped the mirth from my face. It looked like they weren't happy to be there. Neither was I.

Some of them nodded at me. Others ignored me completely. One or two pointed and whispered as they made their way past me. I watched as they left the room through a large set of double doors at the far end. After a while, I was alone.

Even David had left, called away by another person to attend to some detail.

I let out a long sigh, relieved to finally be alone, without a guard. There wasn't much I could do to get out of the situation, but it still felt like a relief. I sat down again inside the wicker birdcage and leaned against the bars, looking up to stare at the ceiling.

"Didn't you think I was coming?" I heard in a familiar voice.

"Aiden? Is that you?" I asked, scrambling to my feet as he came close enough for me to see the reassuring grin on his face and red hair flopping over his forehead.

"Who else? I tried to call your cell phone earlier. I couldn't get off work fast enough to follow you to your apartment. I told my boss I had a family emergency, but then the car wouldn't start. When I finally got to your place, the door was standing wide open and your friends were just coming to their senses. Mia told me what happened." He began looking at the lock on the cage door, as if he could do something about it.

"Is she okay?" I asked.

"She's got a heck of a bruise, but she's otherwise fine. She's worried about you. Mike and Leann are, too. They said David must have taken you, and they kept trying to figure out where you were. I figured I'd better start at Evangeline's, and as I left, my cell phone rang."

"Bert must have made it to a phone," I said, as he fumbled with the lock.

"That's right, he did. I was headed there anyway, but he was able to show me where the portal was. When I got there, he started calling the others."

I started to giggle, fighting hard to be quiet about it. The cavalry coming to the rescue would likely be wearing a Grandma sweatshirt with yarn and kittens, have long grey hair, and see conspiracies behind every corner. I wondered if Stanley would try to bug the lollipops out front to see if they had anything to do with the Kennedy assassination.

"What's so funny?" he asked.

I explained. He grinned at me, but went back to what he was doing. He pulled out a set of lock picking tools from his pocket and went to work.

"How is it that you can use lock picks but you can't chew gum and walk at the same time?" I asked. I'm sure I was giving him a look of disbelief, because no way was he going to be able to unlock that door. I'd be surprised if he didn't drop the lock picks all over the floor in a minute.

He smiled. "I can't in the real world. In a magical realm I'm not clumsy, and I've practiced. Don't worry, I've practiced *a lot*."

He must have. It didn't him long to get the lock open and the door swung easily. I was impressed.

Aiden held out his hand, as if I were the belle of the ball, to help me out of the cage. I took it, not sure quite what else to do, and stepped out of the cage into the room. "We can't stay here," I said, looking around to see if anyone had come back. We hurried toward the door, hoping to escape.

We didn't get far.

"Where do you think you're going, little half-breed? And with the evening's prize? How dare you spoil the festivities for our queen?"

We were faced with an eight-foot tall troll, green and ugly in his striped pantaloons and tights, carrying a large wooden club in one hand and a crossbow in the other.

What the hell?

Who was the half-breed? As far as I knew, my parents had been completely one hundred percent Ohio-born, pure American human. I had a sick thought. Were they talking about Aiden?

He confirmed it when he responded to the troll in front of us. "Slinging barbs about my parentage doesn't get you the answers you want, Grechuk. Nor does it accomplish anything when you've been calling me the same thing since we were kids. Come up with something more imaginative, and maybe I'll pay attention. Besides, what do you want with my friend?"

"Your friend is wanted by our queen. By her information, the queen can cause her death. By her death, our queen regains strength and becomes the leader she once was."

"So which side are you on, Grechuk?" Aiden asked, one arm snaking behind his back.

"I'm on my own side, as I usually am. Right now, it serves my purposes to make sure that both of you are delivered to the queen. She put me in charge of security tonight."

"Big step up for you, isn't it? All those dreams you had as a kid of being in charge of everyone finally coming true for you? You get to bully someone around without consequences. Must be a real thrill to know you finally reached your potential, isn't it?"

"Aiden, maybe it's not a good idea to poke at the troll. Maybe we should be nice and ask if he'll let us by." I was tugging his sleeve, trying to get him to dial it back a bit. No use ticking off the thing standing between us and the door in the interest of an old playground rivalry.

Grechuk laughed, a deep belly laugh that sounded wrong coming from around the tusks sticking out of his mouth. "Aiden Half-Breed, you should listen to your friend. Not that I will accede to her request, but it's much less likely you'll die if you approach things her way. Still full of bravado, aren't you? You haven't changed much since we were young."

"Aiden, who is this?" I asked. Was there something we could use to convince this guy?

"When we were younger Grechuk was always a bully, and now he's got a position where he has a royal sanction for it. But he could always be persuaded to let something go, if you had the right price for it."

"The only thing sufficient is the Holder. If you give it to me, I'll think about it."

Aiden turned to look at me. "I don't have it. Do you know where it is, Janie?"

Aw, crap. I shut my eyes and shook my head, willing my face to go blank. Now was not the time to tell him I'd figured out the secret, which was sitting in my pocket, poking me in the hip with every step. "Maybe we could overpower him. There are two of us," I whispered.

Before Aiden could shake his head, Grechuk laughed again. "Miss, I can hear every word you say. It's no use arguing. Of course, if you two want to take that route, I can wait here until you're done planning, and listen to what you're going to do before you even try. Let me promise you that it won't work."

Better to try a different tack. "Why do you want the Holder, Grechuk? You can't do anything with it."

"I would give it to my queen, of course. You humans are so ridiculous, looking for hidden meanings behind every turn of phrase. I meant what I said. If I help her return to power, my standing goes up. It's that simple."

Aiden chuckled. "You say that like humans are all liars and cheats and thieves. As if the faerie courts aren't worse?"

"We do not lie. We do not break promises. We leave that to the humans."

I remembered Aiden's warning earlier in the week that I shouldn't make any promises to someone with magical abilities. I was taking it seriously now. "Aiden, what do we do now?" I whispered.

"I'm working on that one," he whispered back.

"Work faster."

CHAPTER FORTY-TWO

We stood there, both of us frantically trying to come up with a plan for how to get past Grechuk without getting hurt. That club looked heavy and I didn't want to know what it would feel like. I wasn't coming up with anything good. I assumed Aiden wasn't either; he didn't say much.

I heard a buzzing noise. The door that the others had gone through earlier opened slightly to allow a small light, no bigger than a light bulb, to fly through and head straight for Grechuk's shoulder. The buzzing continued, getting louder as the light got closer. I couldn't make out what the noise meant, but Grechuk listened, and then swatted the light away.

Aiden leaned over, whispering. "That must be Flit. She's a pixie, like the ones we freed that wanted to illuminate the path to the hut you went to, but Flit's always been a favorite of the queen. And she toadies up well to keep her place as a favorite. She's one of the queen's spies."

Grechuk interrupted Aiden with the announcement, "You will come with me. It is time you made your appearance in court, and you, Half-Breed, make your apologies to your queen for the disrespectful way you left. You shouldn't do that without her permission, and you know it."

Okay, so now I was really over my head. I hadn't thought about appearing in court. My jeans and button-up shirt would stand out like a sore thumb against the finery of the people who'd walked past me. I didn't know the customs or the rules or even the protocol. I knew I was going to screw this up.

Aiden grabbed my hand, and squeezed it tight before letting it go again. "Just trust me. I'm on your side, Janie."

I didn't have much of a choice. I was disappointed he hadn't shared his background with me, but then I likely wouldn't have shared something that made me so different from everyone else, either. I had to admit, in most cases, I did try to keep friends from meeting Evangeline;

taking friends to the fundraiser wasn't the kind of thing I normally did. Aiden had done nothing but help me every time I turned around. And even if I could get past the troll and follow my own trail of pebbles back, I had no idea how to re-open the portal. I needed Aiden to get home.

I nodded at him.

"Grechuk, what's the agenda today? Is it a High Council meeting, or just the queen's personal court?" Aiden asked. I was glad he did. I didn't know the difference between the two, but I would never have known to ask.

"It is a meeting of the queen's court. The High Council cannot convene on such short notice, but there is a High Council summit coming up soon. If the queen can consolidate her power before the High Council summit, she stands to take over the Council and the entire magical realm. Some of us would do anything in our power to help her achieve that goal."

Yikes.

Okay, two thoughts rolled through my brain.

First of all, this was a bigger scope than even I had realized. I knew Evangeline was a control freak, but I'd had no idea just how power hungry she was.

Second, there was no way in hell I was giving her the Holder. Breaking the binding meant she would have to kill me, if Aiden and the others were to be believed. And I couldn't care less about her power if the price of it was my life.

Aiden pulled out a wicked looking dagger that had me thinking Crocodile Dundee's giant knife looked like a toothpick. *Okay, way too many '80s movies for me lately,* I thought. I wasn't quite sure where he'd hidden the thing, but the metal in the blade gleamed in the soft light of the room. I wondered if metal affected him the same way; I noticed there was no metal in the grip that I could see, but he'd helped carry the trunks out of Evangeline's house without a problem.

Grechuk didn't look happy. "You insulted the court when you left, and you do so again, now, by bringing metal into our lands. You hereby forfeit any rights you may have had as a guest, Aiden Half-Breed. Instead, you have just earned your way into bondage with the mortal behind you."

Bondage, my ass. They meant to kill me.

"I'm not here to assert guest rights. I am here to ask for a fair hearing for this mortal, who has been brought here other than by her own accord. I claim her rights for her by offering metal and blood." He pricked his finger with the tip of the blade, leaving a drop of red on the point. "You know the laws, Grechuk. Mortals must appear of their own free will for the court to impose its wishes upon them. If she is here under duress, she may request a hearing to determine whether the court has rights to keep her."

Grechuk pondered on this. I wasn't sure what it meant, but suddenly, there was hope that I might get to leave. I nodded furiously behind Aiden's back, trying to confirm was he said. Finally, Grechuk nodded. "You are right. She has a right to a hearing, but you do understand the deciding body will be the queen herself? I believe she will rule against you since it suits her purposes."

I wasn't sure that was an improvement, but I'd take whatever I could get. Besides, maybe there would be enough time for me to ask Aiden how such a hearing would go, and get advice. Since he knew what was going on, I hoped he could represent me. I was sure I'd make a mistake that I couldn't take back.

Aiden tried to put away his dagger, but Grechuk insisted he would not be allowed to take it into the room where the court was gathering. They did some negotiation, finally agreeing that Aiden's knife would be taken back to the real world and tossed through the portal. The blood would be preserved on white linen cloth for presentation in support of my hearing. I voiced the request that Grechuk promise no being would be targeted by the tossing of the knife through the portal. I had a terrible visual image of Grechuk seeing Bert, throwing the knife at him, and then claiming it was an accident. He agreed, on the condition that we go back into the cage without argument so he could take our requests to the queen.

Aiden agreed. "Why are we agreeing to get back in the cage?" I asked, under my breath.

"Because I can't win a physical fight with him and if you play by the rules, you have a chance to get out of here without any strings attached. It's the only way to leave without spending the rest of your life running and hiding from the queen," he whispered back, as Grechuk re-secured the lock and left us alone.

As soon as Grechuk was gone, I had to say something. "You're insane to trust him. How do you know he won't kill us himself?"

"Listen, Janie, I'm not kidding. The hearing is actually a good thing. Your best shot of getting out of here in one piece is not in giving up the Holder, which doesn't help you, but to convince the rest of the court that Evangeline has broken a promise. It's an unforgivable sin in the eyes of the faerie court. They can hide the truth, but they are not supposed to tell an outright lie or break an oath. They can find loopholes to get out of them, but they cannot break promises. Can you think of any promises your stepmother has broken?"

"Aren't you risking a lot? What if she never broke a promise? You've got to have a better plan than that!"

"That's Plan A," he said.

"Please tell me there's a Plan B. I think we're going to need it."

He didn't say anything right away. "I'm working on it."

Great.

I didn't know whether to laugh, to cry, or to grab his shoulders and shake the tar out of him. I settled for a calmer reaction. "So, what's going to happen at this hearing? How much time do we have to prepare? What do I need to know?"

"Well, the first question is whether you, in any way, agreed to come here with your stepmother. If you agreed, then we've got to come up with something different."

I went over the whole thing from the time I was grabbed, kicking and screaming, from my apartment to being thrown into the trunk of a car and injected with something to waking up in the basement tied to a chair to resisting them and trying to get away as they dragged me through the portal to leaving the trail of pebbles for Aiden. Nope. I didn't remember anything that even resembled agreement or acquiescence.

He agreed with my assessment. "Okay, so if we can convince them of your involuntary appearance, then the next step is to figure out what promises she might have made you, and what promises you might have made her."

I couldn't think of a damn thing. My brain was melting down, and nothing came to mind, no matter what I thought of. "Well, I did promise to do certain chores around the house when I was a kid," I suggested, and sat down on the floor of the cage.

"Did you do them?" He sat cross-legged in front of me. Honestly, there wasn't really room for much else. We could both sit down, but stretching our legs out was impossible.

"She made sure of it. If I tried to get out of them, she assigned extra chores, including crazy things that didn't seem to have any purpose, like stripping feathers off their quills, or scooping water into a bucket, and then I wasn't allowed to eat dinner until they were done. I didn't want to complain to Dad, so I did them without making an issue of it most of the time. Especially after the feather thing. I could taste them in the back of my throat for weeks."

"Did she make any promises to you?"

I couldn't think of a single one off the top of my head. Then, all of a sudden, it came to me. "She made a promise to Dad."

"What's that?" he asked.

"Well, when he was dying, she promised to take care of me as if I were her own."

He grilled me on her promises to Dad as he died, promises I'd made after his death that I'd forgotten about, and everything I'd done to keep up my end of it all. How was my promise to meet her for brunch every week going to keep her from figuring out the Holder was in my pocket and taking it from me in order to kill me? I hadn't worked that one out yet.

Aiden leaned back against the bars of the wicker cage, and I wondered if it was hopeless. Even so, I had to ask him the question. "Aiden, why do they call you Half-Breed?"

He sighed. "Because my father was from the magical realm, and my mother was completely human. I don't have any overt magical abilities, but I have trouble in the real world. It's why I'm such a klutz there."

I just stared at him.

"I spent my early childhood years with my mother, but after I learned what magic was, I spent my teenage years with my father.

When I turned twenty-one, I had to choose which realm to live in, and I chose the real world. I didn't want anything to do with the court life, which was what my father was grooming me for."

"Who is your father?"

"He's Evangeline's tailor." He sighed. "I haven't seen him show up yet. I hope he's not here. He was very angry when I left."

"Would he help us?" I asked.

"Not if it would lose him his position and standing in the court. Last time I saw him, he blamed me for bringing down his good name." He leaned his head back, looking at the roof of the cage.

A deep voice boomed across the room. "And your return will only remind my queen of my loss of stature and embarrassment when you turned your back on your rightful place. I no longer call you my son. You deserve nothing."

Aiden stood up and turned around. I peeked around him to look at the red-haired gentlemen I'd seen earlier in Victorian clothing. The overcoat was gone, but the richness of his waistcoat and vest was easier to see now, fitting his trim figure like a glove. No wonder he looked familiar; he was an older version of Aiden himself, but the red hair was tamed and orderly, his clothing was immaculate, and he didn't once trip on the walk across the room to our cage. Despite his harsh words, I heard a note of longing and sadness in his voice. And he wasn't alone. Grechuk was standing right behind him.

"Hello, Father," Aiden said.

"You are a disgrace. I will no longer acknowledge you in court, and will no longer be your protector." He spit in his son's face.

I couldn't put a finger on it, but it seemed to me like it was a performance of some kind. Something in his voice or in his eyes told me Aiden's father was covering something up.

Aiden watched his father walk away, and his shoulders slumped in disappointment. I reached my arm up around his shoulders; he would have been too tall for me to do so if he hadn't been drooped over against the bars of the cage. He leaned against me, and I could feel him shaking, but I couldn't see his face to tell if he was crying. I know I would have been in his situation.

"Aiden, you've been more than a friend to me. I've had to learn we can't choose our families, and sometimes we just have to rely on ourselves." I hoped he knew I was talking about my stepmother. I couldn't have predicted her behavior toward me had this purpose; as a kid, I'd just thought she didn't like me because I took some of Dad's attention away from her.

"I know," he said. "And my mom's great. I came to terms with the idea my father would react this way the next time I saw him, but that doesn't mean it isn't a slap in the face when it really happens." He stood upright, and I saw him wipe the wetness from his eyes and the spit from his face before he turned around. "But enough about my problems. Let's talk about the procedure for your hearing. You need to know how it works so you can convince them to let you go."

I listened to his lecture on procedure, knowing that he needed to concentrate on other matters, but something in his last statement bothered me.

He'd said let *you* go. Not let *us* go.

Aiden wasn't expecting to be able to leave the magical realm with me.

We'd have to see about that.

CHAPTER FORTY-THREE

Aiden hugged me. I did feel better, as if he wouldn't let anything bad happen. After all, he had raced in after me when he knew he wouldn't be welcomed by his father, and he expected me to leave him behind to face whatever punishment my appearance and escape would earn him. That had to mean something. Was it a measure of his principles, or his feelings for me?

The half-magical thing did bother me, but there was no evidence he was working against me. It wasn't like he'd ever lied about it; I'd never asked how he knew about magic, or pressed him about his background. I wondered who his mother was, but it didn't take long for me to figure it out.

I leaned back from his hug to look at his face. "Your mom is Doris, right?" I felt smart for actually figuring something out for myself. I'd felt pretty stupid lately at all the changes in the last week.

He grinned. "You got it. She's great, but I worry about her safety. I was gone long enough that people don't always remember I'm her kid, so I don't call her Mom in public. She understands; it's not a bad thing to be cautious. I just don't trust my father. And they had a huge argument when I left the court the last time."

He was lucky to have a parent who cared so much for him still alive. Dad had been like that, but I didn't have him anymore. I would have given just about anything to have a mom like Doris, and I wondered if my mother would have been the same if she were still alive. I sank into Aiden's hug, trying not to think about anything, especially anything Evangeline-related.

"What a pretty picture," I heard in a familiar frosty voice a few yards away.

I turned and saw my stepmother, arms crossed over her chest in a classic annoyed-Evangeline pose. Aiden jerked back, stepping away from me when he spoke.

"Queen Eva, I do apologize for not recognizing you and paying proper respect when I visited you in the mortal realm. You are certainly looking lovely and younger than ever."

"I can hardly take offense when I hid from you under a selective glamour spell. My stepdaughter was the only one able to recognize me."

I swallowed hard. Was that why the boys had thought her house smelled like magic, and I hadn't noticed?

Evangeline preened in her court attire. She'd always been imposing, but now she was wearing a floor-length violet gown with a cinched-waist corset, and a lush mink-lined robe hung from her shoulders. Jewels dripped from her ears and draped lavishly around her neck, and her hair was loose and wavy around her shoulders with the sides pinned back under a heavy gold jewel-encrusted tiara. She looked like the dictionary definition of the word *royal*.

"Evangeline? Or should I call you by a title?" I asked.

"Your half-breed ally knows the proper court etiquette. I trust he can guide you. I should have known you had someone helping you, Janie. You've never paid enough attention to social niceties to know the rules on how to request a hearing, or even how to ask for something diplomatically. In fact, I'd rather counted on it, but I hope you know it doesn't matter in the end. I'm the queen. I'm the one who will rule on your hearing. You can't possibly believe I would rule in your favor unless you tell me where to find the Holder."

Yeah, right. But then again, where had the key come from? I'd seen a lot in the last week, but most had to do with Grimm's Fairy Tales, stories my father had read to me as a kid. I didn't remember a key in those stories. Wait a minute. I hadn't remembered that book, or Dad reading it to me before just now.

The memories began to pour over me, flooding back in a hurry, as I remembered stories and bedtime tales from my father, time spent with him at the zoo, my first day of school, my first recital, and on and on. I had to fight my way free from the avalanche of memories and hoped my expression hadn't given me away. I suddenly had an urge to touch the key in my pocket, but suppressed it in time for her next statement.

"I don't know what you hope to accomplish by this hearing, but we'll have it started in ten minutes. Prepare yourself. And don't think being my stepdaughter earns you any special favors. Believe me when I say I have no connection with you other than wanting you to tell me where to find the Holder."

Gulp.

The memories were still coming. I remembered the day I'd met her, the day we moved into her house, and the day I broke her Waterford crystal vase. Strangely, there was a part of me that was convinced all three events happened on the same day.

She distracted me from the memories by sweeping out of the room, her robe trailing the ground behind her. She seemed born to be royalty. She had that sense of entitlement, an air of absolute certainty her statements and orders would be obeyed without question. I wondered what Dad had seen in her, and then I wondered what she had seen in Dad. As much as I loved him, he'd been a rumpled college professor who was always buried in his books and research, not really someone who would've been at home sitting on a throne at her side. There was only one explanation for them being together; Evangeline's grand plan to get her hands on the Holder.

Aiden interrupted my internal monologue with a question. "Do you have a plan for the hearing? If we're starting that quick, you won't have long to come up with whatever argument you're going to use. I'll take care of the first part, formally requesting the hearing and stating the grounds for it, but no one is allowed to represent a mortal in a court dispute with a royal. You'll be on your own."

Well, that answered my question about whether or not he'd be able to represent me. I could only hope I'd be able to ask him questions if I got an idea later. I was sure I'd violate some esoteric rule if I couldn't.

"I'm not sure yet, but I can't let her win. Not just because she'd kill me, but do you honestly think her having all that power is a good thing?"

Aiden grabbed my upper arms. "Listen hard. Jacob and Wilhelm Grimm bound her powers for a reason; she wiped out entire villages and towns. She killed anyone who amassed enough power or knowledge to stop her. She became consumed by it, wreaking vengeance on mortals who sought to drain her power. Even her own court participated in the binding ceremony your ancestors put together because she was draining all of their powers as well. It was a giant vacuum, so the royals saw the Grimms' plan as the lesser of two evils."

"What do you mean?" I asked. My arms were going to bruise from where he had hold of me, but he definitely had my attention enough to stop the flow of random memories bombarding my brain.

"If they silently backed the Grimms against their queen and succeeded, they could ensure they would not live under her tyranny forever; she wouldn't be strong enough to hold that much power against them. If they attempted to bind her themselves and failed, they would be tortured for eternity, since many of them are immortal. If the Grimms failed, they could blame the mortals. The Grimms could die, so they could not be tortured forever. It was the best scenario they could think of, so they took the brothers' plan seriously."

That didn't sound good. "So they were looking for a human scapegoat? How is that a good thing? Or are you just warning me to watch my back?"

"They actually don't hate humans. They find them amusing. They take humans by trickery, by promises, and by outright volunteers. They don't seek to wipe you out; but remember, they're always looking out for themselves first."

"What do they want?"

"If you find an excuse for the court, a way to defeat her at her own game, they won't stand with her. They'll have to follow the rules, but give them an out, a way to go against her where they don't lose face, and they'll take it. As long as it's an easy win for them, they'll follow a path Evangeline can't argue with."

"How do you know that? How long's it been since you've been gone?" I asked.

He gave me a dirty look, one eyebrow slanting like an angry red exclamation point over his eye. "I know this court, Janie. I had friends here, once. And there's probably a dozen or more of them, including my father, who can sense it when someone of faerie is telling a lie. They sense it in different ways; some can taste it, others can smell or see it, but they know when it happens. I can't sense a subtle shading of the truth, but I can tell when someone tells a blatant lie when I'm in the magical realm."

There it was again, the reminder that Aiden wasn't completely human. Much as I knew it was an issue to consider another day, it made it hard to see him the way I'd had just a few hours ago. I was definitely attracted to him, but was I sure that I was okay with the not-totally-human thing? I shoved the thought aside. A few kisses and a comforting hug did not a future create. I was getting ahead of myself.

He let go of my arms, and I leaned up against the bars of the cage as I thought over my options, trying to come up with a game plan for what was coming up.

And then it struck me. I knew exactly what I would argue before Evangeline's court, and how to get the faerie court to back me on it. I grilled Aiden on procedure for a few minutes, but we didn't have much longer than that before Grechuk came to fetch us for the hearing.

It was time. And I had a plan.

CHAPTER FORTY-FOUR

Grechuk unlocked the cage and let us out without tying or otherwise restraining us. I was glad. I didn't think a roomful of immortal magical faerie royals would let us escape if my plan blew up in my face, but it felt good to have that be an option, even if it was an unlikely one.

He opened the double doors for us, and stayed at the door as he ushered us inside. If Grechuk was guarding the door, there was no doubt; it would be impossible to slip past him unnoticed. There went my desperate hopes for an escape route.

We entered a large ballroom, filled with over a hundred beings dressed in finery similar to what Evangeline had been wearing; everything was made of sumptuously flowing velvets and silks and brocade. I'd never thought of clothing as anything other than stuff to put on so as not to be naked, or what Evangeline spent too much money on. These guys had fashion down to a science, and every single one of them looked like their clothing had been hand-tailored to fit them perfectly; there wasn't an uneven hem or missed button in sight. I wasn't an expert by any stretch of the imagination, but I knew that whoever worked on their wardrobes definitely deserved an Oscar for costume design. I wondered how much of it Aiden's father had done. Whatever his failings as a father, if he'd made these outfits, he was very talented.

The further I got into the room, the more I realized not everyone looked like a human. There were seven short green men with heavily wrinkled faces and long white beards—I recognized them from the museum. Here and there were human-sized animals, walking on their hind legs, and talking as if they were men and women out for a special evening. I saw a fox, a hedgehog, a wolf, and a donkey all wearing the same rich fabrics and well-tailored clothes, with tunics and tights and pointy-toed shoes. There were several beings with wings, and a few with horns, and a woman with a blue tinge to her skin, who never said a word to anyone.

Evangeline sat upon a throne on the raised platform at the far end of the room, facing the doors we'd just walked through, and the man standing to her right banged a long, heavy staff on the floor. The crowd stopped their socializing to watch me walk across the room to her throne, Aiden at my heels.

When I got close to the dais where her throne sat, Aiden announced my claim, and then I addressed her formally, as he had instructed me to do.

"Queen Eva, my stepmother, I come before you as a mortal, to request a hearing on the basis that my presence here is not of my own volition." I was nervous; my heart beating a steady tango in the back of my throat didn't help matters much. I knew one thing, though. Once I got out of law school and began practicing law, no court appearance would feel as scary as this one.

She leaned forward. "Such a request entitles you to a hearing under our laws, stepdaughter mine, decided by the court. Who is it that compelled your appearance here today?"

"You compelled my appearance, through the actions of your ally, whom I know as David. Your son, I believe." He was skulking around near the platform, wearing similarly well-tailored clothing in crimson and black. His hair was loose, cascading over his shoulders, but it was tucked behind his ears, showing off their pointed tips.

I'd wanted a sibling for years, but I certainly did not want one who would come to my house under false pretenses and kidnap me. I laid out the circumstances of my abduction for the court, and felt reassured by the collective sharp intake of breath behind me. I swallowed the sick nervousness in my mouth, then asked, "Is David even his real name, or is there another name I should use when discussing him in court?"

"I named him Hansel, for a mortal whose imagination impressed me and to remind me of the mistakes that killed my own mother, so I do not make the same ones," Evangeline said.

Hansel . . . who tricked a witch of poor eyesight with a chicken bone to postpone his own death, and got away with his sister Gretel by shoving the witch headfirst into an oven. Yeah, I could see why she didn't want to suffer the same fate. I wouldn't want to be shoved headfirst into an oven, either.

Of course, I was hoping she'd make all different mistakes. In fact, I thought she already had.

A man with a horn on his forehead stepped forward. "I have questions for you, Janie Grimm, to test the willingness of your appearance here."

Aiden had warned me about this possibility, and told me to tell the absolute truth. Some of the royals could detect falsehoods, and there was no way to tell if that was limited to just magical beings, or all beings when they were in the magical realm.

"I will answer truthfully," I said. I assumed my promise to do so would also bump up my credibility a bit, given their fixation on promise-keeping.

"Did you or did you not invite Hansel into your home willingly?" he asked.

"Hansel did not introduce himself with his true name, and led me to believe he was something other than what he was. Under those false pretenses, I invited him into my home without duress. Had I realized his intention, he would not have been invited to the house or welcomed inside. Once I realized his purpose, I attempted to bar him from my home by slamming the door on his hands."

David's hand was bandaged. I saw him realize the entire court was looking at the white cloth wrapped around his fingers, and he quickly hid it behind his back.

"Are you alleging that he lied to you?" the man with the horn asked.

"I am alleging that my invitation was made without knowing the truth, not that he committed an actual falsehood. At most, he gave me a wrong name, and then allowed me to believe he was someone other than who he was, and then entered my home for purposes outside the bounds of the invitation that was extended." I had no idea if he actually used the name David for any other reason, so I couldn't allege he'd lied about that, either.

Because I could not prove he actually lied, Aiden had advised me it was smarter to go this route. Actual falsehood was grounds for permanent death among the royal court; to expose the queen's son to such a possibility was too big of a risk before the hearing itself had been formally granted before an audience. Also, my honesty here in not overshooting my evidence would hopefully convince them I was telling the truth later, when I got serious about accusations against my stepmother.

"What was the invitation? Was it a qualified invitation?" A lady in a gossamer blue gown, with pale wings on her back, stepped forward, her voice no higher than a whisper.

"It was; it was a group invitation to the members of my study group to meet at my home for dinner and to study. There was no invitation beyond that, and only one member of the group has ever been invited over for any other purpose. That person was not Hansel, but a person who was a friend long before the group was formed. On that day, the friend did not receive an open invitation for the day in question, and did not overstep the invitation given. The invitation was only for the purpose of the meeting."

I heard murmuring behind me as I faced my stepmother again. Was I winning them over, or was it too soon to tell?

"Did any of the others overstep the invitation?" A man's voice behind me asked.

"That friend did not overstep the invitation. In fact, she arrived early and offered assistance with hostessing duties, but never once tried to do anything besides prepare for the meeting and make sure I was ready. The others arrived on time, prepared for the meeting." I didn't want to use Mia's name, after Evangeline's statements in the basement about going after my friends. I'd have to do something after I got out of this mess to make sure my friends were safe. I just hoped Aiden had some ideas, because I was fresh out.

I pinched the bridge of my nose, to get my attention span back on track as I turned back to Evangeline for the next question. I caught Aiden winking and nodding at me out of the corner of my eye as I turned back. I must be doing all right. Maybe I did have a future as a trial lawyer.

One of the other ladies to my right spoke up. "How did you know your brother wasn't trying to protect you from something?"

I stared directly at Evangeline. "I just learned he was my stepbrother on my way here. I had no reason to believe I had a brother. Your Queen was married to my father for twelve years and neither she nor my father ever mentioned there was a stepbrother. I have no reason to believe my father even knew about him, but I have no way to prove it, one way or another, since he died six months ago. If I didn't even know I had a brother since no one ever mentioned it, and even my stepbrother himself never brought it up, why would I give him the benefit of the doubt? A brother I didn't know about was protecting me from something I didn't expect? And if he was there to protect me, wouldn't he have at least told me I was in danger when he showed up at my house? He didn't."

The lady who had asked the question called out softly, "I agree."

I was surprised. I didn't think any of them would throw any overt support my way from Aiden's description of their motives when the Grimm brothers had bound Evangeline's power, but I'd take whatever support I could get.

Evangeline looked unhappy. She wasn't smiling, and I was starting to see an emotion on her face I had never seen from her before: fear. She looked scared, as if I was starting to back her into a corner. I hoped that I was.

"Very well, Janie Grimm, you have ten minutes to choose an advisor in your hearing."

"I don't need the ten minutes."

"You've chosen an advisor?"

"Yes. I choose Aiden, son of Geoffrey the Tailor of your court." Aiden had told me his father's name before we'd come inside.

She laughed at me. "You choose the Half-Breed to help you state your case? You do understand he has not been present in court for years?"

"I understand, but he has given me valuable advice in the past that has proven sound and I trust his guidance."

"Aiden Half-Breed, son of Geoffrey, do you accept this request made by Ms. Grimm?"

He stepped forward. "I do."

Evangeline cocked her head to the side. "So be it. The court will take a brief recess prior to the hearing. I would like to speak with my stepdaughter and my son in private. I would ask her advisor and his father to join us."

The court bowed in one fluid motion, bending over at the waist and curtseying with the grace learned from years of practice, and the gentle hum of multiple conversations told me they were intrigued. There were no seats in the room, but people began to mill about, talking amongst themselves, and otherwise paying attention to something other than Evangeline.

She motioned to Aiden and me to follow her into an anteroom. I didn't figure I had a choice other than to follow her, so I did.

CHAPTER FORTY-FIVE

The minute Evangeline got the door closed behind me; I could tell she was unhappy. A part of me wanted to do the same thing I always did: find a way to make her happy enough to leave me alone. The rest of me knew it wasn't possible.

"I have a proposal to make," she said.

"I'm listening."

Aiden, his father, and David, er, Hansel all stood silently.

"If you give me the Holder right now, I will announce we have resolved this dispute and you will be allowed to go free. Your friends will not be harmed. Apparently, threats against them do not work on you. There is a measure of ruthlessness I admire in you, Janie."

I was disgusted with her. "Evangeline, I will tell you I now know what the Holder is, and where it is, but I won't give it to you, or give you any information that will lead you to it. My friends would understand you cannot be allowed to have it."

"And what of this half-breed? Does he understand he is the one special person you would do just about anything to save? I'm not stupid. It's written all over your face. Would you give it up for him?" She laughed. "Have you given it up for him?"

I caught her double entendre, but refused to respond to it other than the blushing heat I felt rising to my cheeks. I didn't dare look at Aiden. I was sure he was blushing just as furiously, even though we were innocent of what she was implying. "He doesn't know where it is, or what it is. He cannot help you."

She reached out and grabbed his wrist, twisting until he cried out, and I heard the sick crunch of his arm breaking. Geoffrey gasped as his son cried out.

Aiden groaned as she snapped bone. "Janie, if you really do know, don't tell her. Don't worry about what she might do to me. Remember what we told you about it. Aaargh." He grunted as she twisted the broken pieces, presumably to shut him up.

It was hard not to reach into my pocket and hand it to her, to save him from further pain, but doing so would give her the ability to kill me and take over the world.

"No, Evangeline, I won't do it." I felt tears on my face as I said it.

Geoffrey stepped forward. "Janie, give it to her, please."

Evangeline's fingers twitched, freezing him in place, with tears falling from his eyes.

She turned her attention back to Aiden and slapped him across the face, over and over again. I saw his eye swelling, and tried to stop her, but she pushed me away. She ended up punching him in the mouth instead. It split his lip, and I saw it bleeding.

"Are you sure you won't give it up to save him?" she asked. "You did not react like this when I slapped you. You must be in possession of the Holder."

It felt like I'd kicked myself in the chest when I said it. I felt like I was betraying him, even though I knew he understood; he'd told me not to do it. Tears fell, hot and fast on my cheeks as I whispered, "No. I won't do it."

She kept hitting him, until I yelled to stop it, and even then I had to grab her by her hair and hit her myself to get her to stop.

"No one strikes the queen!" she yelled.

Aiden's father was watching the entire exchange, his face white, but he couldn't move from where he stood, thanks to my stepmother's magic. "It will all be all right if you just give the Holder to her, Janie," he said.

"No," I yelled. "Everything is NOT all right. She's beating your son!"

Evangeline stood up, her normally perfect hair mussed from the yanking I gave it trying to get her to release Aiden.

Geoffrey whispered, "I announced in court that I no longer have a son, as he made a choice not to affiliate himself with his rightful place at the side of the queen. Surely my loyalty buys me a boon, my queen. You said as much when I announced it." Evangeline released her magical hold on him, and Geoffrey dropped to the ground, crawling toward us on his hands and knees.

I wanted to tell him he did not deserve the son he had, but that wouldn't have helped the situation. My heart went out to Aiden, who was wiping the blood off his lip with the tail of his shirt, but I was missing something here. Geoffrey's perfectly groomed exterior was slipping, his face wet with tears and his eyes red with emotion. I realized that Geoffrey's position, as hurtful as it was to Aiden, had been done to protect him, not to hurt him.

Aiden didn't see it; he was still struggling to get away from my stepmother. "It's okay, Janie. I made my peace with my father's position a long time ago. He's stubborn enough that he won't change his mind unless he sees the light in a way that cannot be overcome. Luckily for us, the rest of the court is more pragmatic than he is."

Evangeline stamped her foot. "I'm still the queen around here, and I make the rules. I can rule that you are not entitled to a hearing, and have you both put to death."

"No, you can't," I said, yanking again to try to get Aiden released. "You already announced I have the right to a hearing. Revoking that now means you have broken your word. And, if I remember correctly, from the legends I've been told of and your statements earlier, you cannot hurt me while I'm in possession of the Holder."

Her eyes went wide at my confident statement, but she didn't contradict me. I had her over a barrel, and she knew it. She grabbed Aiden's hair and yanked hard, as she also pulled again on his broken arm.

Geoffrey finally got to his feet and ran toward his son, trying to release Aiden. "Let go, my queen. You've lost. And I claim a boon for my service to the court. You must release my son."

"I thought you disowned him." She said, tugging again on Aiden's arm.

Aiden cried out. His father dropped to his knees. "My queen, even if I disowned him, he is still my flesh and blood. I cannot stand here and let you hurt him. I have rendered you long years of faithful service. I request a boon in repayment. You used my son to obtain Ms. Grimm's compliance and it has not worked. Do not torture him further without purpose."

Huh. I actually believed him. I wasn't sure what Aiden's reaction would be to his father's plea, but Geoffrey sincerely sounded like a man who would do anything to protect his son.

"Now, stepmother, you really have no choice. You must allow the hearing, and abide by the decision you made earlier. If there is no right to keep me here, in the magical realm, you must let me go. You granted me the right, before your own court, to have an advisor. I chose Aiden. If you beat him to the point he can no longer be my advisor, then you are foresworn as well. You wanted to play by your own rules; you are now stuck with the consequences of those rules."

Evangeline leaned down to grab the front of Aiden's shirt again, cocking back her fist to strike him. To his credit, he didn't flinch. Instead, he just looked her square in the eyes.

"She's right. If you are forsworn, and proven so, you forfeit your crown, the claims of your heirs on your throne, and can be stripped of power by the court."

Geoffrey again tried to pry Aiden out of her grasp, but she backhanded him across the room. "How dare you interfere with the actions of a royal, Geoffrey Tailor. You know better than that. After you kicked your son out of court, I thought you were loyal, but I see now you were just protecting him. I will deal with you later. Count on it."

He tried again to intervene and protect his son, scrambling to his feet, calling his son's name.

"What is a crown in comparison to what I gain by getting the Holder? If I give up the crown, I'll have enough power to regain it by force if I get what I want." She dropped the grasp on Aiden's shirt, and he stumbled back, away from her. "Have your little hearing, Janie. And after you lose, you will serve me until you give me the Holder. Believe me when I say I will make your time with us as unpleasant as possible. Geoffrey, I will deal with you and your son later."

Her hands began to crackle with magical energy, like hand-held lightning building up between her fingers. Her hair fanned out with static electricity, making her look like a psychotic troll doll with a fork stuck in an electrical socket.

This did not look good.

Her fist was still raised in the air, as if about to punch someone, when I saw her throwing it forward, a handful of raw magic crackling and popping as she prepared to toss it in Aiden's face. I jumped in front of him, fully prepared for it to hurt like hell.

I barely felt it. It rebounded on her, and knocked her off of her feet, blowing her backwards into the wall behind her. A knock on the door sounded.

"Queen Eva, is everything all right? The ten-minute recess is over, and we heard a struggle. Shall we call your guards?" a concerned female voice called through the door.

My stepmother gathered herself, and tried to smooth her hair back into place. It wasn't behaving. I could have told her that she needed to get her hands wet to even start getting it under control with the huge amount of static electricity from her magic making it stick up all over the place, but I didn't feel like being nice to her at the moment. I was proud of myself for not making a snarky comment. Instead, I turned my back on her to check Aiden, who had collapsed on the floor, cradling his arm. He gave me a weak smile and grimaced when the smile stretched his split lip.

"Well," I said. "I think we have a hearing to get to." I took Aiden's hand and helped him to his feet, squeezing the hand of his uninjured arm hard enough to show him how scared I was even though I was putting on a brave face for everyone else. He squeezed back, a reassuring pressure giving me courage.

My stepmother was pissed. She looked like she'd sucked on an entire lemon tree as we walked past her and opened the door to head back into the ballroom with the other court members.

It wasn't a win, but right then I'd take every reassurance I could, and my stepmother was shaken. I was starting to feel like I could actually pull this off.

CHAPTER FORTY-SIX

The ten minutes turned into twenty before Evangeline finally took her throne. Her hair was still wild and crackly from the magical electricity she'd tried to use earlier, and her eyes were red and wide, but she took the throne with the regal bearing of the queen she was. If I wasn't terrified of what might happen next, I would have been impressed with the recovery of her composure.

When she finally called everyone back to order, my stomach was a knot of butterflies trying violently to escape the confines of my abdomen. No time to throw up from nerves now.

"Well, Ms. Grimm, you called the hearing. It's up to you to show us there is no legal basis to keep you here," Evangeline called out.

I swallowed hard. "Some of my allegations are such that we might be able to agree on the underlying facts. With the Queen's indulgence, we may be able to shorten the hearing if we can come to some stipulations."

"What sort of stipulations?" she asked, a sly grin on her face.

Gee, I was glad I could amuse her. "Well, you've already agreed that you're my stepmother. I think we can both agree your marriage to my father was legally valid in the mortal realm, under the laws of the State of Ohio."

"I would agree to that."

"Ceremonies for a mortal wedding usually include promises to love, honor, cherish, and obey each other. Did yours?"

"Yes."

"Would you also agree you were married to him for twelve years?"

"I would."

"And that I was a child from my father's first marriage, which ended with the disappearance and death of my mother prior to your marriage?"

"I agree," she said. "Get on with it."

"You agreed any assets of his from before the marriage were mine, didn't you?" Not that he had much but the house I'd already sold to pay my law school tuition. It was still worth saying. The only asset I might have been able to argue about would have been a portion of his retirement account, but I hadn't pressed the issue at the time. Since she'd agreed to pay the rent, I didn't feel it was worth going after.

"Yes." Did I hear her hesitating on that answer?

"Would you agree that your marriage to my father, Robert Jonathan Grimm, was ended by his death?"

"I would."

I couldn't come out and accuse her of my father's death. For one thing, I couldn't prove it, even if I knew the truth. And even if I had proof she had caused it, I had no proof she had done it intentionally, so I kept going with the slow establishment of facts. "Do you remember a day, about a month before he died, when the letter came announcing my acceptance to law school?"

"I do."

Now here was where it was about to get tricky. "On that day, my father asked you to make a promise to him. Do you remember what that promise was?"

"He asked me to take care of you." She was squirming in her seat.

"Actually, I remember his request being a bit more formal than that. In fact, I remember it almost *verbatim* because it seemed so bizarrely worded at the time. He didn't speak that way normally, did he?"

She hesitated.

I stepped back and grabbed for Aiden's hand. I didn't really want him to do anything, but I needed the moral support. I was about to climb out on a limb, and I wasn't sure it would hold me.

"I'm not sure," she said.

The crowd began to hum, muttering between themselves at her statement. I turned to see if I could catch any of their eyes, but they weren't looking at me. Instead, they were all locked on Evangeline. She, on the other hand, was picking at a seam on her dress, staring at her lap, and refusing to look anyone in the eye. I wondered if Aiden's statement about court members who could sense a lie meant they had to make eye contact with her, but I had no way to ask. Did it mean they could tell her answer wasn't the complete truth or not?

"Stepmother, as I remember it, my father asked you to transfer all promises made to him to me, to take care of me as if I was your own child, and to support me with anything I needed financially while I was in law school. Do you remember these promises?"

"I remember," she whispered. The buzzing in the crowd behind me grew louder.

"You agreed, but you asked me to make a promise in exchange, didn't you?"

"Yes," she said, nodding her head.

Suddenly all those contracts terms from class began to make sense. It was as if a light bulb had turned on, and, as suddenly as the flicking of a switch, my brain was brimming with understanding. I was talking about a bilateral contract, with promises on both sides, each dependant on the performance of the other to continue the obligations of the contract. I had relied on her promises for financial support, and I'd followed through on my end. "You asked me to meet you for a weekly brunch, starting with the week after my father's death, so you could be sure to find out if there was anything I needed."

"That's true."

"Stepmother, did you have another reason for asking me to meet with you?"

She didn't answer right away. When she finally did, she spat the words out. "I. Am. Not. On. Trial. Here. You should produce witnesses and evidence and stop trying to get me to provide your sole case. If you cannot do so, we can end the hearing right now, and come to some agreement for you to stay here with us."

Not on your life, sister.

I was rapidly coming to the conclusion she'd known all along she was slowly cursing my father, and when he was dead, she thought she had found a way to slowly curse me as well, until I came into possession of the Holder. Too bad for her I had no intention of giving it up.

"I have just one other issue to ask about, stepmother, and then I will do exactly as you suggest. I will produce witnesses."

She glared at me. "Get on with it, then. Ask your stupid questions."

"Did my father know you had a child when you married?"

"No."

The crowd took in a collective deep breath. Aiden leaned in, hissing in my ear. "They're not going to like that. Hiding a child is not something they will understand; they are proud of their ties and their lineages. That's going to hurt her in the eyes of her court."

"Did he ask you about whether or not you had a child?"

"Can you prove my answer, one way or another?" she asked.

Well, she had me there. I couldn't prove it. I thought for a few minutes, and decided to call a witness. "I would call my stepbrother, David, also known as Hansel, to the stand."

I don't think anyone was expecting that one. This was the aforementioned precarious limb I was going out on. I'd set up the background as best as I could without subjecting myself to questioning. I'd gotten agreements to just about everything I was going to ask her about, and now it was time to start making some serious allegations.

David wasn't in the room, as he'd been sent on an errand for his mother. Aiden explained to me that since I had the right to the hearing, they would wait for him to return. I felt like I was going to throw up. I wasn't sure David's answers would do what I wanted them to do. And I hadn't told Aiden my plan.

While we waited, Aiden's hand slid around my waist. "You're doing fine, Janie. Whatever you're planning, it seems to be working so far. Keep going."

Yup. That was the idea. I hoped he'd forgive me for what I was planning to do next.

CHAPTER FORTY-SEVEN

When David finally came back in, two members of Evangeline's court walked him to the front of the room, where Evangeline sat and where Aiden and I stood.

"Do you prefer to go by David or Hansel?" I asked.

"I like David better. I've always hated the name Hansel," he said in a mild-mannered and harmless voice. Evangeline looked like she was ready to rip his head off. Some part of me found it amusing to see her getting so upset, since she never did so when I was living with her, or at any time I'd seen her in the mortal realm.

"David, the queen is your mother. Do you have a title you go by?"

"I'm technically a prince, but I don't need you to use the title. Ask your questions."

"Has your mother ever provided financial support for you?"

"Yes. In fact, she still does."

"Are there strings on her financial support?" I hated this line of questioning. I didn't know exactly what he was going to say.

"Well, I follow her orders. I owe her respect. I fulfill my duties as a member of court."

"Has she ever threatened to withhold that support from you if you failed to live up to those actions?"

"She doesn't have to. I owe her duties because of her rank, not because she gives me money." The court was silent as I asked the questions; they seemed to be hanging on every word.

Okay, that wasn't working. Time to change direction. "Has your mother ever sent someone to kidnap you from your home under false pretenses?"

"No." He gave me a dirty look.

"Has your mother ever ordered that you be injected with something to make you lose consciousness? Or done so herself?"

"No."

"Has your mother ever tied you to a chair in your own basement?"

"No."

"Has your mother ever threatened to kill or torture or hurt your friends if you don't do what she wants you to do?"

"No."

"Has your mother ever planned to kill you?"

Evangeline stood up from her throne, her hands clenched in fists at her side. "How dare you? You can't prove I ever planned to kill anyone."

"Did you?"

The court sucked in its collective breath. My stepmother looked up at the members of her court. "That's not germane to this hearing."

I wasn't sure how I could fight that statement. I didn't know the rules of evidence for this hearing. What was I saying? I didn't know the rules of evidence for courtrooms in the mortal realm. Evidence class came next year. Besides, if I pressed her, she could claim some plan from some court intrigue or war or ruling from hundreds of years ago and I couldn't say otherwise.

"Thank you, David. I would call Aiden Ferguson as my next witness."

Aiden looked shocked. His father objected. "He has no standing here; he is not a member of this court."

"Neither am I, and yet I have the right to a hearing on whether or not I stay here permanently. If it is my life, then shouldn't I be able to call any persons with knowledge about the case, regardless of their standing with this court? Obviously, if a mortal cannot present their case, then how can you say they are here by choice if their choice is unfairly made or their court ruling was made without all of the evidence?"

I ignored the shocked look on Aiden's face. He probably wouldn't have looked quite so confused if I had told him I would call him as a witness. Oops.

Evangeline didn't move. After a few minutes of waiting for a ruling and not getting an answer, I went ahead on my own. "Aiden, do you have a job?"

"Yes," he said, and named the restaurant.

"Do you work on Sundays, during the lunch shift?"

"Yes." Comprehension was dawning on his face. He was beginning to understand what I was doing. "I work the lunch shift every Sunday, and have for the past two years."

"Do you remember seeing me at the restaurant with my stepmother?"

"Yes."

"How often did you see us there?"

"Every Sunday, starting about six months or so ago."

"Did I miss any Sundays?"

"Not a single one."

Evangeline crossed her arms over her chest. "What does this have to do with your hearing, Janie? This hearing is supposed to be about whether or not we have the authority to keep you here, not about whether or not we have brunch."

"Actually, stepmother, the two are related."

"I don't see the connection, and I'm the one you have to convince."

I stepped forward, speaking directly to Evangeline, but hoping my voice carried enough that every member of the court could hear me clearly. "My stepmother, Queen Eva, you have forsworn yourself with me. You have broken the promises you made to my father when you married him, promises to love, honor, cherish, and obey him. You have not honored him, as you kept vital family information from him before and after your wedding. You did not honor him, or cherish him; you used him for your own ends. You have broken the promises you made at my father's deathbed, so you did not obey him. I have kept my part of those promises, and I relied upon your promises in the decisions I made in my everyday life."

"I did not break promises to you!" she yelled.

"You promised to care for me as if I was your own child, yet you had me kidnapped, drugged, tied to a chair, and threatened harm to my friends if I did not do as you wished. Your own son has testified you do not treat him that way. Therefore, you have not treated me as your own child, and have broken that promise to my father."

The court behind me was silent, an eerie silence that made me think my strategy was working, so I kept going. "You promised to provide me financial support."

"I paid your rent, and gave you extra spending money."

"Yes, you did. But you required me to do something in return, something you do not ask of your own son: the weekly brunch I have attended, without fail, since I promised you after my father's death. Again, you have not treated me as your own child."

"What are you trying to say, Janie?" she asked.

I heard muttering in the background. "You never intended to treat me as your own child when you made that promise to my father, did you?"

"How can you say such a thing?" She seemed hurt, but I knew it was an act.

"Your powers were bound by the Grimm Brothers, my ancestors, and as long as our bloodline is alive, you cannot break the binding. I think you married my father, not out of love, but to try to obtain the Holder of the Legacy, so you could destroy the last of our bloodline and restore your power."

"So?"

Oh, my. She hadn't denied it. I hadn't expected her to be so blatant about it. "Unless you've been planning to kill Hansel, your plan to destroy my bloodline involves treating me differently, by planning to kill me. You've now broken your promises to me, and to my father. You have only ulterior motives in holding me here, against my will, until I give you the Holder."

"Are you saying you will give it to me?" She came down off the raised platform, storming at me.

It took everything I had not to take a step backwards, away from her, but I couldn't bring myself to even appear to back down from her. "I will not give it to you. And if you and your court rule that I must stay, I will never give it to you. I may lose my sanity, but you will not obtain it. And if you require me to stay here, I will not die, so my bloodline does not die out. You cannot win, regardless of the outcome of this hearing, stepmother. Accept it, let me go, and move on with your life."

The court was buzzing behind me. I knew that I'd won.

"I cannot!" Her voice magnified itself into a booming megaphone.

Just those two words were enough for my eardrums to pop. I worked my jaw in a circle, trying to release the rest of the sonic pressure that had built up from her voice.

Before I could realize what she was doing, she grabbed me by the throat with one hand and lifted me off the ground. It didn't hurt, but I was definitely having trouble breathing. I kicked my legs, trying to connect with her somehow, hoping if I could throw her off balance she would let me go. I reached up, clawing at her hands with my fingernails, trying to get her to release me. Out of the corner of my eye, I saw her reach for Aiden, grabbing the shoulder above his hurt arm.

Despite knowing I was in the magical realm, and that the Holder was in my pocket protecting me from Evangeline, it was way too easy to panic at the inability to breathe. I heard Aiden yelling, and saw him reaching up to grab her hand away from my throat, but I had other items in my pocket, beyond that precious golden key.

And both of my arms were free.

Aiden's father grabbed for his son as my right hand slid into the back pocket of my jeans for the screwdriver. My left hand searched for an ink vial in the left front pocket of my pants. That left the key hidden my right front pocket.

While Evangeline tried to throttle me, yelling about ungrateful young people and unappreciative court members, I raised the ink bottle to my mouth and yanked out the cork stopper with my teeth.

I poured the ink directly onto her face at the same time as I rammed the screwdriver into her neck as hard as I could. My arm vibrated from the impact, but once the point of the screwdriver broke skin, it slid in easily. If she'd been mortal, it would have killed her immediately. From the stories I'd heard from Doris and the gang, it still could, but she was a powerful faerie witch; she was still alive, just in a whole lot of pain.

Her face smoked and blistered, as if I'd thrown acid on her skin, hissing like a steam kettle as she let go of my neck. I coughed hard, trying to get more air into my lungs.

She collapsed onto the floor of the room, her courtiers beginning to circle around her, but careful to avoid the spilled droplets of ink spattered on the floor. My own hand was purple across the back of my thumb and wrist where it had spilled. I tasted the sick, metallic taste on my lip where I'd bit the cork to yank it free. I wondered if I had an ink stain on my mouth.

My stepmother was writhing in agony on the floor, but no one made a move to help her, or to relieve any of her pain. There was a part of me that was glad, and another part of me that was sickened at their callousness. Not even David was coming over to comfort his mother. Was it because she was covered in something akin to poison to the rest of them, or was it that she'd alienated all of them so thoroughly it just didn't matter to them anymore?

The other members of the court descended on her, grabbing at her hair and her arms and legs, restraining her as they tied her up and gagged her. I could still hear the muffled shrieks and groans through the cloth they shoved in her mouth. Grechuk ordered the wicker cage that Aiden and I had been in earlier to be brought into the throne room, and Evangeline was unceremoniously dumped inside, the ink still smoking as it burned the skin on her face.

As I watched my stepmother being treated like a criminal, one of the court members came up to me, his heels clicking together as he bowed before me. "I don't wish to cause offense, but it is a grave crime to bring metal into our court."

I sighed. "Sir, may I remind you I am not here voluntarily? If I had known I was coming here and it was my own choice, I might not have had these items on me. As it was, I had no plan to be here, and I've been in fear for my life and safety. If you're going to blame anyone, blame those who brought me here without telling me of their plans and asking my cooperation. I promise you I have no items that could cause such harm to any of you other than what you have seen me use here today." God, I hoped that was true. I didn't know whether the Holder could cause them any harm, but I didn't want them to know it was in my pocket. "The only thing left is another partial bottle of ink, like I just used on her face."

A gentleman with a crooked hat and wearing a monocle stepped forward. He looked like he was the same age as my father had been when he died. "Janie, you proved your case to the entire court. You won. The faerie courts have no claim to keep you here permanently. Your stepmother will lose her crown, and will be incarcerated for your protection. She will be punished according to our laws for breaking her promises. You are free to go, with our thanks."

I looked up and saw the other members of the court, who stood behind him, nodding and smiling at me. They began to come forward slowly, shaking my hand and thanking me, kissing my cheek, but carefully avoiding the side I'd thought might have ink on it. I'd have to wash my face carefully the minute I got back.

One of them asked, "Is that ink?"

"Yes, iron gall ink. It has actual metal in the ink itself," I told him. "You're going to have to really scrub to get that off of her. It stains."

Two other court members were dragging the wicker cage containing my stepmother away. One of them reached into the cage and pulled the screwdriver out of her neck, and she screamed as they yanked it free. Aiden's father handed it back to me as he gingerly avoided the metal tip by touching only on the plastic handle. I slid it back into my pocket, ignoring the blood that would surely stain my jeans. I felt better having it in my pocket, but felt the need to put it away since the other members of the court were staring at it like it was a poisonous snake.

"Ms. Grimm, I'm not sure you know exactly what you have accomplished here today," Aiden's father said, bending low over my hand. "My name is Geoffrey, and I am pleased to make your acquaintance."

Aiden's jaw dropped. I had to remind myself he hadn't seen his father's reaction to Evangeline's hurting him; he'd been too preoccupied with the breaking of his arm and the punches and slaps and hair pulling to notice his father begging the queen to let him go.

Geoffrey grimaced. "Son, I had to disavow you as long as Eva was on the throne. She had compelled my obedience by magic, and by making threats against you. Now, however, I do believe she will face some serious consequences. Being forsworn is one of the gravest crimes that can be committed in our court. The fact she has broken promises will strip her of most of her court backing, if not her throne.

I, and I'm sure others, are grateful to you. None of us wished to see her get the binding lifted."

"Thank you, sir," I said, not ignorant that my automatic response was due, in large part, to Evangeline's constant nagging with regard to manners.

"I'll walk you out. I'd like to talk with the woman who has inspired such loyalty from my son, as well as freed the court from the queen's influence."

Oh, goody. What was that supposed to mean?

CHAPTER FORTY-EIGHT

Geoffrey escorted us out of the gingerbread house, and down the path toward the portal. On the way, he apologized to his son. Aiden didn't say much other than to acknowledge his father's remorse in hurt disbelief. I was sure he just needed time.

Finally, Geoffrey asked if Aiden would talk with him another time about the decisions he had made. I kept my mouth shut, until it began to look like the peace offering would be rejected.

"Aiden, I'd give anything to have my father back for just one more day. Meet with your father and talk. You don't have to agree to any more than that, and you don't have to be best friends, but at least think about what he's saying, and take the time to talk about it." I walked ahead of them, following the path of white stones I'd scattered without waiting for them.

I heard some yelling behind me, but I tried not to listen. They had emotional stuff to shovel, and it really wasn't my business.

Before long, I slowed down to let them catch up. I didn't want to get lost.

"Janie, hold up," Aiden huffed. "I have some news."

I stopped completely. "What's up?"

I saw Geoffrey running up behind his son, followed by two other court members. Aiden didn't pay them much attention. "It's my understanding the court wishes to extend their apologies for the actions of their former queen, and to inquire of what you might be in need of."

Did I ask them for rent checks for the rest of the school year? Did I ask them to give me back my father? I just stood there, unsure of what to say next.

Geoffrey jumped in. "This isn't a joke. You shouldn't have been brought here by force. Most magical beings who take a mortal into their world are taking trespassers or voluntary visitors. And our queen's actions also stripped you of the support of your only parental figure."

"What's your point?" I said, not sure what he was driving at.

"Your stepmother promised to give you financial support, and her promise specifically to you was to pay your rent, right?"

I nodded.

"Well, what if we helped make sure you had a roof over your head for the rest of your life? In fact, there's some support for the idea that it's your house anyway. We agree that you are owed reparations for her actions, and you are entitled to anything your father would have been owed for the breaking of promises to him. For this reason, you are to be awarded your stepmother's house. We will make sure you get the needed paperwork in the mortal realm."

I was flabbergasted. That solved the housing issue neatly, but did I really want to live in Evangeline's house? Then again, if there was a portal leading to this gingerbread house, and possibly to Evangeline herself, maybe it was a good idea not to sell it or rent it out. Maybe living there, I could keep an eye on it. It was worth a thought. If nothing else, I could always borrow against the house to cover living expenses through law school. Or I could possibly get a roommate? I had options.

I turned to Aiden. "Is there anything I should be concerned about with this offer?"

He shook his head. "It's genuine."

"Sir, on the condition that there are no strings on the house, I accept."

He sighed. "Everyone will be grateful to hear it. We all felt we were in debt to your ancestors, and didn't realize what was going on with your father. To find out she broke her word to him, and you, is the ultimate crime, and we do not wish to have our names besmirched for being untrustworthy."

Aiden snorted, but he didn't say anything else.

Geoffrey handed me the keys to the house. I recognized Evangeline's key ring, and asked about her car, since the keys were on the ring. "We assumed that was part of the house. We have no use for it, and Eva will not be permitted in the mortal realm during your lifetime. It's yours."

I couldn't imagine driving around in an Escalade, but I didn't know what else to say, so I said thanks. Maybe I could sell it.

"At this point, I will leave you," Geoffrey said, opening the portal back to the basement.

I could tell there was more he wished to say to his son, but I didn't think I should push the issue. There would be time for that later. I knew I might have to tell Aiden what I saw his father do to save him if he hadn't noticed it himself. I stepped through the swirling purple air into the basement, and stumbled for the stairs to get the light at the top turned on before Aiden came through. I knew he'd trip over something the minute we got back into the mortal realm, and, with his already broken wrist, that could be a bad thing.

He came back through as I went down the stairs to meet him, and wrapped his good arm around me in a hug. I hugged him back, grateful to be alive, and to be out of the magical realm.

Aiden asked, "So, did you really figure out what the Holder was?"

I nodded. "It's a small golden key. It was in Dad's iron trunks. He had it the whole time."

Aiden pulled back and looked down to catch my eyes. "That makes perfect sense. The Grimm Brothers always ended their story collections with the tale of a Golden Key that opened a small trunk, but the story never told us what was in the trunk. Some scholars theorized that the opening of the trunk was the opening of the imagination, but it sounds like it was a clue for future generations."

"I didn't know that. The only way I figured it out was because I had it in my pocket when Evangeline was hitting me in the face, earlier. If she couldn't hurt me when I was in possession of the Holder, it was the only thing that made any sense. That key had to be it."

He took my chin in his hand and turned it side to side, looking for bruises or marks. "You don't look hurt."

"I wasn't. And when she grabbed me by the throat, it didn't hurt either."

"If your father had the Holder, how did she manage to curse him?" he asked.

I explained my theory about the Holder only working on the youngest member of the Grimm family, which was me.

"It makes sense." He wrapped his good arm around me again, and pulled me in closer.

I leaned my head on his chest and enjoyed his arms, or rather his *arm*, around me. "Either way, we made it through it all."

"Yes, we did. And I have a question for you, before we go upstairs to find Bert and call the others to let them know."

"What's that?"

"Will you go out with me on Friday night? As in, on a date? I was thinking dinner and a movie."

I didn't answer right away. There were a lot of questions in my mind; the half-magical thing, the loss of my stepmother no matter how much I'd hated her, the ownership of the house, whether I had the ability and the focus to finish law school, and everything else. Would I be able to have a normal life now, or would magic rear up to bite me again? I could hear Bert yelling at the top of the stairs that he couldn't open the door and could someone please come tell him what was going on? Life was never going to be easy. I couldn't dictate or organize how my future would go; I would have to take some chances.

"That sounds good. I'd be happy to go out with you, Aiden."

He let out the breath he'd been holding, and leaned down to kiss me. His lips touched mine and I knew I was home, safe, and finally protected from my evil stepmother.

And I knew I'd made the right decision by saying yes to Aiden.

ACKNOWLEDGEMENTS

Special Thanks go to the following people:

To the Dayton Area Novelists Group, for outstanding critique. Thank you for believing in this book enough to make it bleed. I'm sure the wait staff at the restaurants for our meetings had no idea what to expect when we showed up for another DANG meeting. Also to the Mechanicsburg/Springfield Writer's Group; you guys have no idea how much confidence you have given me in my work. Thank you.

To my parents, Alvin and Karen King, for teaching me that I can do anything I set my mind to as long as I'm willing to work for it, and for reading to me as a kid, which taught me the value of good stories told well, including some of the Grimm tales referenced in this book.

To my grandparents, Loren King, Dorothy (Hartzler) King, Merlin Woodruff, and Mary Jane (Clyburn) Woodruff for outstanding examples of love, commitment, and perseverance, and for showing me that a dream can become a reality with hard work and dedication.

To my brother, Alex King, and my sister, Ashley Ballard, for picking on me enough and putting up with the torment I'm sure I put you through. I'm glad I have you, and all the family memories to draw on in my writing.

To the real "Jake" and "Bobby", my brother in law, Jake Ballard, and my cousin (by marriage), Bobby Jones, for having a sense of humor enough to allow me to use their first names. Yes, you guys are more than just funny guys with trucks who know the good stories.

To Blake, my nephew, for making me laugh at things I'd forgotten about being a kid.

To Ray and Daniel Westcott, for giving me reasons to smile every single day.

To Jenna Bennett, Kit Ehrman, Julianne Lee, Elizabeth Bevarly, Julie Kagawa, Butch Wilson, Jamie Mason, Steven Saus, Elizabeth Vaughan, Heather Leonard, and many others I've probably forgotten for telling me that I had the writing ability to get there, even if I hadn't quite made it yet. Even if I've forgotten to name you, I'm still grateful.

To my music guru, Chris Mickles, and his wife, my sounding board, Audra Mickles. Thank you for brainstorming, ideas, music, world building, and lots and lots of fun tabletop gaming.

To Dr. Matt Teel, former head of all things fantasy at Urania, the speculative fiction imprint at Musa Publishing, for seeing potential in this book and going the extra mile to assure me that the book was good, and to Jaime-Kristal Lott, for all her work in the editing process. It was truly a pleasure to work with you both. Also a special thanks to James O. Barnes at Loconeal Publishing for believing in the book after Musa ceased to exist.

AUTHOR INFORMATION

Addie J. King

Addie J. King is an attorney by day and author by nights, evenings, weekends, and whenever else she can find a spare moment. Her short story "Poltergeist on Aisle Fourteen" was published in MYSTERY TIMES TEN by Buddhapuss Ink, and an essay entitled, "Building Believable Legal Systems in Science Fiction and Fantasy" was published in EIGHTH DAY GENESIS; A WORLDBUILDING CODEX FOR WRITERS AND CREATIVES by Alliteration Ink. Her novels, THE GRIMM LEGACY, THE ANDERSEN ANCESTRY and THE WONDERLAND WOES are available now from Loconeal Publishing. The fourth book, THE BUNYAN BARTER, will be available in 2015. Her website is www.addiejking.com

72818355R00147

Made in the USA
Lexington, KY
06 December 2017